Andrei Livadny

Edge of the Abyss

Respawn Trials

Book One

Thank you FOR your support and inspiRAtion! They mean so much to me, AndRei Livadny.

MD
BOOKS

Magic Dome Books

Respawn Trials
Book # 1: Edge of the Abyss
Copyright © Andrei Livadny 2019
Cover Art © Vladimir Manyukhin 2019
English translation copyright © Sofia Gutkin 2019
Published by Magic Dome Books, 2019
All Rights Reserved
ISBN: 978-80-7619-045-0

Also by Andrei Livadny:

Phantom Server LitRPG Series:
Edge of Reality
The Outlaw
Black Sun

The Neuro LitRPG Series:
The Crystal Sphere
The Curse of Rion Castle
The Reapers

Respawn Trials LitRPG Series:
Edge of the Abyss

Expansion: The History of the Galaxy (A Space Saga):
Blind Punch
The Shadow of Earth
Servobattalion

Short Stories:
You're in Game!
(LitRPG Stories from Bestselling Authors)

You're In Game-2
(More LitRPG stories set in your favorite worlds!)

Table of Contents:

he Legend of the Guardians states:

ne who is pure of heart and desperately needs help, will always receive it.

Chapter One

THE UNEXPECTED PHONE CALL came late in the evening. I was still awake and answered at once. "Hey. What's going on?"

My nephew and I got along quite well, although he hadn't called or visited as often over the last few years. He was all grown up, with his own life now.

He said hello and then proceeded to breathe heavily into the phone without even asking after my health.

"Denis, why don't you get to the point?"

"I need your help."

"Tell me," I said and limped over to the window. The street was obscured by an autumn drizzle. The edge of the metropolis had crept right up to the village and the low clouds were snagging on the tips of the rising skyscrapers. The old house that I had inherited from my parents would soon be slated for demolition, and there was nothing I could do about it.

"I've been invited to join an expedition. For three months. Somebody needs to keep an eye on the apartment... I've also found a side job, you see, a pretty good one. I don't want to lose it."

"Any more details? Where's the expedition heading to? What kind of job? Of course, it's no trouble for me to water the plants and feed the cat."

"I don't have a cat, you know that! The work's simple, from home. Nothing heavy. You'll fix your health up, too."

"Interesting. What kind of side job provides medical treatments as well?" I smiled distrustfully.

"I can't explain in two words. Can you come over?"

"What, right now?"

"Yes. I'm short on time. I kept dragging it out, hoping to find someone else to replace me, but it didn't work out. I'll call you an air taxi right now and pay for it. Will you help me out? My flight to Irkutsk leaves in three hours."

"Fine. We'll talk when I get there."

"Thank you! See you soon." He disconnected at once, probably to avoid any additional questions.

Denis had graduated from university the year before last. He had majored in Geology but, unfortunately, rapidly developing technology had made his profession redundant. All the corners of the globe were being carefully watched from orbit and the search for mineral resources was performed using powerful computers and scanners. The same thing had happened in many fields of human activity. Of course, machines weren't capable of completely replacing us, but they were faster and more effective at solving highly specialized problems.

In summary, Denis couldn't find a job in his field and for him to receive an invitation to join an expedition was an unmissable chance to launch his career.

My nephew's small rental apartment was located on the 102nd floor of an enormous living complex. As I ascended in the high-speed elevator, my ears became blocked several times from the change in pressure.

"Hi, come on in!" Denis was clearly happy to see me. "I didn't interrupt any of your plans, did I?"

"Oh, what plans?" I waved him away. "What sort of expedition are you going on?"

"A private one." He replied vaguely. "If everything goes well, they're promising to employ me as per my specialization. I simply couldn't miss a chance like this."

"Why didn't you call me earlier?" I sat down in an armchair and looked around. The modern apartments are fully automated. All the furniture is inbuilt so there are no separate rooms. The required piece of furniture comes out of the wall or descends from the ceiling. It's called 'transformable space' but I think it looks empty and uninviting.

The only thing that stood out in Denis' apartment was a VR capsule made from dark tinted plastic, through which I could see the twinkling of indicator lights. It stood on a massive base and was slightly tilted, about 30 degrees relative to the floor. I'd seen such devices before. They were being heavily advertised over the last few years.

"You see, everything was only decided last night!"

"Okay. What's the side job? What exactly would I need to help you with?"

"Are you familiar with virtual reality?"

"Computer games, you mean?" I raised an eyebrow. "I played them in my youth."

Denis shook his head reproachfully. "Man, you've really fallen behind the times," he said and touched a sensor. Something hissed in the wall, a recess opened and a tray with two disposable cups extended towards us. I didn't touch mine — coffee this late in the evening was a bit over the top.

"Computer games are the ancient past. They've been replaced by full-scale virtual reality. It's basically an endless world where you can live."

"Live?" I smiled skeptically. Truth be told, I had heard something similar but had not taken it seriously.

"You'll understand if you try it yourself," Denis looked at me with obvious hope.

"Where's the capsule from? It costs a lot of money,

right?"

"I took out a loan and I'm paying it off little-by-little."

"I thought you couldn't find a job?"

"Yeah, so this is my job," he touched the convex side of the VR capsule. "Two to three hours a day and it's enough to live on."

"And what do you do in there?"

"I perform various tasks. They're quite simple. I've left a brief description of what you'll need to do. Have a read of the instructions file, I've set it up so that it will automatically download as soon as you... well, I mean, my character, will enter the game. Help me out, please? I've got nobody else to ask! Here's the access chip to my account. The automated system in the VR capsule will adjust all the necessary settings. Believe me, you have nothing to worry about, it's all completely safe. The system will fine-tune your body at the same time. The life support system inside is top notch."

"Fine," I glanced at my old-fashioned analog watch that I wore out of habit. "Your plane leaves in an hour. You're not going to miss it?"

Once I was alone, I sat back down in the armchair and took a sip of cold coffee. My sleep had evaporated anyway. I glanced at the VR capsule with some alarm.

I wasn't against progress but I also wasn't a slave to the latest gadgets. Everyone had heard about virtual reality, of course, it was all they spoke about on the spherovision these days, but I've always been skeptical about this kind of information. I reckoned all the fuss was just advertising for these very expensive 'immersion' devices. Honestly, how could anything replace real life?

I'd been through the Asian Conflict and had been wounded twice, once seriously. After several years spent in hospitals, I was forced to retire. Yes, I had fallen behind the times. My brother — Denis' father — was working on the Mars Project and was currently about thirty million kilometers away from Earth, on his way to the Red Planet. As far as I understood, VR capsule technology was first developed for long-distance space flights and only later adapted for commercial use.

The doubts, wariness and a growing sense of curiosity made me skim through the instructions.

It seemed quite easy. Finishing off the cold coffee, I undressed and caught my reflection in the smoky plastic of the VR capsule. What was I waiting for? It's not like I was leaping into the line of fire.

A familiar chill formed in my chest. Seriously? Could I be afraid?

The motors hissed softly. Two segments moved apart and down, sliding along the sides of the capsule. The interior reminded me of a solarium. The bed looked firm, with a block with lots of openings at its head.

I climbed inside and lay down. It was uncomfortable. How do people put up with this for several hours?

The first impression turned out to be false. The hard surface suddenly changed its properties, becoming pliable and conforming to my shape, as if I was sinking into a thick, gel-like mass.

A sharp hiss came from the head of the bed. Ten flexible servocontrollers suddenly shot out of the openings and wrapped themselves around my body. I felt the touch of numerous sensors, the sharp, almost painful prickling over my temples and back of the head. I jerked automatically and tried to sit up but the cords held me tightly. The outer segments slid back into place, cutting off the light. A spicy scent sent my mind to sleep in a few seconds.

My eyelids felt heavy. A belated panic flashed through my thoughts. Denis never mentioned anything like this. He didn't really tell me anything!

...

Physical data does not match the last account records.

Bioscanning will commence and VR capsule parameters will be adjusted.

Please wait.

...

My muscles twitched involuntarily. There were occasional flashes of pain. The tingling in my temples turned into stinging.

...

Testing is complete.

Life support parameters have been adjusted.

Feedback (immersion) level has been reduced to 25%.

Please note, you perceive fewer sensations and receive less experience at low feedback levels.

You can always increase the sensory level above recommended but you are responsible for the consequences (see item 213.2 of the User Agreement).

Welcome to the Edge of the Abyss virtual reality!

...

I was expecting anything but birdsong and simply froze in the first moment due to emotional shock.

The view from the town wall was incredible. I was surrounded by the predawn light, the rough stone was cool under my hand and the respawn circle glinted around me, but it was the birdsong, once so familiar and then completely forgotten, that pierced me to my core. It was as realistic as if I had been transported back to my childhood.

The air was clean. A gentle breeze stirred the leaves and carried the scent of freshly mown grass.

It's hard to explain the gamut of emotions that I felt. My surroundings didn't feel fake. Digital reality had exceeded all my expectations.

I took deep breaths. The meadows, groves and scattered hills, the floodplain covered in morning fog —

the whole landscape bewitched me.

I didn't hear the footsteps and didn't even notice the shadow until a sharp blade touched my throat and I heard a whisper, "Don't move or I might accidentally cut you."

My reflexes would have probably kicked in in the real world. I would have broken the jerk's arm, but I unexpectedly felt completely helpless here and stood still, my eyes bulging.

"Three seconds. You're free."

I turned around. A young guy stood behind me, dressed all in black.

"Don't get aggro," he said quite conciliatory. "I'm leveling up my Stealth skill. Why'd you freeze? Are you lagging?"

I didn't understand a word of what he'd said.

"Contact tech support," the guy suggested and disappeared, melting into the shadows as if he'd never been there.

The respawn circle (located on the fortress tower) lit up with a string of unfamiliar symbols and the figure of a well-built warrior appeared among the flickering glow. His armor was splattered with blood. Ignoring me, he rapidly headed to the stone steps leading downstairs.

"How come you're so early today?" A guard stopped beside me. He held a torch in one hand, while the other rested on the pommel of his sword.

"I couldn't sleep," I answered automatically.

"Remember our agreement? You owe me five coins by this evening."

I wanted to ask, 'what do I owe you money for?' but then stopped myself. I didn't know what Denis did in this world. He had left me very sparse instructions.

"What if I don't manage to get so many?"

"Then you won't enter the town at night," the guard snapped back. "If you can't pay, make sure to finish your business before sunset!"

"Sure, I will." There was no point in arguing. I had to figure it all out first. I strongly disliked his dismissive tone, however, and the scornful way he had said 'business'.

"That's better."

The respawn circle lit up again. An attractive young elven woman appeared.

Elusive_Wetta. Light Elf. Detective, Level 29.

"Hi, Dan," she nodded to me like to an old friend. "So, you're stuck in the sandbox? Still working as a mule?"

I simply shrugged, unsure of how to answer.

"Well, cheer up. One day you'll save up enough for a normal account and then you'll be able to play properly, instead of running errands for those assholes."

She left and I turned back to examine the town.

Anchor. Capital of this province. Location status: safe.

A small castle rose in the center of the hill. Two

defensive walls encircled it below, while one- and two-story houses formed quarters, divided by twisting streets.

I descended the stone stairs, proceeded down the street to the nearest square and looked around. The traders' stalls were still closed. Time here seemed to match the time in the real world.

To avoid drawing the attention of the occasional pedestrians, I sat down on the worn front steps of a building and tried to call up the interface.

I succeeded after a few attempts.

...

Dan_23214, Human race, Warrior class.
Current level: 10.

...

I glanced through the character's main characteristics. Why go into the details? I'd just stand in for Denis and not level up anything. I noticed that Dan had a clear imbalance towards Strength and Stamina, while other characteristics were at baseline.

Okay, what else could I find out?

An advertising block suddenly appeared in my field of view in response to the mental query. The system was persistently encouraging me to switch to the new tariff plan.

It turned out that Denis had a Trial account. I focused my gaze and received a hint. The first month was free, then fifty credits per month. Restrictions were that you couldn't develop your character beyond level

11

20 but you could level up peaceful professions, for which certain skills and abilities were unblocked. Access was possible from any device. The Trial account (for introductory purposes) could be used not only by the registered user but also by their family members, whose social contacts were automatically confirmed.

The next type of account, which the system was encouraging me to switch to, was a Standard account. Access was only through a VR capsule and the single restriction was that a character could reach a maximum of Level 100. The monthly fee was 500 credits. No way! That's a solid amount of money in the real world!

The subscription fee for the Advanced account was 1,000 credits. There was the ability to transfer game currency... I didn't read any further since this obviously wasn't for mere mortals.

Following the links, I proceeded to study matters of interest. I was greatly surprised to find that millions of people all over the world owned a Standard account, according to the game statistics. I didn't think there were that many rich people.

Aha, so VR capsules could be rented! It turned out that residential districts in megacities had special entertainment centers where equipment rental was quite affordable for the average user.

My nephew sure led a strange life. He didn't have a job and yet had taken out a loan to buy a VR capsule, rather than just renting it. I glanced at the prices. The cost of the budget model started at 10,000 credits. The numbers didn't add up in my head...

Fine. I'll figure it out later. There must be an explanation. But why doesn't Denis pay for a Standard account, staying on the Trial one instead?

Attention, you have a message!

The letter icon flashed. I opened it. As expected, the letter was from my nephew.

Hello. I'm fine. I'm guessing that you've logged in already. The most important thing is to play on low level. Don't accept any quests, whatever you do! Keep an eye on the character's progress. If you think that you're about to go up a level — kill yourself. If you get to Level 11, you'll lose the protection and other players will be able to attack you. Believe me, even safe locations are full of hardcore players and dropkicks.

If you've got any questions, shoot me a line.

Dan.

Perfect timing. What did he mean by 'kill yourself'? Jump off a wall?

I noticed that the sun had risen and it was time to get down to business. The town was gradually filling with people. Stalls were opening and pedestrians appeared on the streets.

I found the list of tasks in a separate folder. Places

were marked on the map. It was suggested that I visit several stores and then make a foray beyond the town walls. The reason wasn't yet clear.

The first control point was located nearby, only a hundred or so meters away. With the semitransparent minimap hanging in the right upper corner of my vision, there was no way to get lost. I followed the winding streets. Some were paved while others were mired in mud, creating a typical medieval environment.

The mark on the map matched the Alchemist's store. I pushed open the door and entered. Judging by the frame, a player stood behind the counter.

"Hey there, Dan. Here," he passed a heavy bag over to me. "Tell Hulk that the next batch will only arrive the day after tomorrow."

That was the end of the conversation. Seeing that I was still shuffling my feet, the merchant called Miserly_Borg raised an eyebrow. "Is there a problem?"

"No, no, nothing."

"Then why are you standing here? Get a move on! Time is money!"

How rude and confusing. I could hear the same dismissive tone as in the guard's voice.

I simply shrugged and exited the store, deciding to avoid asking any questions for now.

The day was warm and bright. It was so realistic that it sent shivers down my spine! My mood improved again. I headed to the next spot marked on the map, staring at everything as I went past. Nobody paid me any attention. Stopping at the Smithy, I spent a long time watching the craftsmen, fascinated by their work. Where could one see such a thing in the modern world?

I visited two other shops and received some food supplies and a dozen vellum scrolls. That's it. My inventory was full and the weight was close to maximum.

So, Denis works as a courier here? Sort of like a delivery service? None of the merchants demanded any money from me for the goods. Now I understood why Denis had spent all the available points on Stamina and Strength when he created the character.

I checked the map. Yes, I'd finished all the tasks in town and now my route lay beyond the wall, first along the road and then down a forest path. I had to reach a marker in a small clearing before midday. It was going to be a long walk.

I strolled through the forest, admiring its beauty and breathing the dizzyingly clean air. The level of authenticity in the digital world continued to astound me. The scarcely visible path gradually led me deeper into the trees. I began to come across mossy roots, shadows gathering overhead among the dense branches. I felt like I was in a national park, a place that no longer existed in the real world. Now I understood why most players rented VR capsules. It was a completely different level of perception! All the senses: touch, smell, the breeze, taste... I picked a berry, tried it and spat it back out. It had a bitterly sour taste.

...

You have sustained mild poisoning (10 seconds — 1 HP/sec).

Would you like to obtain the Herbalist skill so that you can identify plant properties?

...

I selected 'No'. My nephew had explicitly asked me not to level up the character, which meant that he wanted to get Dan_23214 back in the same state as I had received him.

Well, I was fine as it is. In the gray reality, I had forgotten the very word 'nature' as cities grew rapidly in size, throwing tentacles of communication towards each other and the technosphere sucked up all the resources, turning whole regions into wastelands. It made this world look even brighter and more attractive. This world had a ban on technology. It had been replaced with magic, which I hadn't seen any evidence of so far.

I was deep in thought, admiring my surroundings. Like a child, I examined the thicket with unfeigned interest, touching the tree bark and feeling its texture.

So unbelievably real!

Even the fatigue was gradually making itself

known. Another realistic aspect of immersion, since I hadn't gone on any extended walks in a long time. Oh, and I'd stopped limping! I couldn't feel the effects of my injuries at all.

I focused on three indicators in the interface. One was showing the current number of HP (health points). The second and shortest one showed the amount of mana (mental energy). The third bar was currently wavering in the middle. This was my physical energy, known as Stamina in gaming slang, which was spent on every action but quickly regenerated. The Stamina parameter was responsible for it.

My thoughts were interrupted by a noise. Someone was crashing through the undergrowth! What was I supposed to do?

While I was trying to think of something, an enormous bear entered the small clearing. The surrounding frame was red, with a skull symbol. The mob exceeded me significantly on all levels!

I stood still, hardly daring to breathe. My only weapon was a dagger. Even my distant knowledge of gaming was enough to mentally curse Denis for his carelessness. Daggers required a high level of Dexterity while Denis had spent all his points on Strength and Stamina! He's just a mule! I looked around and spotted a thick tree branch on the ground. Maybe if I grabbed it and used it as a club, I would inflict much more damage than with the teeny knife?

This was a grave mistake. Getting into a fight with

an adult brown bear turned out to be a stupid idea from the beginning. The difference in our levels was too great but I had been startled by the bear's sudden appearance. My reflexes kicked in — there's a reason people say that the self-preservation instinct manifests as two extremes — fight or flight.

Grasping the heavy branch, I received several messages at once.

...

You are overloaded (you have exceeded the maximum transportable weight possible with your current characteristics).

Your mobility is reduced by 50%.

You cannot effectively use the club (you lack the Heavy Crushing Weapon skill).

...

"AAAAAH!"

I discarded the useless branch and bolted away.

...

You have used a war cry. Your Strength and Stamina have temporarily increased by 1. The aggro radius of the NPC enemy has increased by 10 meters.

You have attracted the attention of the adult brown bear.

...

A spine-chilling roar sounded behind me.

The mob became completely enraged for some reason. A crushing blow of its paw snapped the pine trunk where I had stood just a second ago. A sweet woody scent filled the air.

I ran at breakneck speed, crashing through the blackberry brambles. The prickles tore at my skin and clothes. System messages appeared one after another. Luckily, the message window was located in the lower part of my field of view so the signs didn't obscure my vision.

...

Outfit durability is reduced by 20%. Protection from physical damage reduced by 2 points.

You are injured. Bleeding 30 seconds (1 HP/sec).

...

The bear's roar sounded closer and closer.

The thicket suddenly ended. I found myself on the steep shore of a relatively narrow but turbulent river. A mossy log lay over the rapids. Quick, to the other side!

I was roughly halfway across when I slipped, lost my balance and fell. I felt a chill in my chest, there was a fountain of droplets and my breath was knocked out of me. The strong current immediately began to drag me over the rocks.

...

Injury from falling 25 HP. Stun negative effect for 10 seconds.

...

The bellowing of the disappointed bear came from behind me. I had passed a bend in the river by this point and was tossed into the deep. I was drowning!

The branches of a weeping willow hung over the pool. I grasped desperately at the thin branches that reached down almost to the water, but they slipped through my hands, leaving only leaves behind.

A shadow flashed through the water and I even managed to read the frame.

Carnivorous catfish, Level 15.

...

The Swimming skill is available. Would you like to select it?

...

NO!

The Stun debuff had passed. I managed to grab the exposed tree roots, cling to them and climb onto the shore.

I lay there completely exhausted, gasping for breath. My clothing was in rags and my whole body was burning. The Life bar had shrunk by two-thirds, taking on an alarmingly orange color.

After a little while, I caught my breath and sat up, my back against the tree trunk. I stretched out my arm — the fingertips were shaking slightly. I listened apprehensively to the sounds of the forest, in case there came the crunch of a branch or the rumble of an animal.

The water gurgled softly, the trees rustled overhead and the birds trilled their songs.

Right, so what do I do now? While my HP slowly regenerated, I opened the location map, first reading and deleting the annoying message,

Life support system recommends: urgent exit.

No way. Firstly, I feel relatively okay. Secondly, I had business to attend to.

I'd lost my way. The route trodden by Denis was somewhere off to the side. Now I'd have to make my own way through the woods.

Oh, and this place was called the Peaceful Forest according to the map. I wondered what the traveler could expect in the Wild Lands, whose boundary was about twenty kilometers north of here!

I should have found a weapon more appropriate for my character! It was too late now to regret my carelessness. I had thought that I would stroll through the forest, breathe the clean air and complete a simple task, combining the pleasant with the useful, but it was not to be.

The leaves rustled as something crawled by. To be honest, my heart jumped at the noise. Keeping completely still, I read the frame.

Adder. Level 7.

It didn't notice me and disappeared among the dense patch of ferns.

I wonder if mobs attack each other? Or do they only attack players?

I approached a witch hazel bush and used my dagger to cut off a long branch. Using a piece of rope that I found in my inventory, I attached the blade to my improvised spear and looked at the result.

A crooked makeshift spear. Cannot be thrown. Stabbing damage 2-5, multiplied by the current Dexterity score. Special attack: deep lunge. Chance of critical hit 1%.

You have successfully created an item. You have gained 30 Exp. The Craftsperson skill is available. Would you like to accept it?

...

I selected 'No'.

I hadn't managed to trick the game with my makeshift spear. The modifier was still Dexterity, which my character had at the base Level (5). Hence, the spear's damage was 10-25, which was the same as the dagger.

Having rested and waited for the Life bar to regenerate completely, I headed into a tangle of ferns, moving in the direction of a wooded hill a couple of kilometers away, where the coveted marker glinted in a small meadow.

I must have met the bear by accident. I had simply been unlucky. I spotted only a few small animals on my way, which I easily avoided.

A withered tree drew my attention at the foot of the hill. It stood out so clearly against the background greenery that a person simply couldn't pass it by. I became curious, of course, so I came closer and saw a circle of yellowed grass and rough-hewn rocks that jutted out from the ground.

...

You have found the location Mysterious Hill.
Quest available: Dried Up Spring. Type: normal.
Find and remove the rock that is blocking the spring.
Reward: 100 Exp, +1 reputation with the residents of the nearby village.

...

I didn't have time to lug around rocks. I had to deliver the goods first and then decide if it was worth coming back here.

A few steps later, I stumbled across some yellowish bones peeking through the moss, as well as a rusted pickaxe with a rotted wooden handle lying beside it.

...

Quest available: The Secret of Forest Hill. Type: normal.
Find out whom the pickaxe belonged to.
Reward: 500 Exp.

...

I didn't disturb the remains. I was intrigued, of course, but there was no time left for a search. Work was waiting and I was running late enough as it is! Yet I still lingered. Something glinted dully in the grass. Interesting... I squatted down and saw a large, teardrop-shaped crystal with a simple amulet beside it, adorned with the stylized image of a shield. I picked up both objects and examined them.

...

You have obtained the Soul Crystal.

Unrecognized artifact. You do not have enough Intellect to determine its properties.

You have obtained the Guardian's Amulet. Unrecognized artifact. You do not have enough Intellect to determine its properties.

The Secret of Forest Hill quest has been updated. The quest type has changed to personal.

Find out if the Soul Crystal and the Guardian's Amulet are somehow related to the miner's remains.

...

I placed the amulet straight in my inventory but examined the crystal, noting that a tiny and delicate flame had sprung up inside from the warmth of my palm. I looked at it more closely. What a strange flame! It was edged in black.

What could it mean? I had no idea. I'd try to find some information about the Soul Crystal later but now I had to hurry!

It was after midday when I reached the forest glade with the marker.

I smelled smoke from a fire and picked up my pace, but then stopped when I heard the voices.

"A hundred gold. Hand them over and we'll go our separate ways. You'll wake up in respawn."

There was a sickening moan in response.

"Hey, Wang, heal her up a bit or she'll kick the bucket before long."

I carefully made my way through the bushes framing the clearing, crawled to the top of a small rise and peeked through a gap in the tree branches.

"Assholes! Let the girl go!" came a voice from a deep hole.

There was a camp set up in the clearing. I stared at the roughly assembled cages. A wounded wolf sat in one of them and a girl about five years old huddled at the bottom of the other: frightened, in rags and with a tear-streaked face.

The three players looked quite average, except that their avatars emanated a strange, misty aura.

"Worry about yourself instead," snapped back *Impatient_Wang, Dark Mage, Level 30*. He was easily distinguished from the others with his long staff and draping garments. He approached the edge of the hole and cast a spell. The red light of the special effect briefly illuminated the unsightly details. I managed to spot the same female elf that had I met this morning. She had landed in a trap and was caught on the sharpened spears at the bottom. The elf's Life bar was almost empty but the mage's intervention had extended her suffering. The healing spell made her HP jump to the middle of the bar and change to a yellow color.

"What the hell do you want with this NPC?" asked *Savage_Hulk, Dark Assassin, Level 30*, as he also approached the edge of the hole. He seemed to be in charge. "Did you accept a quest from the village elder to free her?"

"Have a heart, filth!" The elven woman wheezed out. "She's but a child."

"Yup," Savage gave her a crooked smile. "She's a piece of code wrapped in a soppy avatar," he pointed out. "It's only a game, or have you forgotten that? You've got your quests and we've got ours. You want to free the girl? Not a problem. Another hundred gold coins and she's yours."

"I don't have that many..." The elven woman moaned in pain again.

The third PKer (the usual name for player killers) sat off to the side, beside the fire. *Fierce_Zarek. Dark Warrior, Level 31.*

Is this how Denis earned his money? Nobody would trade with criminals and the town guard wouldn't let them near the town, but this didn't seem to be much of a problem. My inventory was full of parcels of food, vials and parchment, everything that they needed, delivered straight to their forest camp.

"Alright, have a think, maybe it'll make you more talkative," Savage_Hulk lost interest in the female elf and returned to the fire.

"Dan's running late today," noted the Dark Warrior.

"He's still got to take the loot back to town."

Indeed, there was armor, weapons and chunks of some kind of ore laid out not far from the cages.

"You're going to get banned, scumbags," groaned the elf.

"Nope," Savage replied lazily, "Nobody's going to touch us. Even if you write to support, we'll show them our logs. You fell into that hole by yourself. Wang here was healing you, trying to save your life. What's the problem? There's no torture. Plus, we've got Dark auras, remember?"

I didn't understand a lot from their dialog. My body was suddenly flooded with uncontrollable rage. I thought that I'd gotten rid of such feelings long ago and had regained my self-control, leaving the past in the past... but a crimson mist descended over my mind.

The trembling quickly reached my scalp and made the skin there feel too tight for my skull. My fingers clenched the shaft of my makeshift spear.

...

You cannot attack other players while you are under the Aura of Immunity. Reach Level 11 to unblock the PvP option.

...

The message didn't reassure me in the slightest. My heart felt like it was ready to jump out of my chest. I couldn't think straight.

'Breathe in...out... In... out... Think... It's easy enough to die a pointless death... You're alone, unprepared, practically weaponless...' Snatches of thought flashed through my mind. 'Look in the inventory. What did you bring for these jerks?'

I could feel my blood singing in my veins, my heartbeat thumping in my ears.

The scrolls wouldn't help. I didn't know how to use them. What about the vials?

I noticed that the crystal I had found had begun to glow again. The orange flame with the black border leaped and flickered inside.

The letters on the labels grew blurry. I read the names with difficulty. This one would do. And this one.

Now, I had to get a grip on myself and pretend that nothing was happening. I was still trembling. The adrenalin couldn't find a way out.

I crawled backwards, stood up, brushed my clothes off and walked through the shrubs, no longer trying to hide. As I walked past the pitfall, I surreptitiously dropped two large healing potions, a levitation potion and a couple of vials of poison into it. There was no time to read what kind of poison it was.

"Dan, where the hell have you been? You're late!" Savage reproached me.

The elven woman understood everything and immediately sent me a private message.

Thanks. I'll deal with them. If you want to help, free the girl. Grab her and run. There's a path beyond the fire that turns to the right. Follow it. The village elder will protect you. I've dropped a marker.

"You've got a bear around here!" I snapped back. "Level 30, at least! It almost tore me to shreds!"

Savage spat to the side scornfully.

"Fine, drop off your stuff, take the loot and run back. You need to deliver the goods to the trader before evening."

"Yep." I gave him the parcels of food, parchment and vials, then, barely holding myself back from punching Savage in the face, approached the stolen goods. I spotted a morning star among the weapons. Quashing the rage inside me, I focused my gaze with difficulty and read the object's properties. It was the perfect level for me...

"What are you lagging for?" the Dark Warrior was watching me closely.

"Yeah, coming. What an interesting object," I picked up the weapon and pretended to examine it.

A suspicious noise came from the pitfall.

"Wang, go and take a look!" Savage ordered at once.

"She's trying to escape!" Yelled the mage.

Using the moment when they were all distracted, I smashed the morning star into the cobbled-together cages. The wood splintered into pieces. The girl turned out to be a bright one and ran towards me.

...

You have completed the first part of a secret quest, Rural Days.

You have gained 500 Exp.

You have reached a new level.

Attention, now that you have reached Level 11, you have lost the Aura of Immunity. PvP mode unblocked.

The Rural Days quest has been updated. Take the girl to the village.

...

I picked up the girl. Now I had to get out of here!

The freed wolf shot past me like a gray shadow. Wang gave a full-throated scream as the animal sunk its teeth into his ankle, disrupting the casting.

The levitation glow died down in a shower of special effects. I could hear shouts and the clash of weapons behind me but I didn't look back. I ran as fast as my legs would carry me, past the fire and to the right, onto a path that led steeply down the slope.

I wasn't being followed yet but I doubted that the elf would last long alone against three opponents. The girl clung to me, sobbing.

Chapter Two

THERE WAS A LOGGING area immediately beyond the hill, then the path took me to the forest edge and joined a dusty country road.

My strength was ebbing away rapidly. My Stamina was almost at zero. I had to watch the green bar constantly, switching to a fast walk to let it regenerate a little.

"I see him!"

The shout sounded dangerously close, so I started running again.

The road dipped into a narrow valley between the hills. It was damp and muddy, with horse tracks visible.

My chest was hurting. I was out of breath and wouldn't last much longer.

...

You ran for three kilometers without stopping. The Field Athlete skill is available. Would you like to select it?

...

There's no time... I'll sort it out later... The road went uphill again while my pursuers drew closer and closer. With a low-pitched buzz, a fireball shot past me and set the grass alight.

The mage was going to aim better next time. I zigzagged instinctively. There was a splash of flame and clouds of smoke and steam. You missed me, jerk!

Where was the village?!

There! Another three hundred meters... I wasn't sure that I was going to reach the palisade that the peaceful farmers had built around their village. Only one thing cheered me up — the gates had watchtowers and I'd been spotted.

Would they help? As if in response, there came a shout, "Bandits! Bandits! Sound the alarm!"

Arrows whistled over my head, dampening my pursuers' fervor. The local farmers weren't so helpless after all!

The gates trembled and began to open. Men ran out to meet me. They were armed with all sorts of things: plows, axes and pitchforks, but there were many of them! Their frames were yellow, meaning that they were neutral towards me. Their levels were 30 and higher.

Staggering a little, I slowed down to a walk.

There was the village elder. Short, silver hair, walking with a limp. "Granddaughter!"

...

The second part of the quest Rural Days has been completed.

You have gained 500 Exp.

...

That's it... I couldn't go any further.

I fell to my knees. The girl was no longer crying, she slipped out of my arms and raced towards her grandfather. I fell on my side.

...

Emergency exit from virtual reality is recommended with a reduction in the realism level and feedback calibration.

Call an ambulance?

...

With a flick of my pupils, I canceled the recommended actions. I wasn't finished here yet. I wanted to see these bastards getting pitchforked!

But no. Savage and his gang decided not to get into a fight with a crowd of villagers. The mage set alight a wheat field with his fireballs and the Dark players retreated to the forest using the fire as a cover.

The elder approached me. His frame was now green.

"Thank you, stranger. You have saved my granddaughter!"

The message icon blinked. I opened it. It was a note from Savage:

You're dead. Don't think that you can hide out in the village.

I dropped the three into the KOS list[1]. Now the system would automatically warn me if they were to appear nearby.

The envelope symbol appeared again. The message was from the elf this time,

They killed me. Respawn in 20 minutes. How are you?

...

I'm in the village. I got the points for your task. I went up a level.

...

Dan, I can hardly recognize you, but thanks anyway.

A word of advice — kill yourself a couple of times. Or write to support and say that you went up a level by accident. Maybe they'll restore your Aura of Immunity.

...

I'm not going to do that.

...

I caught my breath a bit. The men were putting out the fire, the village elder helped me to my feet and critically inspected my clothes, which were now in

---

[1] Stands for 'kill on sight'. Basically, a personal enemy list.

tatters.

"This won't do. Come, I have some old leather armor. It will fit you perfectly. I haven't seen you around these parts before. What is your name?"

"Dan."

"They call me Craig." Said the old man and his frame immediately displayed his name.

We entered the gates. It was a small village, only about twenty houses.

"What are you defending yourself from?" I indicated the palisade.

"These are dark times," complained the elder. "Sometimes it's bandits and sometimes it's wild animals."

"What kind of animals? Bears? I met one today."

"If only. We hunt those with bear spears. Werewolves have appeared in the woods again," he sighed heavily. "We haven't suffered any for ages. They must have returned to their old den. Maybe you will vanquish them? I have an infusion of a rare root, from days long gone. I have never tried it myself but my father told me that if you drink the potion, the beasts will think you are one of them and won't attack. It doesn't last long, however."

"Where is their den?"

"There's an old cave in the forest. I can show you from afar, if you like, or note it on the map. Will you kill them for me?"

"I'll try."

...

You have received a new quest: Rural Days. Monsters' Lair.

Figure out how to deal with the werewolves.

Reward: 1,000 Exp.

I didn't spend long in the village. As soon as I received a set of old leather armor from the village elder, the surrounding world went crimson.

There was no time to realize what was happening or even get scared. I was suddenly enveloped by darkness with a message coming through it: *Emergency exit*, then I heard a hissing sound and a dull light flooded the capsule.

I lay on the bed, my breathing irregular. The bed of the VR capsule had again become a smooth and rigid surface. A signal was nervously beeping at the head of the bed.

To my surprise, the interface was still there. I could still see the semitransparent icons and a message window.

...

Metabolic correction completed.

Warning, access to the VR capsule has been blocked for 8 hours until the medicines finish acting.

...

In accordance with the User Agreement (item 234.1), you have been implanted with a standard interface module. Data is displayed via contact lenses.

...

I reflexively touched my right temple, where I had felt a strong burning sensation when the game was loading. That's right. I could feel a small swelling beneath the skin, like a tiny ball had been inserted there. I didn't feel the contact lenses but I could still see the icons, although they had grown duller.

I lay there and listened to my body. It ached as if all my adventures in the virtual world had taken place for real. Was it the feedback? My muscles received nerve impulses and tensed according to those 25% of realism?

I was starving. I couldn't remember the last time I had felt so hungry! How long had I spent in the game?

A message instantly appeared.

You have played for 6 hours and 39 minutes.

It is now 12:24 pm. The outside temperature is 12 °C, the forecast is cloudy with some drizzle.

I was shown the menu of the nearest cafe offering home delivery, then I was told that I hadn't logged into my social network accounts since I had registered, invited to use the latest search system, shown the currency rates...

Close!

I wasn't against progress but this was too much.

The last thing I needed was to start getting news from all over the planet! I didn't bother configuring the unexpectedly obtained interface right away but simply switched off the information input.

...

Emergency service notifications and biomonitoring data cannot be switched off.

...

Fine. I minimized the window and clambered out of the virtual capsule. Wash my face, eat and sleep... I had no other desires.

The range of icons before my gaze immediately changed. Now I could see the controls for the smart house. How convenient! I held my gaze on the image of the shower and a wall panel slid aside, exposing the entrance to the hygiene module. I focused on the funny icon for 'rest' and a section of the wall began moving, with a made-up bed descending from the alcove. Perhaps people were mistaken in their fear of neurotechnology?

A minute later, standing under jets of hot water, I felt much better. I was overcome by a pleasant sensation of fatigue, as if I had really gone for a long walk through the forest.

My eyelids were drooping but the feeling of hunger was stronger. I turned off the water and began to look for a towel, which wasn't there. On the other hand, one of the icons in the interface grew slightly larger, as if inviting me to activate it.

I focused my gaze on it. Warm air blew from tiny openings. This truly was a smart house.

I stepped out of the shower and found a set of clean clothes ready on the table. The semitransparent menu waited for me to pay attention to it. I got dressed, ordered and only a few minutes later, heard a hissing sound in the wall. The pneumatic delivery service worked promptly and my late breakfast was served.

I slept for six hours and woke up feeling well-rested and refreshed. First thing first, I walked up to the VR capsule and put in the activation code, but to no avail.

...

Please wait for metabolic correction to be completed.

...

Fine. I decided not to call Denis just yet. I really wasn't impressed by his shady deals in virtual reality but the world itself had made an indelible impression. I wanted to return there. I couldn't help it.

Right, what time is it?

7:07 pm.

The VR capsule would unblock at around 9:00 pm. I should at least find some general information about the project. How do I develop my character? Are there ways of making money that I'd find acceptable?

I washed my face and ordered dinner. I ate slowly,

at the same time studying the information that my online search had produced. Passions were running high online, opposing opinions clashed and nobody held back their emotions as they fought to defend their point of view.

The Edge of the Abyss was the first project using full immersion technology. The incredible realism had won over billions of people all over Earth but had also pushed many away.

The prevailing opinion was that the game was too difficult. A person couldn't increase the level of some sensations but dull down others. Most players didn't want to experience pain but wanted intensity in everything else. Very few safe territories. Poor selection of races.

Frequent demands to switch off the PvP mode. Complaints about cruelty and the domination of Dark characters. *We came here for fun but we keep getting killed by other players!*

A storm of emotions, basically.

Right, and what do the developers say to all this?

There are actually numerous different races but nobody wants to play them. The immersion technology has led to the predictable problem of psychological incompatibility between the human mind and the body it must inhabit if it chooses an exotic character.

Realism in everything. That's the defining feature of the Edge of the Abyss. The developers openly warned about the possible risks and suggested that people start on 10% immersion, which they said was completely safe since a deadly wound would feel like a bruise or a deep scratch, no more...

It looked like the world had gone mad. Everyone wanted to visit the Edge of the Abyss but hardly anyone was willing to look into its depths.

Between the inhabited lands and the unexplored territories lay the so-called Dark Frontier, consisting mainly of destroyed towns united by ancient fortifications where (according to the virtual world's storyline), long-lost civilizations tried to withstand the invasion of the Abyss.

The frontier was controlled by the mysterious Shadow Clans. Some players joined them, mainly fans of hardcore. They were called Dark because of their characteristic smoky aura, which they gained from completing quests...

The timer beeped.

The VR capsule was ready for work but I hadn't yet decided on how to develop my character.

Wait. Why am I clinging to it? I'm clearly not going to continue Denis' so-called work, so perhaps I should create a new account and start from scratch?

Perhaps I will. But today I'll go in as Dan and have a better look around.

"Oh, your potions work miracles, Markusha!"

A hunchbacked old crone was leaning over me, murmuring something unintelligible. The pungent smell of herbs filled the small room. I lay on a hard bench. The light from an oil lamp left Craig's face mostly in shadow. "The spirits have been kind to him and have allowed him back into our world," the wise woman took a step back, adding, "I have done what I could."

The village elder went to walk her out while I sat up and looked around. Yes, this was the room where the emergency exit from virtual reality had occurred. But why did my character remain here instead of disappearing?

A brief hint appeared.

You were being carefully watched by the key NPC of the location.

"You're a tough one," Craig smiled and sat down at the end of the bench. "What will you do now?"

"I'll return to town."

"Just don't forget my request. It's almost a full moon. You need a full moon to kill a werewolf for certain."

"Why?" I was surprised.

"An ancient belief," he shrugged his shoulders and didn't explain further. "You have the potion. We are depending on you. By the way, you can spend the night here. It's dangerous to cross the forest at night."

"No, thank you. I have things to do."

In truth, I felt odd being there. Something seemed to press down on me, as if an evil lurked in the village. I wouldn't be surprised if one of its residents was a werewolf.

I bid the village elder farewell and went out into the yard. The moon floated among cumulus clouds, with only its edge visible. The night was warm and still. A distant and drawn-out howl came from the forest, making my skin go up in goosebumps.

"How do I reach the road?"

The villager guarding the gates opened them slightly and pointed in the right direction.

"Turn left when you reach the fork beyond the hill."

"Thank you."

My plan was simple. The road should be patrolled by the guards. All I had to was reach it. With my leather armor and makeshift spear, I felt much more confident than a day earlier. Moreover, the territories around Anchor were starting locations. The mobs here were no higher than Level 15, except for the rare quest animal, like the werewolves, or the brown bear that I had met by chance.

I could see the fork in the road in the dim moonlight. It was a couple of kilometers to the forest. There were fields all around so I had a clear view of my surroundings. Oh, a cluster of red markers appeared on the minimap. I drew cautiously closer.

...

Wild rabbit. Level 7.

...

Nibbling on cabbage.

There was another one but it looked rather odd. It was larger than normal, with an unusual smoky color. It ignored the cabbage and crept closer to something else, acting just like a predator.

...

???. Spawn of the Abyss. Level 10.

...

It made a lightning-fast jump and there was a squeak. I had enough time to notice a fading frame.

Field mouse. Level 2.

It was hunting other mobs!

...

Creatures that have been to the Abyss undergo random visible changes. Be very careful! If you can study the new species and enter its description into the Game Encyclopedia, you will receive +1 to Fame. Each increase in Fame automatically gives you 25% of the Exp that your character requires to reach the next level.

...

Hmm, quite a promising way to develop! I wasn't in a hurry right now so I could observe the behavior of this strange animal.

The ??? stood up on its back legs and sniffed the air. It wasn't interested in its fellow rabbits. Picking up my scent, it suddenly turned around and began taking huge leaps towards me.

Hit!

...

Ability found: leaping attack (damage 20 HP).

Ability found: spinning attack (damage 25 HP).

Ability found: venomous bite (damage 5 HP + 3 HP/second, duration 10 seconds).

...

I was thrown back several meters, that's how strong it was!

Blood poured down my cheek. The pain was tolerable but the poison burned and my head felt fuzzy, as if I was in a fog. I anticipated the next jump. It wasn't too difficult. The creature attacked in a straight line so all I had to do was prop the butt of the spear against the ground and angle it slightly forward.

...

You have inflicted critical damage!

...

I sure did! The smoky rabbit was pierced through by the spear's blade, twitched and fell still.

The action of the venom finished. The short fight had taken away half my life points but the mutated beast was dead. Examining the body gave me 'a piece of poisoned meat' and a 'strange skin' (properties unknown).

...

You have discovered a new type of creature from the

Abyss. Would you like to name it and enter the information into the Bestiary?

...

Well, why not?

I agreed and called the mob Smoky Rabbit.

The system didn't torture me and offered a possible description.

A normal rabbit that has been to the Abyss and has doubled its Strength and Dexterity points. At the same time, its Stamina has decreased and the number of life points has halved.

Abilities: leaping attack, spinning attack, venomous bite.

Confirm?

...

Sure! It all made sense and there were no errors.

...

Congratulations! Your article has been published. You have received 395 Exp and +1 to Fame.

A new skill is available: Naturalist.

...

I didn't take the skill. I had to first decide in which direction I was going to develop. I was glad of the gained experience, though. I was close to reaching Level 12.

It was time to keep going. My wounds had already healed a little thanks to natural regeneration. My life bar would fully recover quite soon. Wandering through the countryside was interesting but I had to find a suitable weapon, preferably with scaling damage[2] from Strength and minimal Dexterity requirements.

The incoming messages icon blinked. It was a screenshot this time, of the fork in the road and me leaning over the rabbit carcass. The description underneath proclaimed, *Player Dan_23214 discovered a new species of Abyss-altered creature!*

...

I didn't know what this Fame would get me. I suspected that I wasn't alone in this. Others undoubtedly had more achievements. It still felt nice.

I continued my journey in a better mood. The night cool was invigorating.

The plowed fields soon ended and the cart track was replaced by a rather decent paved road. I could see abandoned manors not too far away, along both sides of the road. I couldn't understand why they stood empty. The area seemed peaceful and the location was low level. A place to enjoy life.

It was still quite far to the main road and I was overcome by curiosity. Whom did the abandoned buildings belong to? What had gone wrong here? The gentle breeze made the clouds part and moonlight flooded the area. Why didn't I turn off the road and explore the abandoned buildings?

That's what I did. I found a gap in the decorative

---

[2] Scaling Damage – Bonus damage due to higher scores (above the minimal weapon requirements) of one or more characteristics of the player.

fencing and cut across the fruit garden, heading towards the dilapidated structures, their roof tiles smashed, the doors flung wide open and darkness pooling in the windows.

Weeds grew thickly between the trees. Every step was accompanied by the rustle of tall grass. The minimap was empty, with not a single worrying marker. It looked like the mansion had been abandoned long ago and even mobs avoided this place. Why could that be?

Holding my spear in front of me, I reached the path leading to the house. It used to be wider but the earth had sunk in many places and the stone blocks were lost in the dirt. Interesting... I kept stumbling across overgrown holes that looked suspiciously like funnels. The gaps in the house façade bristled with broken bricks.

I had seen dozens of these abandoned buildings from the top of the watchtower! What had happened here?

The unexpected attack came from behind and to the side, knocking me to the ground.

"Well, naturalist, how does it feel to be famous?"

I tried to leap back to my feet but no such luck! I was under a Stun debuff.

"Tie him up!" Savage_Hulk kept throwing glances in every direction as if this place terrified him.

A noose tightened around my throat and my wrists and ankles were bound as well. There were three Dark players. Impatient_Wang winked at me. He was the one who had applied the magical fetters that didn't let me move. Fierce_Zarek, the Dark Warrior that I had seen in the camp, kicked away my makeshift spear.

"Wondering how we found you? You shouldn't have advertised your achievements! Stupid newb," Hulk spat scornfully. "You thought that I wouldn't recognize the area where you looted that hare on the screenshot?"

"Savage, we really shouldn't hang around here. Let's take him to the road and torture him there. Or crit him now, but you've got to decide quickly."

"I'm not sending him to respawn!"

"Then let's drag him away from here and find a calmer place."

"No. We'll teach him a lesson. One that he'll remember for the rest of his life. Go into the house and find signs of a portal. When you find one, try to activate it!"

"Are you completely out of your mind?" Wang looked seriously frightened. "What if the Shadows start coming?"

"We've got auras! They won't touch us!"

"Yeah, have you checked? Have you?"

"Calm the heck down! Do what I tell you or you can piss off." Savage snarled back.

The Stun had worn off but I still couldn't move. There was no point in talking to these bastards. I'd survive the pain somehow, and learn the lesson too.

Looking at my frame, Hulk pulled out a dagger. The dully glinting blade suddenly grew longer as the metal was shrouded in a black flame. Slowly, with obvious experience, he sunk it into my back, not too deeply, however. Blood spattered and there was a flash of pain. My life bar shrunk by a third.

I clenched my teeth.

"Patient, are you? Stubborn? How long are you going to last?" The blade went in a little deeper and twisted slowly, producing another burst of pain that made my vision darken. "You will delete your account," the Dark player promised. "Or you'll become a dribbling vegetable," he added, pulling the dagger out of the wound and casting a minor regeneration charm. "Take him into the house!"

I kept my teeth clenched and said nothing. I wasn't going to demean myself by talking to such scum. Nobody could convince me that they would somehow be different in real life, turning into normal guys. Even in that distant time when virtual worlds only existed on consoles and PCs, you could tell who was who. Reality with full immersion only made these differences more pronounced.

"Wang, did you find a portal?"

"Over here!" The voice of the Dark Mage came from

some distance away.

I was dragged through a series of trashed rooms. I noted quite a lot despite the pulsating pain. A serious battle had taken place here once upon a time. The furniture had been swept aside and the walls were covered in slashes and burn marks. A fire had also ripped through the building. Frost patterns could be seen here and there, as if the combat magic had left its mark on the columns and friezes.

This used to be a rich mansion. I doubted that it had been developed and built for an NPC. More likely that this used to be the home of a player who had donated plenty to the virtual world. What had caused all the damage?

"Here!" Wang pointed to the sunken floor tiles forming a stone circle. "This is where the Abyss burst through. Listen, Savage, maybe we shouldn't risk it? Who knows where the portal will lead?"

"Cast it!"

"Fine. But if we get wiped out, you owe me compensation. I'm not risking my stuff and they'll definitely drop because of our auras!"

"All right, enough whining, cast it!"

Fierce_Zarek dragged me to the wall and threw me down like a sack of potatoes.

My eyes met those of Savage_Hulk. He must have read a lot in my gaze because he immediately lost it, "What, you think we'll get in trouble? Ha, suck on it. You'll kick the bucket, of course, but not by our hands!

An incredible series of respawns awaits you," he promised balefully as Wang set out black candles and drew a circle of symbols.

"Ready. Move back, you two, and put him in the circle!"

"Where will the portal open to?"

"I have no idea! It's totally random!" Wang bared his teeth in a grin. "Let's hurry it up before something makes its way from over there!"

I was dragged along the floor again and pushed into the dip formed by the sunken tiles.

A purple-black flame shot up silently. I felt like a splinter swept up in a violent torrent. My mind went dark and then came back.

I couldn't see anything. There was the sound of dripping water. It stank terribly and I seemed to be lying on a pile of refuse, barely alive.

Messages flashed before my mental gaze.

...

You have used an abandoned portal, left over from the time of the Abyss invasion.

Contact with the previous point has been lost. The closest respawn circle has been activated.

...

My HP bar was barely in the red. No weapons.

It was pitch black. Grim sounds echoed back and forth.

Hissing. Scuttling steps approached from different directions. My body was pierced by terrible pain as if someone had splashed acid on me and then a large sign appeared before me.

...

YOU HAVE DIED.

You have lost 1,290 Exp.

You have lost an item: makeshift spear.

Respawn in 19:59, 19:58...

Would you like to leave the VR capsule?

Warning, frequent emergency exits lead to increased use of the sensory gel. Don't forget to obtain more consumables.

...

Twenty minutes of waiting? I'll suffer through it somehow. I had no desire to purchase additional consumables. I didn't even know how much they cost.

...

Leave the VR capsule?

...

The sign blinked at me persistently.

I selected 'No'. I had ways to occupy myself since the interface still worked.

I opened the logs and read,

You have moved ????? kilometers.

You have found a new region: (Enter name).

Achievement gained: Trailblazer. Nobody has been here since the Abyss invaded. You are the first (+1 Fame, +5% to land travel speed, +395 Exp).

New quest available: **Survival Environment.**

Find a way to survive and rapidly advance to level

30.

Reward: Your Adaptability will increase by 2 points. Time to complete: 48 hours.

New quest available: **Terra Incognita.**

Explore your surroundings and uncover at least 50% of the map.

Reward: +1 to Fame.

...

I must have missed these messages when I lost consciousness. Oh well. They should be listed in my quest journal. I'll be able to accept them once I respawn.

All right, who killed me? It happened so quickly and unclearly. I turned to the logs again.

...

You heard a noise.

Unidentified creatures.

??? attacks with toxic spit. Damage over time 10 HP/sec.

??? attacks with toxic spit. Damage over time 10 HP/sec.

??? attacks with toxic spit. Damage over time 10 HP/sec.

You have died.

The timer continued its countdown. Why didn't I just

leave virtual reality and to hell with it all?

I'd mucked up the character (in the state that Denis needed it). I went up a level and lost the Aura of Immunity. It was unlikely that the helpless and unevenly leveled up mule could find any work now and he would be easy prey outside the town walls. It would be easier to create a new one.

So why was I digging around in the interface, stoically awaiting regeneration?

The answer was simple — I was hooked. So much had happened in less than a day. I'd plunged into the virtual world like into a whirlpool, hungrily absorbing the incredible realism, feeling young and full of energy again.

I had no idea how it would all turn out but I wanted to get out of the trouble that I'd found myself in, return to the starting location and get back at the Dark ones. That's just to start with.

It was decided. I was staying. I'd see how it all worked and if my first impression turned out to be correct, I'd get my own account. Where would I get the money for my own VR capsule? Only time would tell. I'd solve the problems as they came and in the meantime, I'd use the available access.

No weapons. I doubted that I could kill someone with my bare fists.

00:49

Was I ready?

00:10

Chapter Three

WHAT A CREEPY place. I'd respawned underground, on the shore of a tainted and reeking creek. The thick fumes, gloom and rustling... My nerves were wound up tight.

A long room with a wide crack in the ceiling. The gap emitted a weak light with some plant roots hanging through it.

The respawn point was marked with a flat and roughly hewn stone.

Without moving or showing any other signs of life, I continued to examine my surroundings. My eyes became gradually used to the dimness. Not far from me, on the damp and slimy wall, hovered a revolting-looking creature.

...

Centipede. Level 13.

My throat closed up. Everything looked way too realistic here. I was lying on a mountain of garbage piled up beneath the crack, trying to pretend to be nothing but rags, and with good reason. The creature was close and I was probably within its aggro zone. I wouldn't be able to break through its chitin with my fists. I needed a stick at least.

The nervous tremble wouldn't leave me. Very slowly, I stretched out my hand, feeling the various junk beneath my fingers.

The centipede noticed me after all and curled itself threateningly. Why wasn't it attacking?

Only then I noticed the thin, rapidly fading golden lining marking a circle around me. A hint immediately appeared. Apparently, I couldn't be attacked by mobs in the first few minutes after respawn, but as soon as the aura faded completely, so would my temporary protection!

I hadn't felt so many acute emotions in a long time. Denis wasn't lying, it really was a full-scale virtual reality, a digital world where one could live!

Or die a painful death — I could see venomous saliva drip from the disgusting creature's mandibles. I frantically dug through the junk but nothing appropriate turned up. I was going to be killed by a few venomous spits!

Another mob came scuttling along the wall. My hand touched something solid and a message appeared at once,

You have found the remnant of a rusted sword.

Durability 9. Damage 4-5, multiplied by the current Strength score.

...

I snatched up the weapon and attacked at once. The sword struck the stone wall and produced a shower of sparks. Did the creature swerve out of the way?

No! It wasn't fast enough... It was too flimsy and was sliced in half. I got rid of the second one just as easily. Phew... I took a few steps back, sat down on a rock and breathed heavily. So much stress!

A blurry, hunched over silhouette suddenly flitted through the gloom. Some kind of undead? It was hard to tell in the dark. I leaped up and turned, but it was too late. With a powerful thrust, the zombie drove its spear right under my ribs.

The pain and surprise made me scream and hesitate, and I immediately received two more hits.

The surroundings grew darker and were replaced by a blood-black fog. A large sign appeared:

YOU HAVE DIED.

The time between a virtual death and respawn was not only a serious psychological test but also a chance to plan further actions.

Lines of system messages glowed in the dark.

You have died.

You have lost one level.

Durability of torn clothing: 0.

…

Yep, one of the inventory slots now contained 'rags'.

Well, what did I expect? Savage_Hulk had clearly predicted my near future. He knew that the Abyss portals lead to locations where my character couldn't survive.

I felt mad. They've messed with the wrong guy! I simply wasn't expecting an attack from behind!

I opened the character panel.

Dan, Level 11

Race: Human
Class: Warrior
Life Force 10
Strength 11
Dexterity 5
Stamina 12
Intellect 5
Adaptability 7
Luck 5
Charisma 5
Damage (fists) 22
Effect of the Abyss 0
Mutations 0

Primary skills:

Race bonus +2 to Adaptability
Class bonus +1 to Strength, +2 to Stamina
HP 200/200
Maximum load 55 kg
Dodge Chance 5%
Physical Energy 60
Mental Energy 25
Resistance 7%
Chance of Successful Hit 2.5%
Attractiveness 5

Physical Defense 11+20.3
Agility 5
Faster Regeneration 6%
Learning Ability 5, Mental Defense 12.5
Adaptive Leveling (none)
Chance of Finding Items 2.5%
Possible number of NPC companions 1
Damage (broken sword) 44-55

Secondary skills:

Battle technique + 5% to physical defense when using light and medium shields

I had another ten minutes until I could return to the game.

I should look at my equipment and inventory, see if anything could serve as a weapon.

So, what did I have?

Torn clothing. Durability 0, defense 0.

Old leather jacket (light armor). Durability 25, defense 8.

Old leather pants (light armor). Durability 15, defense 5.

Old leather gloves (light armor). Durability 7, defense 2.

Old leather boots. Durability 17, defense 5.

Interesting how the character's outfit panel was designed. There were slots for everyday garments, so I could wear my rags under my armor.

A quick calculation showed that I currently had 31.3 units of Physical Defense. Twenty of them came from the gear, 11 from Strength and another 0.31 as a Dexterity bonus. Why was I adding up these numbers? Because I was planning to survive. Simply put, my defense would be automatically subtracted from the incoming damage. If, for example, the physical damage from an enemy sword was 50, I would be hit with 18.7 points. With my current HP, I would be able to survive 10 such hits but the 11th would send me into respawn. Things were much worse with my Resistance. Toxins, poisons, bleeding — my character couldn't really cope with any of this. Seven percent of resistance was too low. I would have to evade venomous spits and other such nastiness.

I was leaning towards the thought that the underground was a simple water drainage system located beneath a large town. The tunnels would surely have vertical shafts that I could use to climb up to the surface.

My mind was glitching. I felt overwhelming terror at times, which would quickly fade away. There were plenty of reasons for fear and doubt. I'd landed in a digital environment whose rules I was not familiar with. Would my life experience help me?

I looked through my inventory again. Apart from my outfit, I had a flask of water, a vial with a potion given to me by Craig for the quest, a stale piece of bread, and the mysterious Guardian's Amulet and Soul Crystal.

It certainly wasn't much. On the upside, I could run quite quickly over short distances since I had good Stamina and the character was carrying only 25% of the maximum load, which also increased speed.

It's decided. I'd explore the nearest tunnel. Perhaps I'd get lucky and find a way to the surface straight away.

The reeking gloom obscured my vision.

I wished I had a torch. I could try and make one out of some branches and rags, but how would I get a fire going in these clammy catacombs? A chilly dampness came from the wide arched doorway. Tendrils of fog drifted along the ground.

The vapors were quite acidic! I got used to the smell but the system messages about the gradual reduction in my outfit's Durability made me wonder if I should be barging straight ahead.

I looked around me. No centipedes so far. The zombie was about twenty meters away from me, digging through the garbage. I couldn't read the frame from here but his leather armor and rusty spear made him a dangerous opponent. I wouldn't head that way.

The tunnels were full of toxic vapors. Why did I think that? My throat started to burn and tickle whenever the light underground breeze carried the reeking miasmas towards me.

A section of the thick brick wall near the respawn point had been shattered. Another tunnel could be seen beyond the uneven hole, which was clearly not part of the rainwater catchment system. I'd leave that tunnel for later.

The fog grew thicker in the meantime. The mustard streaks were no longer drifting close to the ground but rising higher.

Well, let's see what my life experience was good for. Was the digital world realistic enough that a few simple tricks would work here?

I took my ragged clothing from the inventory and dampened it with the water from my flask, thus making a primitive breathing mask. It would filter out some of the poison.

The zombie had noticed me in the meantime. He dropped what he was doing and was watching me from a distance but not yet attacking. Not the best neighbor. There was no more time to waste, I had to get out of here!

Four tunnels led out of the collector. Two to the right of the respawn circle and two to the left. I could discern a faint green glow of unknown origin coming from one of them. Yes, it could be dangerous, but pitch blackness was worse. Forwards!

I took a deep breath, held it and ran as fast as I could. Through the poisonous fog, splashing through the fetid puddles. The light gradually grew brighter. Not even small animals lived among the toxic vapors. My Stamina dropped quickly, and I had to slow down to a walk when the bar got to almost zero. Yep, it was regenerating, but slowly.

I took gasping breaths of air.

...

You have sustained mild poisoning (2 HP/sec).

Effect: dizziness and weakness. Strength has been reduced by 1 point until the effect of the poison wears off. Stamina regeneration is slowed down by 25%.

...

Swaying and holding onto the wall with my left hand, I finally got out of the toxic cloud and found myself... in a dead end!

The tunnel had been destroyed. The roof looked like it was about to collapse at any moment. There were signs of mudslides everywhere. The most impressive sight, however, were the moss colonies emitting the green glow.

The debuff continued to weaken me but the risk was worth it! Now I could make a torch.

There were two types of moss. The first spread out like a carpet. The second type looked more like seaweed, with a profusion of glimmering threads hanging down from the ceiling. I gathered some and wound them around a stick that I had found in the same spot, getting quite a good source of fluorescent light as a result, which dispelled the darkness by about a meter.

I waited for all the negative effects to pass, then held my breath again and raced back.

I was sitting on the regeneration stone and waiting for my strength and poison-affected health to recover. I'd noticed that HP regenerated twice as fast at the respawn point. It was a valuable observation, considering that I didn't have any potions.

Hey, the zombie had crept closer! He was hiding behind a pile of broken bricks, thinking that I couldn't see him. I didn't like having him so close. I really needed to get rid of him but lacked the strength for it right now. His weapon was longer, too. By the time I got close enough to strike him with my sword fragment, he'd be able to stab me several times with his spear, despite the slowness of the undead.

All right, no time to sit around. My Life bar had almost completely recovered and the poisoning had worn off.

To the next tunnel! I held my breath and ran as fast as I could. The handmade torch turned out to be a great help. At least I didn't trip over any rocks underfoot. I rapidly crossed the dangerous part, reached a section of tunnel clean of vapors and immediately spotted an arched doorway in the wall. I stopped to catch my breath, then looked through it. Perfect! A stone shaft with rusted brackets led upwards.

Without waiting for the poisoning to pass, I start climbing, having secured the torch behind me.

I saw a rusted grate. Excellent, I'm nearly there!

The hinges made a long screech and debris showered down on my head. I lifted the barrier up a little and looked outside. It was dark and damp. Another underground level?

I'd find out in a minute, as soon as I recovered some Stamina.

I sat on the floor and looked around me. The room appeared abandoned, like it hadn't been used in a very long time. A stone gutter ran up at an angle, ending at a nailed-up archway. Pale rays of daylight could be seen through the gaps.

I used the sword fragment to lever several boards loose. I'd made it!

"Guards!" Came the sudden female screech. "It's a necro! It's coming from the old sewerage system!"

I heard the clatter of boots and jangling of weapons. I was almost blind after the darkness in the dungeon.

"Get ready to fire! Burn the monster!"

"Wait, it looks human!"

"What human? Can't you see his green aura? He's a necro for sure!"

Whom were they talking about?

"Hey, guys, I haven't got a necrotic aura. My moss is glowing!"

"Burn the monster!"

I recoiled instinctively and tumbled down the sloping gutter just in time. A fireball knocked out the remaining flimsy boards and the roaring flame scorched the stone walls, leaving soot behind.

"Hey! I'm just lost!"

My voice was lost in the thunder. The spinning, smoldering sparks went out and something burst open with a sharp twang and a shower of icy fragments. Frost rapidly spread along the walls. Oh, so if I hadn't been burnt to a crisp, I'd be killed by the ice? The town guards were terrified of the underground for some reason and weren't willing to take the risk. They must have had good reasons, but what was I supposed to do?

"Block the entrance!" came the order. "Quickly! Fire and ice aren't going to stop it."

Damn. It seemed like they had taken me for a highly dangerous monster.

The ground shook. Elemental power was being used. High-level mages must have joined the patrol surprisingly quickly, as I doubted that the average person was capable of such a thing — the walls suddenly lost their solidity and began to melt as if the stone had turned to wax.

I didn't have time to retreat into the shaft. There was a crunch of bones, an instant of unbearable pain, and a system message appeared among the crimson darkness:

YOU HAVE DIED.

You have lost one level.

I must have lost not only a level but also consciousness because I didn't remember anything from the twenty minutes between death and revival. I came to in the respawn circle.

A reeking creek gurgled quietly. Rats squeaked among the piles of refuse.

A centipede stopped in a corner of the vaulted ceiling but wasn't yet reacting to my appearance.

I lay without moving.

The stench no longer caused me to retch as I had gotten used to it. But if this kept going, the sensory realism would be the end of me. The aftermath of the pain kept me paralyzed but I was in no hurry to get to my feet. I surreptitiously inspected my surroundings. The familiar zombie was sitting with his back to me, stolidly digging around in the packed garbage.

My eye was twitching. There was a nervous tic in my cheek. My wheezy breathing sounded too loud in my own ears, loud enough to make that freak turn around...

What a great reality we have invented. The very embodiment of kindness and civility, we're intelligent creatures after all, right? So why did our imagination create such things?

Away with these thoughts. Philosophy wasn't going to help me here. It was just my nerves.

I sat up with a groan and checked my inventory. I hadn't dropped anything during my virtual death. The sword fragment and the handmade torch were still there. I looked at the moss threads wrapped around the stick and tried to read their properties.

I thought the game would inform me that my low Intellect didn't allow me to identify the item, plus the fact that I lacked the Herbalist skill, but the system unexpectedly offered a pop-up hint.

Crooked handmade staff.

Additional: weak necrotic aura. +10 response from

the undead. -50 response from any living creature. 1% chance of recovering a small amount of health when striking an enemy.

Warning: prolonged use of the item may project the aura onto its owner. Effects have not been studied.

...

I threw away my handicraft with fear and disgust. I would be more careful in the future.

The pain in my chest wouldn't go away...

The aura surrounding the resurrection stone hadn't yet faded when a system warning suddenly appeared:

Session time allowed as per medical indications has run out.

Additional metabolic correction required.

Forced exit commenced.

Apologies for the inconvenience. During the time that you undergo medical procedures, your character will remain protected at the resurrection point.

Chapter Four

IT WAS ALREADY evening in the real world.

I didn't feel too good, that was true. I was tired. My muscles were aching. I didn't know what exactly the metabolic correction system was doing to me but I couldn't see much benefit from my time in the VR capsule.

I needed to get a good night's sleep. Tomorrow was another day. I took a shower and was just about to have supper when I heard a suspicious noise. A quiet whine, as if a servomotor was idling somewhere.

I listened carefully. The sound seemed to be coming from the front door. The indicator lights were green on the security panel so could there be a fault in the system?

They say that full immersion in the digital space doesn't affect a person in any way. What utter crap!

After hours spent in the virtual capsule, I was still on edge. The stress from the virtual deaths still hadn't let go of me. I didn't feel safe, as if Denis' apartment was an extension of the underground.

Who was it scratching at the door?

I hadn't removed the contact lenses so I connected to the security camera through the smart house control interface.

As I thought. Three young men, strangers, were in the corridor. Two were glancing around, clearly nervous, while the third squatted down by the access panel and was trying to break the electronic lock using a compact device.

The camera's microphone was working and I could hear their hushed voices. "We shouldn't have come... We've sent him to be rekilled[3] and that's that. Why take the risk?"

"Dan owes us money now!" Hissed the guy trying to break the lock. "We missed the caravan because of him!"

"Since when?"

"He helped the elf woman escape and she reported us! The town guards would have never gone into the forest otherwise!"

"And since you can't get to her, you've decided to take it out on Dan, is that it? Use your head! This isn't VR. If we get arrested here..."

---

[3] Rekill – a player's death immediately after respawning.

"Wang, shut up! I owe five grand in real life now! The caravan was not supposed to reach the town. He's ruined all our plans."

"What do you expect to get from Dan?"

"We'll see. How long is this going to take?"

"We could have just buzzed the door. We used to party together!"

"Ha, like he'd open the door for us! I bet he's sitting inside and shaking in his boots! How much longer?"

"Here, I've opened it!"

The front door jerked aside. The three guys pushed their way into the apartment and stopped to stare at me.

"Where's Dan?"

"He's gone for a walk."

"And who the hell are you?"

"Not anyone you should worry about. I suggest that you leave before I call the police. You're not going to get away with just a warning for breaking and entering."

"I'm gonna snap your bloody arms!" One of the guys pulls out a rubber truncheon with a taser. "Sit down and shut your trap!"

"Or what?" I stirred him up on purpose. They didn't see me as a worthwhile opponent. Fools. I thought the blond, sturdy youth of about twenty was Savage_Hulk.

"You've asked for it!" he charged at me but his strike landed on thin air while the discharge from the taser only damaged one of the apartment's subsystems. Sparks flew from the wall and tendrils of acrid smoke began to seep from a barely noticeable gap in the paneling. The fire alarm started screaming at once.

"Let's get out of here!" Wang shouted.

"Oh no, you don't!" I ripped the police truncheon out of Hulk's hands and the rest was all on automatic. Wang got zapped with the taser and went limp, I struck Savage on the shin, making him howl with pain and collapse without reaching the door, and I stopped the last guy, who must have been the Dark Warrior, with a powerful stun to the head. He wavered, his gaze growing dull and looking like he was about to faint.

"Would you like to talk now?"

"You're dead! You're so dead!" Savage hissed.

We didn't get a chance to have a heart-to-heart. I was going to call the police myself, but the keepers of the peace responded surprisingly quickly. A patrol car must have been nearby and my 'helpful' neighbors had obviously heard the disturbance.

The police acted by the book, I must say. They handcuffed me first. Right out of the shower, wearing only my boxers and with a cudgel in my hands, I must have looked highly suspicious, while the three young men groaning on the floor appeared to be the victims at first glance.

I didn't resist arrest. We'd sort it out soon.

"Why are you injuring people, Andrey Dmitrievich? They came to visit a friend and you attacked them. Have you been drinking today? Have you taken anything? You don't look very well."

"That's not how it was, Captain. They broke into the apartment."

"Really? The three victims are reporting the opposite and they're not contradicting each other. There is no record of a break-in as the discharge destroyed the security system. I think you did that on purpose. By the way, where did you obtain a police taser? It's not something one can buy in the store."

This was looking bad. I was literally being set up. I couldn't figure out why the captain wasn't interested in finding out the truth and was taking the side of the Dark players but I lost all interest in talking to him. I would just be wasting my time.

"I have the right to make one call."

He raises an eyebrow. "To your lawyer?" He was practically laughing in my face.

"Something like that. Give me back my communicator. I won't say another word. One call and you can lock the cell."

He gave me the communicator with a dismissive gesture. "I'll be present for the conversation."

I shrugged and dialed a number. It took a while for

the person on the other end to pick up the phone since it was the middle the night. "Max? Did you recognize my voice? Good. Police Precinct 214. Come at once. Yes, problems. Got it, I'm an adult. OK, I'll be waiting."

"That's it?" The captain became wary. "Who is Max? Your drinking buddy? Another army veteran?"

"You'll see soon enough."

The lock clicked and the barred door slid aside with a rustle.

"Out you go," Max Pekhov, my old platoon commander, shook his head. "You haven't changed at all, Andrey. You're still as reckless as before."

"Rich boys?" I shook his hand and nodded subtly in the direction of the 'victims'.

"Nope. This has nothing to do with the golden youth. They're the offspring of local gangsters. Come on, I'll drive you home and we'll talk on the way."

"We need to drop by my nephew's apartment first."

"What for?"

"I have to collect the access chip to his account."

"You surprise me. Have you gotten hooked on VR?"

"It's a matter of principle."

"You haven't fought enough in real life?"

"Max, stop nagging. Thanks for getting me out of that mess. I'll sort the rest out myself."

"No, you won't."

"Meaning?"

"Not here. The walls have ears."

Yeah. Some popular expressions have become literal in this era of high tech.

"Fine," I decided not to argue.

Our paths diverged several years ago, during the Asian Conflict. We kept in touch but rang each other only rarely. I never returned to the forces after my injury. Life had scattered us far and wide.

The sky above the megacity had turned a predawn gray. An old, unpretentious CUV stood idling in the parking lot, a little way from the patrol cars.

I got into the back seat and Max sat in front. The driver turned around and stretched out his hand in greeting, "Alexei."

"Andrey," I said and shook his hand.

"Max, where are we going?"

"To the Enthusiasts Avenue and then we'll see."

"Okay," the car pulled smoothly out of the parking lot and I sensed a real beast hidden under the hood of the unassuming CUV. Clearly a supercharged engine, custom built.

We drove to Denis' apartment, I took the chip and wondered what to do with the broken door.

"Don't worry," Max noticed my hesitation and patted me on the shoulder. "I've already sorted it out. The technicians are coming, they'll fix the lock and alarm the apartment as well. It won't do to leave the capsule unguarded," he sat down in an armchair. "So, tell me, how did you end up in the Edge of the Abyss?"

My story was pretty short, as you know. It only took five minutes.

"A word of advice?" Max looked at me, his eyes narrowed.

"Yeah?"

"Don't go back into VR."

"Why's that?"

"Because of the level of realism. Not many can handle it, trust me."

"Can you explain?"

"You only die once..." he glared at me. "This phrase is no longer true, don't you see? Everything is different there. You die and are reborn, again and again."

"I'll manage."

"Are you sure?"

"No, I'm not, but I intend to try again. I've got some unfinished business. I can always reduce the sensory level."

"That's what everyone thinks. That's what the developers want you to think. In reality, the reverse is true: even at 10% percent of realism, frequent respawns can send a person mad."

"Then I'll try not to die!"

"So, persuading you is pointless? All right, it's your decision," he shrugged. "You've got the chip? Let's go, it'd be best if you lie low in the real world for a few days."

"Wait. Thank you for your help, but why do I need to leave?"

"Let's go, don't get stubborn now. The local thugs have found out your address and they won't leave you alone. They'll send someone better."

"Seriously?"

"Times change quickly," Max smiled crookedly in response to my surprised look. "Criminals are striving to get into the digital world. It's much simpler there. Almost no accountability since everything is part of the gaming process," his lips twisted in a grimace again. "You've seen it yourself. They won't stop at anything. If someone gets in their way in VR, they'll find them in the real world."

It all sounded quite persuasive. Max obviously knew what he was talking about and wouldn't be joking about such things.

"All right. Let's go."

We went out onto the street and got into the car. Alexei immediately drove out of the yard and joined the flow of vehicles.

"How do they make money in there?" I resumed our interrupted conversation.

"Oh, on everything. For example, low-level locations have a lot of paid items, such as expensive outfits on weak characters. People hunt them down and kill the players, mainly by using high Luck scores or special abilities in case of drops. The obtained equipment ends up with the merchants. The end goal is to sell stolen goods and convert game currency into real money."

Considering the amount of jargon coming out of my old platoon commander's mouth, he'd spent a while in the Edge of the Abyss!

"Isn't attacking another player in safe locations punishable with an account block?"

"It is," Max agreed. "However, there are many ways to trick an inexperienced player into PvP mode, causing them to break the rules and become a justified target. Anyway, a player is under the Aura of Immunity for the first 10 levels and then they have to protect themselves. Don't forget that the Edge of the Abyss is virtual reality, meaning it fully imitates real life."

"Without any laws?"

"No, why? There is an acceptable PvP range. It is calculated simply as the level of your character +20. There are no bans within it, except that you might end up with a negative aura and ruin your relationship with the local NPCs. Basically, anyone can choose whether to remain in town and be protected by the guards, join a powerful faction or risk going off alone beyond the town walls. Most people take that risk. The Edge of the Abyss statistics show that millions of users log into it every day from all over the world. People want fun."

"And land in a meat grinder?"

Max only shrugged. "There is an excess of blood and virtual deaths. Almost nobody sticks to the 10% realism that the developers recommend. The digital space presents too many temptations for the modern person. This world turned out to be harsh but it is the result of our actions, which can't be denied."

"You mean there's no way to fight the Dark players?"

"No, why? You can, using the game's methods. Which is the surest way, actually."

"I don't understand."

"Capturing and controlling territories. Creating truly safe regions, where a Dark aura is no good even for quests."

"Is that what you're doing?"

Max hesitated but then nodded. "I'm a member of the Mongoose Clan. We ensure safety on our lands."

"Can I join you?"

"No, not yet."

"Why?"

"Firstly, I don't decide who gets to join. Secondly, your level of realism is too low. Our test for respawn is at least 75% of immersion. Thirdly, a player needs to have a Standard account and be at least Level 40 to join the Clan."

"Why is it so strict?"

"Would you take complete newbies into battle with you when your regular enemy has a hundred kills and can put up with pain that you can't tolerate?"

I was silent. The sensory realism really did change everything.

"Don't feel bad. I'll give you recommendations for

upgrades and permission to log in on our lands. You'll be able to take a good look around, try yourself against mobs and only then decide whether you want to stay."

"Thank you for the offer but it won't work. Unless I can delete a character and create a new one."

"Why?" Max was surprised.

"I'm somewhere in the Dark Frontier right now. Savage and his gang sent me there using an ancient portal."

"Why didn't you say so before?" Max perked up.

"What's so special about my situation?"

"The Dark Frontier is located beyond the Wild Lands. Not many have been there since the Abyss invaded. We tried to organize a raid but we haven't reached it so far. I'll be blunt, information from your map would be very useful. Frontier items are priceless!"

"Right. It's easier to draw water with a sieve than farm there. My character has already dropped to Level 9."

"What was your level before?"

"Level 12 when I landed there."

"Are you willing to log in again?"

"I'll try."

"Then keep it together. We'll get to you. Do you have a recording of when the Dark players opened the portal?"

"No, there was too much going on."

"That's a shame!" Max was genuinely disappointed. "You certainly know how to find trouble," he chuckled.

"As I've said, people don't change with age."

"Where are we going?"

"To be honest, we're just doing circles right now."

"Are you trying to decide whether to take me to your secret base?" I felt hurt.

"Don't sulk. It's not my base, it belongs to the Clan. I'd sent a request and was waiting for a reply."

"Did you get it?"

"Not yet. Lex, let's head to our place," he told the driver. "Circumstances have changed."

"No problem."

We turned sharply, circled around the old city lanes for a while, making sure that we weren't being followed and then headed to the center of the megacity again. Thankfully, it was still early morning and there was no traffic.

"May I see the account information?" Max asked.

"Here," I gave him the chip.

He activated his personal nanocomputer, entered the login and password that I gave him. Max's eyebrows rose in surprise. "How long have you been playing?"

"Less than a day if you add up all the sessions."

"Yet you've already received a personal mission and related artifacts!"

"Do you mean the crystal and the amulet?"

"Yup.

"What's so special about them?"

"They're unidentified items. Which means they're from the Abyss."

Alexei pulled into a parking lot while we were talking.

Holographic ads glowed on every side. There was a great number of cars despite the early hour.

Mainstream Digital Entertainment Center.

"Seriously? This is your base?" I must have looked completely baffled.

"Mongoose is a combat clan," Max replied. "Renting a fully-equipped center gives us a lot of advantages."

"For example?"

"We don't destroy families and don't place our loved ones in danger. We work in shifts. A day in the capsule, two days at home. When we need everyone online, for example, for a raid or an attack on our lands, there are enough capabilities here. This place has everything, from back-up VR capsules to rest zones."

"So, players from other regions can't be members of your clan?"

"There are other centers. Sorry, I can't answer many of your questions right now."

We made our way inside through the service entry. We passed along the internal second-floor balcony above the dancefloor and bar. There were a lot of people below us and it was impossible to tell who had come to party and who was relaxing after a combat shift.

"In here," Max opened an inconspicuous door. We found ourselves in a long, radial corridor. "This is the guest wing," Max said curtly. "This is your room, I'll leave you to settle in while I make my report. Get some sleep. We'll talk later."

I followed his advice without too much musing. It had been quite a night. I was utterly exhausted.

I was woken up by a dual tone.

"Open."

The door slid aside and Max walked into the room.

"You've had quite a snooze," he smiled broadly and sat in the armchair. "Time to get up and wash your face!"

"Right. You're giving me orders now?" I tried to joke. I actually felt quite tense. My life had changed so abruptly.

I came back after about 5 minutes. The small table between the armchairs had dishes laid out on it. A light breakfast.

"Have you got any good news for me, Max?" I took a sip of the juice and was surprised to find that it was real juice.

"It's all quiet at Denis' apartment so far. Considering that you refused to work as a mule for the Dark players, your reputation is in the positive with our clan."

"Max, I have a request. I know the information is out there on the net, but I don't have time to dig through the flood and separate fact from fiction.

Explain what's going on, will you?"

He nodded as if had expected the question. "What exactly are you interested in?"

"Why is the world called the Edge of the Abyss? Who are the Dark ones? Where does their aura come from and what advantages does it give them?"

Max took a sip of his coffee. "Have you head of the Land of the Chosen?"

"No."

"Ten years ago, it was an elite private club for very wealthy people. The first full-scale virtual reality and, to access it, fully immersive capsule technology. A sensory realism of 100%, plus it was a fantasy world set in the pre-industrial age with an untouched biosphere. A digital Eden, basically. There was a large dollop of magic, mysticism and alchemy added. It contained a leveling up system, boundless territory for exploration, stunningly beautiful towns — all for a small number of users, who had absolute power in that world."

"So how did they share it?" I couldn't help but ask.

"They didn't, initially," Max replied. "Their paths didn't cross at all, unless they wished it. Each one had their own town and endless space, as well as thousands of NPC subjects, who were generated by neural network technology."

"What's the problem, then? There's a reason why you started with this, right?"

"Do you remember the beginning of the Asian

Conflict?"

"A rhetorical question. It was scary. Personally, I thought the nuclear strikes were a realistic option."

"You weren't the only one. That was when the Land of the Chosen began to show signs of strain. When the global economic crisis hit, compounded by the fear of possible nuclear strikes, many financial empires collapsed. You remember how it happened. Sudden bankruptcies, currencies soaring and crashing, defaults..."

"To be honest, I wasn't really interested in the global economy in those days. We were right in the thick of it. Have you forgotten?"

"No, I haven't," Max touched his personal nanocomputer bracelet and the holographic image of an elderly man appeared in the air between us. "Ernst Goodman. Founder of the first digital shelter. He had lost his fortune in the space of a few days and people say he was suicidal before he found a way to fix his situation. Goodman owned one of the islands in the Land of the Chosen. It was all that he had left. When the conflict escalated and the world balanced on the edge of a nuclear war, he bought a bunker that nobody wanted, left over from the Cold War. He took out a loan, bought a batch of VR capsules, and offered anyone who wanted to save themselves a place in the Land of the Chosen."

I snorted.

"His plan worked," Max continued. "He got his

fortune back within a few weeks. Places in the VR capsules cost an astronomical amount but the fear of what was coming was stronger and all the available spots were snapped up. The idea was picked up at once since the owners of the digital worlds were the richest and most influential people of the world. The continents and islands of the Land of the Chosen were populated at an incredible rate. It turned out to be an incredibly profitable business. The manufacture of VR capsules had been perfected and put into production by that point. The plan was to use them for long-distance space flights. By the time the Asian Conflict reached its peak, the population of the digital world was several dozen million people. Global tensions rapidly found their way into virtual reality and the digital Eden began to arm itself, with the first clans being created. Things didn't progress to large-scale confrontations as the Asian Conflict was finally resolved, but full immersion technology had reached the masses. When the hysteria subsided, it became clear that the past was not coming back. The exclusive club for a select few became a densely populated virtual space. People didn't want to abandon it."

"I was recovering in hospital at the time."

"And I had quit and was trying to find a way to make a living. We were lucky, in a way."

"Lucky?!"

"The Land of the Chosen was hacked. You won't find any official information about this, only rumors on shady forums.

"The Abyss is a virus?"

"I'd put it another way. The Abyss is content that has been altered. Nobody knows the exact date of the attack. There were no obvious glitches but there were gradual NPC mutations. Cults of the Abyss appeared in some regions. The NPCs started praying to some sort of Shadows. Then came the catastrophe. A section of the digital space disappeared. Portals appeared in other zones, from which poured forth disfigured but incredibly strong creatures. The Land of the Chosen underwent an emergency shut down. They avoided a lot of casualties that way. They wanted to completely freeze the project but it didn't work. Over a billion users all over the world had given away all they had for a place under the digital sun. If access was taken away from them, mass rioting would have swept through the Earth in days. A multinational management corporation was urgently created and given control of the project. They tried to recover the Land of the Chosen but the rollback didn't work."

"So how did they find a solution?"

"Strong NPC factions were introduced by the developers. They wiped out the beasts that had invaded and closed most of the portals, but they couldn't move past the Dark Frontier, a mysterious network of empty towns and crumbling fortifications surrounding the heart of the Abyss. That's all I know."

"Did they find the hackers?"

"No, but everyone knows it was done by the New Asia conglomerate. They couldn't accept their defeat in the real world. The digital zones belonging to them were going to be annexed but instead they disappeared, swallowed up by the Abyss. No one's found a way to stop mutations among the NPCs. It's impossible to delete the defective content without destroying the virtual world. Some believe that the Abyss was created using gaming techniques."

"Gaming? Is that even possible?"

Max nodded, explaining, "The initial co-owners of the Land of the Chosen had enough power and the right to alter the digital space using 'magic' within their own territories. Many of them occupied quite senior positions in the New Asia conglomerate. That suggests certain things, doesn't it?"

I finished my juice and was silent for some time, trying to process what I had heard. Then I asked, "Where do the Dark players come from?"

"Players with Dark auras appeared about six months after the Abyss invaded," Max replied. "They had reloaded the reality by that time, corrected the leveling system and created safe regions where small groups of users could gradually explore the Wild Lands and even reach the edge of the Dark Frontier. In those distorted forests and deadly dungeons, and sometimes among the ruins of abandoned towns, live mutated NPC characters. If you have reached Level 30 and use 50% of realism, they will speak to you and offer you a

test and a reward for the *future belongs to the Abyss.*"
Max quoted with a crooked grin. "Meaning that it has
always existed and will soon swallow everything up
again."

"What's the point of it all, Max? What advantages
does the smoky aura give people?"

"It's all relatively simple and practical, like in real
life. The Dark players are rewarded for killing other
players. They gain experience, unique weapons,
apparel and abilities that they cannot get any other
way. But first, you must dedicate yourself to the Abyss.
For that, you accept a task, for example, obtaining a
certain item. The player follows hints but eventually
discovers that this trinket (always a different one) is a
sacred object in a small village somewhere. Hence, the
dilemma. They won't give you the item willingly. You
can't buy it. You can only steal it or take it by force.
There are no other options. You must decide. Many
think, 'Oh, what's the big deal, an NPC village, they'll
respawn. Meanwhile, I'll complete the quest and get a
pile of goodies that I've been promised.' It's easy to
become a killer in the digital world. I guess the usual
moral brakes don't work."

"Yup. Seen and heard it myself. 'It's only a game
and the NPC is just a chunk of code, nothing more'."

"Exactly. One minor detail, though. A child always
gets in the way, who must be murdered."

"A humanity test?"

"More like an inhumanity test. Yet many pass it.

They turn away or close their eyes. Remember the phrase in the classic? 'I'll pray for my sins later'," Max curled his hands into fists. "But it's not so easy to wash the blood off your hands, even if it's virtual. As soon as the task is complete, you get a smoky aura. Many don't return to complete the quest but a day passes, then another, yet the aura doesn't dissipate. You can no longer enter normal towns with it. You can't discard the item that you obtained from the inventory. Any player or NPC has every right to send you for respawn. I'm just stating facts, I'm not feeling sorry for them. There are some that delete their character. Others become bandits and form gangs. And some return to the Dark Frontier. As a reward for the first murder, they receive a fully-fledged Dark aura, which adds points to their characteristics, gives them the ability to use items, outfits and weapons altered by the Abyss, and unlocks a dark magic branch on the skills tree."

"And there's no way back?"

"Theoretically, there is. There are cleansing amulets out there, but nobody has found one yet. Dark players take the side of the Abyss. We don't know their real hierarchy yet. Nobody has traveled further than the Wild Lands so far, and those who reached the Dark Frontier either deleted their accounts or switched to the Dark side. There is another category, however, the most detestable, in my opinion. Savage_Hulk and his gang belong to it. They get to Level 30 and head to the Frontier. They accept the mission and obtain the aura, but serve only themselves and not the Abyss."

"What's the advantage in that?"

"Once they obtain the aura, they don't need to worry about their accounts. They won't get banned because they now belong to an 'enemy faction'. Dark players can be eliminated face-to-face but that's it."

"And nothing can be done?"

"That's not true. But we have to use gaming methods, as I've already said. We don't let them set foot on our lands. We protect new users and players with peaceful professions. Fifty percent of realism is a lot, believe me. Death is still death, and after a dozen respawns it begins to terrify."

I nodded, deep in thought. "What about me?"

"Do you truly want to stay?" Max narrowed his eyes. It was a familiar look. We had been through a lot together.

"After everything that you've told me? Yes, I do!"

"Justify why."

"I won't. It's not something I can explain. To live the remainder of my life in front of the spherovision when I have an alternative? Max, don't act dumb. You know me."

"Fine. Let's consider it a rhetorical question. But there are complications."

"My health's still good."

"That's not what I meant. We would like to ask you not to get a new account. You'll remain Dan."

"Why?"

"Your inventory contains unique items with hidden abilities. None of our people received the Secret of Forest Hill personal quest, although they went there alone and in groups. There is no dry tree and no remains. There are no rocks or the dried-up spring either. You've been to a place generated just for you. And the deciding factor is that your character has been teleported further than any of our explorers have been."

"Will I get support?"

"Here, yes. But not in the Edge of the Abyss. It's impossible. The section of underground that you have discovered hasn't helped us in any way, we haven't been able to find it so far. You will have to level up and escape from there on your own. But the Clan is willing to pay for the information. Any discoveries that you make will increase your reputation among us. You can join the Mongooses as soon as you find your way back. Now, about the real world. It's dangerous for you to return to Denis' apartment or to your own. You'll stay here for now. We'll provide you with a VR capsule.

You have a lot to think about. If you come back alive, you'll have payment and stars on your shoulders. And if you perish, well..."

The door opened suddenly and a guy of about eighteen entered the room. He was holding a nanocomputer tablet.

"Hi. Are you Dan?" he glanced at me.

"Didn't anyone teach you to knock?"

"Oh, sorry, I was thinking about stuff. You're Dan, right? I'm here about your character."

"Andrey, let me introduce you to Sasha, he's our analyst and tactician."

"Yeah, nice to meet you." A section opened in the floor and another armchair rose from the recess. "Right, fellows," he sat down. "The character has some crap skills but he'll live. I checked the logs. I estimate the overall level of the undergound as 25+. It's pretty passable. I reckon it used to be just a normal set of subterranean locations for a large town. Dan's Stamina is pretty good, you just need to quickly level up your Adaptability and you'll be fine."

"I get killed." I reminded him.

Sasha deigned to look up from the tablet. It was weird, he seemed to be focusing over my head as if he was looking for a frame.

"Andrey, despite all the 'respect your elders' crap that I get hammered into me here, don't be a newb, OK?"

"I wasn't the one who created the character."

"Yeah, but you're the one playing. Can I continue?"

"Go on."

"OK." he focused on the tablet again. "This is what we do. We increase the realism level to 50%. This will allow you to accrue additional experience points. Your goal is to go up 5 levels and get your Adaptability to 12 and then you'll be the king of this dump."

I choked on my juice.

Max was listening in silence. My eyelid was twitching while he was trying not to smile. He was enjoying this.

"What's wrong?" Sasha asked in surprise as if these few sentences were a detailed lecture that could explain everything.

"I'll kick the bucket. It will be incredibly painful! There's a zombie with a spear hanging around. I've only got a broken sword. Why do I need to level up my Adaptability? Can you explain properly, since you're a specialist?"

"Like Luck, Adaptability affects all characteristics. But while Luck is random, the effect of Adaptability is quite predictable. Many simply underestimate it. Basically, when the character was created, the five available points should have been spent on Adaptability, then additional progress bars would have appeared beside each characteristic in the interface. They fill up gradually and don't reset to zero if you die. It's called 'adaptive leveling'. Meaning that the fastest-growing characteristic is the one being used the most in that particular moment. If you carry heavy loads — your Strength increases. If you climb trees or shoot a lot with a bow and arrow, the additional bar next to Dexterity will gradually fill up and," Sasha snapped his fingers. "bingo! you get +1 for that characteristic. Get it?"

"Now I do." I nodded.

"Adaptability actually has lots of hidden

advantages. As soon as you get it to 12 points, you'll be able to use certain items and equipment that aren't typical for your class, and when your Adaptability reaches 15, you'll have the option to create a multiclass character."

"Multiclass?" I asked in surprise. "What for?"

"When you meet a Warrior of the Abyss, you'll understand why. We'll discuss that later. Right now, we need to quickly get you up 5 levels. You're a former soldier, right?"

"Yup."

"Then I don't see any problems," he concluded cheerfully. "You know how to group together correctly? You know what rolls are?"

I nodded curtly.

"Your opponent has a spear," Sasha continued. "Which means that he has two types of attack: stabbing lunge and spinning strike. You simply avoid the stabbing move. The mob is vulnerable at the end of the forward lunge. You jump back to get out of range of the spinning strike, then find the right moment and attack. I saw in the logs that you were killed with venom as well?"

"Yup. Centipedes."

"Super!"

I couldn't understand what he was so happy about.

"You can buff your weapon," Sasha explained patiently. "Smear the centipede along the wall with your first hit, then dip your blade in the slime and it will inflict additional poison damage for a period of time. The zombie's weak spot is its neck, so you need to go for the throat or the base of the skull from behind. This is called a critical hit. During a crit, your sword will produce 150% of the base damage. Get it?"

"I get the general gist. I'll have to try it out."

"All right. Get your Adaptability to 12 and then we'll discuss what you need to do next. Remember that the virtual world isn't simply realistic. You can use different events to your advantage. Anyway, go and experiment. For more detailed instructions, I'll need the logs and video of your next session."

"Well?" Max asked when Sasha grabbed his tablet and ran off to continue his other work. "Will you risk it?"

"Yes, I'll try one more time."

"In that case, here's an additional chip and a personal nanocomputer," he gave me a thin bracelet and added, "Wear it on your wrist. In normal mode, the information is displayed on your contact lenses or as a holographic tablet, whichever you prefer. When you're using the VR capsule, the chip allows you to create a personal digital space."

"What do I need it for?"

"The gap between a virtual death and respawn is twenty minutes. You can spend that time in comfortable surroundings. It relieves stress. Each member of our Clan has such a chip. It helps if you have to spend several days in a virtual capsule, during a raid, for example."

"Can you explain how it works?"

"You'll have access to a builder and will be able to create a virtual room with a familiar interior. You'll also be able to expand your personal space if you have enough imagination. You'll work it all out yourself, it's very straightforward."

"So, I won't need to leave the capsule at all?"

"In theory, yes. But I don't recommend abusing that option. It's better to exit, have a proper meal and a proper rest. One more thing, you have internet access in your personal space. If you need to get some advice or find information on the gaming forums, you can safely press 'log out'. Just don't leave your character in dangerous spots."

He touched a sensor on a wall control panel. A section of the floor moved aside and a VR capsule rose up.

"Ready to begin?"

I was silent.

"Then dive in," Max patted me on the shoulder reassuringly. "Fifty percent of realism is very motivating, trust me!"

Chapter Five

I GOT UNDRESSED and lay down in the VR capsule. The whine of the servomotors no longer made me nervous. The sensors wrapped around me body, the gel shifted slightly and the segments began to close.

That's it. I was on my own now.

The intro came and went.

...

Welcome to the Edge of the Abyss!

...

Max was right, the heightened realism was very motivating. Smells were sharper, my trembling was more pronounced and the rustling coming from the darkness sent shivers down my spine.

My fingers tightly gripped the handle of the broken sword. The pile of refuse ran down to the stone gutter and a centipede lay in wait on the wall. An involuntary tremor ran through me. Calm down. If I started to panic, I'd be sent to respawn again.

Reassuringly chanting "none of this is real" to myself didn't help in the slightest. I felt fully immersed in the gloomy dungeon setting as I heard the hiss of the venom dripping from the disgusting creature's mandibles. I began to understand why the Edge of the Abyss maintained a billion users. Where could one experience such a thing in the modern world without paying for it with one's life?

The sound of footsteps, snuffling and the rustle of collapsing garbage. Someone was creeping up on me from behind. My recent opponent, I bet!

I rolled and leaped up, striking as I spun around. The sensations were incredible as if I was young again!

My muscle memory was correct but game mechanics came into play and my character had a very low level of Dexterity. The strike was slow and inaccurate.

Damn it! I jumped backward, avoiding the retaliatory thrust.

Sasha was right. The zombie attacked with his whole body rather than just his arm. He was pretty clumsy and off-balance. The momentum drew him forward and forced him to bend over, leaving him vulnerable.

That was my moment!

Yeah, I wish. The sudden spinning attack sliced

through the air. The rusty spearpoint almost slashed across my throat.

Shit!

The centipede arched its body and spat venom at me but missed. I was in constant motion, avoiding the attacks and trying to control the situation but without much luck. A sudden pain pierced my leg. A huge rat had sunk its teeth into my ankle!

I flung it away with my sword and limped to the center of the arched hall where the lighting was better and there was more room to move. The zombie followed me, breathing noisily and watching me without blinking as it waited for me to trip or get distracted.

It was a bit too quick-witted for a mob!

The piles of refuse that had accumulated below the crack in the ceiling started to move. Rats, at least ten of them! I must have disturbed their nest.

There was no way that I could deal with all of them. I need to run, but where? Toxic vapors continued to trickle out of the tunnels and only the break in the brick wall looked more or less safe. Although, how could I be sure?

There were no other options. Were there?

So many rats. They were large, stocky creatures of Level 6-7. I could take any one of them if it had been by itself, but they were social mobs and attacked as a group.

I needed to clear the central hall any way that I could, without dying myself. The gap in the wall was not a solution. I didn't know what lurked in the depths of the labyrinth. I had to survive! This was really important. Having experienced the heightened realism and previous respawns, I wasn't sure that I could return here again and again when I already knew that I was doomed to fail.

I changed my strategy. I grabbed the shredded shirt from my inventory, poured water on it like last time and pressed it to my face as I dashed into the toxin-filled tunnel, the one that was a blind alley.

There was the green glowing moss that absorbed death energy. I spun on the spot. A whole pack of rats were chasing me!

I swiped at them with my broken sword. Got 'em! The quickest ones died. The vapors really sapped their health. Many didn't even make it out of the poisonous fog.

The toxin affected me too but to a lesser extent. I was alive, at least, and the zombie was too cautious to follow me.

Several more rats leaped out of the gloom. One collapsed before reaching me, its paws twitching helplessly, and I killed the others without too much trouble as their Life bars were at a minimum.

I caught my breath, desperate to get away from there. Now that I knew about the necrotic energy, I could feel the unnatural cold emanating from the walls. But why was it focused right here?

A good question. I inspected the moss, looking for

something unusual beneath the soft carpet covering the stones, but in vain. I couldn't stay in this tunnel for too long. The piercingly cold energies were clearly unsafe. I needed to return to the central hall. The rats following me had all perished thanks to the vapors but that blasted zombie was probably waiting for me near the exit.

I suddenly felt incredibly tired. My thoughts became apathetic. I wanted to sit down on a mossy boulder, close my eyes and forget about the gloomy atmosphere as I found peace, no matter how brief.

I obeyed the urge. I sat and meditated, reassuring myself that rest was necessary to regain my Stamina and regenerate Life points.

The strands of moss hanging down from above started moving, reaching towards me and softly sliding over my shoulders to slip down along my body and wind around my arms.

I started, shaking off the haze in my mind and leaped up, ripping the glowing threads.

So that's how they fed? They mentally lulled their victims to sleep, cocooned them and dragged them up the ceiling?

I looked up. Bingo. There were cracks in the ceiling through which the carnivorous plants grew down. Beside the cracked masonry, I could see a collection of dully glowing cocoons of various sizes, which dripped a bitter juice. I bet there weren't even bones left over from the prey.

A system message appeared as soon as the thought came into my head,

You have discovered a hitherto unknown type of plant altered by the Abyss. Would you like to name it, describe it and add the information to the Game Encyclopedia?

Reward +1 to Fame.

...

I thought for a second and then agreed. I'd be unrecognizable in the image but it'd be like a message to Savage that I was alive and continuing to develop successfully, even gaining more Fame. Plus, the eliminated pack of rats had given me 1,200 Exp. Twenty creatures worth 60 experience points each. The heightened realism had really bumped things up. I was close to going up a level.

...

You have access to additional information gained from experiments. Do you want to add it to the description?

...

I agreed again. Perhaps my Wiki article would save someone from a horrible death or warn them against using the glowing threads. This was the result:

Carnivorous moss. Found in the dungeons of the Dark Frontier. Has the ability to mentally lull its prey to sleep, cocoon it and slowly kill it.

Can be used as a source of light with care. The makeshift torch has a weak necrotic aura which is

projected onto its owner (+10 response from the undead and -50 response from living creatures).

...

You have gained 375 Exp. Your Fame has increased by 1.

You have reached a new level. You have one free characteristic point. Would you like to spend it?

...

I increased Adaptability like Sasha had recommended.

I'd have to find out what the benefit of Fame was when I got the chance.

...

Recommended skill: Naturalist. You will be able to study new types of plants and animals more quickly and effectively, and to note their special features.

...

I declined for the moment. I understood that a character's development had to be carefully thought through and planned.

The short break really helped. Firstly, I regenerated my Stamina and HP. Secondly, I made a discovery and gained a level. Thirdly, my mood improved. Moreover, a very tempting idea had come into my head but I would have to prepare before I could carry it out. At a minimum, I needed to deal with the enemies lurking near the respawn point.

I took a risk, exited the game for a short while and called Sasha. "Hi. I've got a question."

"Yeah?"

"How do mobs respawn?"

"What do you mean?"

"Let's say I kill all the enemies around a respawn circle, how soon will they reappear?"

"The typical interval for NPCs is four hours, but if there are no other players nearby, the location responds to you. It's simple, the mobs will only respawn if you die or if you leave the dungeon for ages and then return."

"Got it, thanks."

I returned to the game. This meant that I had a chance to clean up the hall. The most important thing was not to rush or I'd need to start anew.

I ran through the toxic fog again.

I rolled when I reached the edge of the cloud — just in time as the zombie was waiting nearby and jabbed forward with his spear but missed me.

I leaped to my feet and cast a glance to either side. The centipede was far away and I couldn't see any rats.

My opponent had already turned around and was advancing towards me. He had a strange nickname, *Jeber_Arium. Level 12.* There was a sinking feeling in my stomach. Shouldn't an NPC be labeled differently? Something like Ancient Zombie, Level 12?

What could a player be possibly doing here, especially looking like this?!

I probably didn't look any better, wearing my shabby leather armor, my face smeared with dirt and wrapped in rags like a mummy. A fragment of a rusty sword in my hand. I wonder how he perceives me?

Jeber_Arium attacked. Remembering Sasha's advice, I avoided the stabbing thrust, leaped to his side and chopped twice with my sword.

What a howl! There was genuine pain in that scream. Damn it. Could he really be a player?

I rolled over a mound of compressed garbage. My 'combat acrobatics' (if one could call my desperate attempts to avoid being hit that) were rapidly using up my Stamina so that I was almost exhausted. The muscle memory that Sasha spoke about was there but I was out of the habit of moving like this and hadn't practiced in a long time... I became disoriented at times and the somersaults brought on waves of dizziness.

I suspected things weren't going to end well,. My opponent hadn't landed a single hit but he'd preserved his strength. The inflicted damage had taken away about a third of his Life points. The long spear let him keep me at arm's length. He thrust the spear forward as soon as I paused.

My Dexterity level left a lot to be desired. I got caught at the next short roll. The zombie predicted my move and imitated a stabbing attack but then switched to a spinning strike.

The tip of the spear slashed through my right shoulder. Blood gushed from the wound and the zombie didn't waste any time, performing a series of spamming attacks that produced a Shock debuff.

Here it was, the true price of realism! I could have handled the pain if I was on the recommended 10% but not on 50%. My legs gave out from under me.

Everything swam before my eyes. The menacing, hunched-over figure blurred. I was rapidly enveloped in a reeking gloom and a second later, the pitiless thrust pierced my chest and my mind went dark.

...

YOU HAVE DIED.

75 Exp lost.

...

The VR capsule opened with a rustle.

Max and Sasha helped me drop over the edge and dragged me to an armchair. A door opened and someone else ran inside. I wasn't thinking clearly but I could feel the person give me an injection.

"Well?"

"He'll live. Did you idiots put him on 50% of realism?"

"We recommended it," Sasha grumbled.

"Like I said — imbeciles! You're destroying people with your accelerated leveling up! Is he having a cuddle party in there? No? Then what the hell? No more than twenty-five percent! Let him work for it slowly, let the experience dribble in bit by bit but without any fatalities, got it?"

"Yeah, we got it."

"Hey, it's all good..." My mind cleared a bit and I decided to interrupt.

"Sure, buster," the unfamiliar guy just shook his head and left. It seemed like these incidents weren't a rarity for him.

"You did well," Sasha got comfortable in the chair opposite me. "Avicenna's right, we'll have to drop the realism. I watched the recording. I'll jot down a leveling up plan for you. You're a quick one. You'll aggro the rats and then draw them into the toxic cloud. You'll quickly gain three levels that way. Meanwhile, I'll figure out how to kill Jeber."

"Is he a player?" I asked hollowly.

"Yup, but don't worry about that. Talking to him is pointless. He's a 'drowner', I bet."

"A what?" I took a sip of mineral water.

"He played a lot at high realism levels and went nuts. He doesn't leave the VR capsule and has forgotten about the real world. He must have been a relatively successful player but bit off more than he could chew and entered a hardcore location. He must have died again and again, losing levels as he went. Right now, he's not that different from an NPC."

"But he's a person!" I exclaimed.

"He WAS a person," Max clarified gloomily. "You occasionally meet them in the game. For him, the dungeon is the only reality. He's forgotten everything else. I'm not sure if he's capable of normal communication at all. Usually, you can't get through to them. You're just going to have to kill him."

I was silent. We'd see about that.

Over the next few hours, I got acclimatized to the gloomy atmosphere of the Dark Frontier dungeon.

It was gradually turning my stomach. Hanging out at a garbage dump and leveling up using rats was not what I'd call enjoyable.

"Come on, chill," Sasha had developed an optimal route for me and explained what I had to do, based on yesterday's recording. "Farming's always like that at the start. Suck it up."

I had insisted on keeping the level of realism at 50%, though.

I didn't cross paths with Jeber since he was not in the habit of wandering through the tunnels. He mostly sat on the shore of the reeking creek and tried to fish something out of the murky water.

I had no food. No clean water. I constantly raced through the toxic fog, drawing hordes of rats after me, all to gather crumbs of gaming experience. Wasn't that just a reflection of our normal, fussy lives?

...

You are suffering from thirst.

You are suffering from hunger.
Your Stamina has been reduced by 10%.
Speed of natural HP regeneration has been reduced by 10%.

...

Where was I supposed to get food and water? There was plenty of rat meat but I wasn't yet ready to eat it raw.

It had grown noticeably darker. The muted light seeping through the crack in the ceiling was gradually fading. It must be evening up above.

The night was for monsters. This was particularly relevant for the underground.

The thought produced an ironic smile. My old, long-forgotten attitude to life was coming back to me: I grinned recklessly at a huge rat that had followed me through the toxic cloud and plunged my sharpened sword fragment into its brazen snout.

One shot!

I was surrounded by a weak golden glow. I had finally gone up to the next level!

I returned to the resurrection circle and dispatched the centipede but got slightly poisoned myself and had to wait for my Life points to recover.

According to the leveling up plan, I had to collect a pile of rocks, annoy the rats from afar and drag the next pack through the toxins.

It took a whole hour to go up another level.

Pure hardcore, no fun. It was more like exhausting

hard labor. I was tired, I had breathed in heaps of fumes and my leather armor had lost half of its Durability and was covered in dirt. My face stung and my arms were covered in scratches.

My Life bar flickered at half-full. It kept increasing slightly due to natural regeneration but then dropping from time to time due to the poisoning. I decided I better wait until the debuff wore off.

I sat exhausted and breathing heavily. My throat was parched but I wasn't going to risk drinking from the puddles.

The darkness gathered around me so that I could see faint reflections of a pulsating, deep violet glow through the crack in the wall. Could it be the portal through which I was sent here? I hadn't had time to see anything before my instant virtual death and then I had woken up in the respawn circle.

It was worth checking, even if to just glance at it from a distance. The farming was done for today anyhow, since I doubted that I could level up effectively in the dark. I didn't have night vision and it would only take one wrong step or a trip and I'd fall or simply get gnawed to death.

The muted glow went through curious changes in color from lilac to almost black.

It had to be the portal! It was probably located in one of the tunnels that I hadn't yet explored. I guessed that its gleam was barely noticeable during the day, when enough light came through the gap in the ceiling.

I was going to risk it. I was thoroughly sick of the dungeon. There wasn't a single safe corner here where I could leave my character and exit cyberspace. Max thought that I only had one option, to farm non-stop until I could confidently kill any mob that I encountered, but where was the guarantee that I wouldn't meet even stronger opponents on the surface?

I needed alternative exit routes, so there was no reason to sit here and wait for sunrise. Onwards, to explore!

I crossed the creek, stopped and listened carefully.

The quiet steps paused immediately. Was Jeb creeping after me? I glanced behind me often and briefly spotted the hunched-over figure. He didn't seem to be planning an attack but who knew what was on his mind?

The hole was wide and uneven as if an explosion had blown out a section of the wall. Chunks of brick protruded from the edge like broken teeth. Apart from the emitted light, I could hear something resembling a child's cry coming from the tunnel depths.

My surroundings changed dramatically as soon as I climbed through the gap. The low stone vault was supported by thick columns that reminded me of melted candles. The comparison was due to their gently undulating shapes and the yellow streaks covering their surface. I touch one and a hint popped up,

Amber gum. A rare alchemical and magical ingredient. Highly valued for its properties. Gradually

absorbs elemental forces, which can then be released. Used to strengthen weapons (elemental damage), create levitation and flash potions, as well as to power certain devices created by dwarves.

Amber gum is difficult to obtain as it is found only in very dangerous places with strong energies emitted by the Abyss.

...

I understood the warning but this didn't change my plans. I tried to break off a piece of the amber gum but my sword fragment wasn't a suitable tool for this. I did manage to find several small fragments of the unique mineral at the bases of the columns, though.

The crying and wailing grew louder. The cave floor began to slope downward. It was covered in a network of wide cracks, emitting... a black flame! Yes, I had been right. It wasn't smoke, it was fire, purple in the center and charcoal along the edges. It fell back and flared back up again, casting forward long, flickering tongues.

I circled around the most dangerous areas and tried to cross the cracks in places where the effects of the Abyss were least noticeable. My face and arms started to tingle.

A wide fissure crossed the farther cave wall. The pulsating light was coming from there.

...

You are observing a unique phenomenon. Would you like to add its description to the Game Encyclopedia?

Reward +5 to Fame.

...

I stopped, unsure. The smoky rabbit and a colony of carnivorous moss was one thing. But a place where the Abyss had erupted, with large deposits of amber gum and something mysterious ahead of me, was information of a very different kind. My logic was this: there was a lot of gum here. If I published my Wiki article, people would start looking for me. Many would want to get their hands on my map.

Delay publication.

The system didn't insist and so I kept going.

Chapter Six

THE FISSURE WAS SHORT and led me straight to the next cave.

I hid behind an outcropping of stone and observed the scene in front of me.

Up ahead stood a half-destroyed dwarf village, which was obvious from how squat the structures were. I could see it clearly from my higher position. It was an incredibly unusual and creepy place. In the center, where the market square used to be, glittered an oval-shaped mass of black-purple energy, pierced by bright streaks of red and green.

Terrifying creatures wandered through the streets. The crying and wailing were coming from the underground inhabitants, their bodies twisted and fused together. How could I accurately describe them? Imagine that a mad, enraged sculptor had slammed his creations together, combining several figures into one shapeless mass, with fragments of bodies, arms, legs and heads sticking out of it. This terrible creation continued to survive and moved around however it could.

There were dozens of these fused, mutilated balls of flesh. Some emitted a green aura (I now understood what the city guards were so afraid of), plumes of smoke came from others and yet more were surrounded by a dull reddish glow with streaks of darkness.

...

You have found a working Abyss portal.

+10 to Fame (if a video is published).

You have found sentient beings altered by the Abyss (name the mutated species).

+15 to Fame (5 for each species if the materials are published in the Bestiary).

...

I replied 'Delay publication'. There was a lot to think about. I first had to find out what were the benefits of increased Fame versus the risks.

Many things now made sense. I could see what Savage_Hulk had been counting on. My character would have certainly experienced a succession of short and extremely painful resurrections in a place like this. Best case scenario — I would have gone mad, which is probably what had happened to Jeber_Arium.

I had been lucky. When I died, I had been

resurrected in the closest respawn circle that was located away from the grim portal. The wastewater collector no longer seemed so revolting. Everything is relative.

In the meantime, things were changing in the cave. The portal began to glow a little brighter and a violet clump of energy appeared in the center, surrounded by black lighting. A moment later, a projection was cast from the almond shape onto the wall, with the stone surface disappearing!

Warrior figures stepped out of the new tunnel. They were much higher than normal human beings and were encased in armor, with their helmet visors down and their faces obscured. The squad moved confidently forward, ignoring the twisted lumps of flesh. The indigenous inhabitants of the cave showed no aggression. On the contrary, they cowered closer to the ruins, afraid to get in the way of the aliens.

There came a dull sound and pack animals followed the first squad. They were enormous lizards, boxes and parcels stacked high on their backs. The drivers were tall, humanoid creatures dressed in loose robes that obscured their figures. The caravan moved slowly and unhurriedly.

I counted thirty lizards, about ten drivers and twenty warriors. I couldn't read their frames but they were red in color. All I could discern were the skull symbols, which indicated their high level of hostility towards humans.

You have discovered a previously unknown NPC faction.

*New quest available: **On the Path of the Abyss**. Find out as much as possible about the network of portals and the creatures traveling through them.*

Reward: varies depending on the discoveries made. Unlimited time to complete.

...

The clump of energy in the center of the portal refocused. The tunnel closed but another one opened in the opposite wall. The caravan disappeared into the darkness, the guards following close behind.

The projection faded a moment later and the stone looked solid again.

Something viscous dripped from the ceiling and fell at my feet, eating a hole in the stone as it hissed and emitted toxic smoke.

I slowly looked up.

Damn it!

The ceiling was covered in enormous centipedes, also altered by the Abyss. I saw the same '???' in their frames as I had seen in the game logs. So that's what had sent me into respawn!

...

You have discovered a new type of Abyss-altered creature! Give them a name and a description.

Reward +1 to Fame.

...

Postpone!

You have been poisoned.
Damage 10 HP/sec.
Duration — unknown.

...

Without waiting for the next venomous spit, I rushed back to where I had come from. The creatures wandering aimlessly along the streets of the destroyed dwarf village spotted the movement and three balls shot off in my direction. One was woven out of greenish necrotic energies, the second hummed with fire and the third left behind a smoky trail.

I slipped through the fissure, ran through the cave with the amber gum, reached the reassuring dark of the collector and headed for the respawn circle but collapsed before I could get there. The strong venom was quickly eroding my health.

Everything swam before my eyes.

I felt feverish and my thoughts were all jumbled together.

...

You are suffering from severe poisoning. Your Strength, Stamina and Dexterity are temporarily reduced by 3 points. Find the anti-venom.

...

Where? What did it look like? My strength was slipping away and I was horrified by the effects of the venom.

I could hear a vague rustling in the gloom. There came the sound of creeping feet. Of course.

Jeber_Arium wouldn't miss his chance now. He was going to kill me, the bastard...

I could see the zombie out of the corner of my eye. He sidled up to me, clutching a rusted dagger in one hand and something gross that he'd found in the pile of refuse in the other.

I tried to crawl away from him but realized to my horror that I was as helpless as a baby. The debuffs caused by thirst, exhaustion and poisoning had made me an easy target.

He leaned over me. "Weak..." his whisper raised goosebumps on my skin.

The rusty but sharpened dagger touched my lips. Fear flooded my mind, erasing the fatigue but clearing my mind for only a second. I was still weak as I felt Jeber lever the dagger to unclench my teeth and rapidly stick something revolting in my mouth.

My jaw cramped as my mouth was flooded with bitterness.

...

You have used a clump of healing moss. The poisoning has been neutralized.

...

Well, I certainly hadn't expected this! I had been preparing to die another painful death.

Everything kept swimming before my eyes while Jeber_Arium didn't waste any time and opened my mouth again, pushing something slimy inside. I was going to be sick!

I couldn't spit the thing out. It dissolved in my mouth and another system message appeared before my blurry gaze.

You have eaten a puffball.

You are no longer hungry.

You are no longer thirsty.

HP regeneration speed has increased by 1%.

...

A few minutes later, I managed to raise myself off the ground, crawl to the wall and sit there, leaning against its rough surface.

An unexpected turn of events, to put it mildly.

Jeber_Arium stood hunched over by the stream and wasn't even looking in my direction.

The pity he'd shown me... was it an echo of his past personality or had he really changed his attitude towards me?

It was an important question. If we became friends, I'd be able to exit cyberspace without worrying about my character. It would also be easier to level up, as well as looking for a way out of here.

Once I felt better, I hobbled over to the respawn circle. "Jeb, come here and we'll talk!"

He didn't even turn to look at me. Back to being completely withdrawn.

Alright, I wasn't going to insist. I had to be careful with him.

What were my chances of getting out of here? There were only two unexplored tunnels left. Circumstances were forcing me onto a certain path. Publishing my discoveries in the Game Encyclopedia would help me to go up to the minimum required level. I did wonder what the 'price of Fame' was though.

There were still a couple of hours left until the rats respawned so I started looking.

The necessary information was clear and easily accessible.

Fame was one of the secondary characteristics, clearly undervalued by the modern community of the Edge of the Abyss.

One could increase Fame using different methods. For example, 'Famous Explorer', 'Famous Naturalist', 'Famous Warrior', and as the opposite, 'Famous Conqueror', 'Famous Thief', 'Famous Assassin', etc.

The second component (determined exclusively by the actions that led to the Fame) directly affected the obtained effects and bonuses.

Any discovery could be used in different ways.

Option 1: You find previously unknown plants or creatures, discover new locations, activate new respawn circles but don't share the obtained information. You won't gain any Fame points, but you can sell the information from your map or travel diary (where all the important gaming moments are automatically recorded).

Option 2: You publish your discoveries in the Game Encyclopedia. The Fame and Experience points (25% of what is required to advance to the next level) are added immediately. When you obtain 25 points of Fame, you get the option to broadcast your adventures live (which can be a source of income). When you gain 50 points, you receive an Aura of Fame. Representatives of any NPC faction will then refrain from attacking you immediately but will try to get a closer look at you (this doesn't include wild creatures).

Five hundred points of Fame allow you to activate an Aura of Immunity that lasts 2 minutes and takes 24 hours to regenerate. Nobody attacks you when you're using it but any aggressive behavior from you will immediately dispel it.

One thousand points of Fame make any NPC faction that you meet neutral towards you and allow you to travel safely through their lands for one hour. After that time, only key NPCs in the location will remain neutral to you while the others (including bandits) will respond to you as normal.

The Aura of Fame can have different shades. It's tinted depending on the balance of good and bad actions that you performed to gain this characteristic, as well as your kill rating.

Importantly, if your discoveries lead to a large-scale gaming event, you gain additional Fame points and (optionally) a unique ability (depending on the scale and direction of the event).

The opinions on the forums disagreed completely with the Wiki article. There was one post that I found especially interesting.

I don't recommend leveling up Fame. Firstly, all these auras are complete garbage. Secondly, always being in the center of attention isn't great. For example, you can no longer use Stealth and other similar skills. If you've reached the edge of the Dark Frontier (all the tastiest discoveries are there), it's better to sell the information than to publish it.

I sat and thought it over.

It was indeed a dubious characteristic for a beginner player. The experience (in my case, 375 Exp) that I would get for 1 point of Fame could be obtained from killing rats. But the higher a character's level, the slower and harder the leveling up. I estimated that starting from around Level 50, the 25% became worth it. Surely, if you needed 100,000 Exp to reach the next level, it was nice to get a quarter of them by writing in the Wiki about some weird plant or mob that you've encountered.

It was clear what the admins were counting on. High-level players capable of reaching the Dark Frontier had to be motivated to publish their discoveries. Considering that the content mutations caused by the Abyss couldn't be removed, they needed to be classified as quickly as possible, and under the present conditions, the easiest way to do it was using players.

I was in a unique position but my level was low. It was better to save the discoveries and publish them later, when every point of Fame would provide a sizeable contribution to the development of my character.

As I mused about this, my health bar recovered completely.

There were six hours of darkness left. I still had two unexplored tunnels but I didn't want to venture in there by myself. There was a chance that Jeber_Arium would accompany me and we'd manage faster and easier if we were together.

I looked around but he was nowhere to be seen.

Well, I'd wait until morning. In the meantime, I had some unfinished business to attend to. I headed towards the green glow coming through the toxic cloud.

The dead end illuminated by the luminescent moss still provoked an involuntary tremble, but I wanted to check what was hidden in the cocoons under the ceiling. Perhaps some of the objects carried by the victims had survived?

I took a deep breath and tried to knock down the first of the growths with a long stick that I had found earlier. It tore open and greenish debris rained down on me with a clang of metal fragments. A rotting wooden shield dropped down, nearly hitting me on the head, and shattered against the rocks.

Nothing useful. Fine. Let's try the next one.

After a lot of effort, all the cocoons had been knocked down or split open. My head was hurting and my armor was covered in dirt. There wasn't much loot. My hope of scoring something major hadn't come true. The tip of a naginata, a broken staff, a bow with no bowstring, several arrows, plenty of bones, a silver amulet on a thin chain and a two leather items consisting of a shoulder piece and quite a curious glove, and that was all.

Time to go. The aura hovering over this place was starting to make me seriously uncomfortable.

It was cold and damp by the respawn circle.

Well, let's have a look. I sat on the respawn stone, which looked like an ancient grinding stone covered in runes. The amulet and glove warranted further study.

The delicate piece of jewelry on a thin chain glittered mysteriously. I concentrated on it, trying to read its properties.

...

Thread of Time Amulet. Item for invocation. Hang it around your neck and touch it in a moment of danger. Perhaps one of the ancient creatures that used to live here will respond?

Requirements: Intellect 20.

Warning, if your characteristic is too low or you lack

the skill 'Concentration', the amulet's action is not blocked but occurs randomly. Be careful! Read ancient books about how to correctly perform invocations. If you know and can imagine a specific creature, you will achieve a better result.

...

I thought about it and decided not to activate the amulet. What if it really worked? I wouldn't have minded some help, of course, but the chance of a wonderful intervention was abysmally small and it could cause me grief instead. It would be better if I discovered more about invocations and then decided whether I should risk wearing this thing around my neck.

I examined the glove.

...

Incarnation of Flame. A master artifact made from salamander skin.

Requirements: Intellect 10, the skills 'Concentration 5' and 'Elemental Control 5'.

Item abilities: Favor.

Put on the glove and check if you have the potential to obtain the right abilities.

...

Of course, I decided to try this.

The skin of the mythical lizard had become dry and wrinkled from such long and careless storage. The fingers on my left hand felt like something was gripping them hard but then came the sensation of warmth and

a new message appeared,

You have gained the ability 'Start a Fire'.

Fire has been known to humans since ancient times. You cannot use the powerful magical potential of the item but you can start a fire to dispel the dark and to warm up.

You have successfully used the item's special ability. You have received 150 Exp.

I immediately started looking around for firewood. I was so sick of the chilly dampness of the dungeon! I didn't know if I'd ever be able to use the full power of the glove but the ability to start a fire was a priceless gift.

I gathered some dried twigs and tried to get a fire going.

Jeb appeared on the other side of the creek and watched me from a distance. He was obviously wondering what I was doing but fear and distrust remained stronger than curiosity.

I arranged the twigs in a teepee and stretched my hand out over it, concentrating on the image of fire as my intuition suggested.

Nothing.

My fingers trembled. Perhaps I needed to utter a special word? Or was I rushing ahead and it was better to read some guides first?

My hand was suddenly pierced by a sharp pain.

Glowing streaks spread over the glove and my mind went briefly fuzzy. My Life, Stamina and Mana bars shuddered and dropped slightly but then...

A timid flame licked the gathered twigs, went out, reappeared again and grew stronger, throwing up sparks. The fire gathered in strength and began to emit heat.

Lengthening shadows leaped along the underground walls. I sat down by the fire, feeling blessedly warm.

I sent Sasha a description of the item and naturally asked, 'Is it normal that I can use it?'

A reply came soon after, 'Yep! Such finds are rare! Use them more often and maybe you'll discover something more.'

'But I'm not a mage!'

'It doesn't matter. They're *items*, get it? They're specifically created for character classes that don't possess magic. Different scrolls, for example. Anyone can use them. The amulet and glove suit you fine. Once you raise your Intellect, you'll be sweet! You'll be able to use elemental fire in battle!'

'Right. What about the amulet?'

'Squeeze it in your hand and try to concentrate, then tell me what happens. How's your leveling up going, by the way?'

'I'm planning to get to Level 13 today.'

'Good. Contact me as soon as you get it.'

Chapter Seven

T HINGS SEEMED BRIGHTER in the light of the fire. Without waiting for sunrise, I dispatched two centipedes, then annoyed some rats from a distance, led them through the fumes as had become my habit and finished off the ones that had survived.

...

You have reached a new level.

...

Finally!

Once I spent the available points on my characteristics, the interface revealed the long-awaited bars for adaptive leveling up. The trick was this: the game penalized me for dying by slashing my highest characteristic, which was Strength. The game didn't touch the precious Adaptability so I quickly increased it to the required number.

It was time to check what advantage it gave me.

The nest closest to the respawn circle had been wiped out, the fire was glowing a cherry red and a hunchbacked figure could be seen beside it. Jeb, who had dared to approach the source of light and warmth, immediately became wary when he heard my footsteps.

I waved at him from afar.

Unfortunately, Sasha was right. Jeber_Arium responded completely the wrong way to my friendly gesture. He raised his spear and rushed at me.

It would be terrible if I got killed. I would have wasted the monotonous work of several days.

I felt genuinely sorry for the 'drowned' player. "Jeb, let's talk!"

His response was an energetic thrust.

I rolled away, anticipating the spinning strike that was going to follow. Yeah, his range of moves wasn't very big. I quickly learned how to recognize his few decoy moves.

"Jeb, can you tell me about yourself? How did you get here?"

The questions confused him. He sniffed and slowed down but continued to watch me darkly, waiting for a chance to stab me with the rusty spearpoint.

"Where is your VR capsule?"

That made him angry again for some reason and he attacked me. I got a couple of scratches and managed to smack him with the hilt of my sword. When I realized

133

that things were taking a bad turn, I retreated into the toxic cloud.

Jeber_Arium didn't follow me. He was afraid of the toxins, otherwise, things could have ended badly since there wasn't much room to turn in the narrow dead end, among all the glowing moss. Jeb could have stabbed me to death with his spear, with no chance of avoiding his attacks.

All right. I'd keep trying and maybe he'd talk to me one day.

In the meantime, I opened the character panel and glanced through the results of the short skirmish.

The adaptive leveling was working! The bar next to Dexterity had increased by a couple of percent! Awesome result! All I need was to find a book to read to pass the time between rat respawns and to raise my Intellect.

I ran through the fumes again, expecting an attack, but Jeb had disappeared. On my way to the respawn circle, I managed to find and pull out of the garbage a tree branch that had been carried there by the rainwater.

I sat by the fire. I was tired and incredibly sleepy but it was dangerous to leave my character here unattended.

Should I try to doze here without leaving the VR capsule?

The fire illuminated a small area. I noted a movement in the gloom and grew tense.

No, I wasn't imagining it. Jeb was back. He approached very slowly and cautiously. I took a good look at him. He was no zombie. He was just terribly skinny and dressed in rags.

"Come to the fire."

He understood my speech yet was afraid and sat down timidly by the flames. A minute passed, then another one, and his features slowly relaxed. Jeb put the spear aside and stretched his hands out to the fire. The flames were reflected in his pupils.

Suddenly, a weak, emerald glimmer appeared around the respawn point.

I looked more carefully and a hint appeared,

Safe zone.

...

Jeb no longer felt hostile towards me! He sat and stared at the fire, the closest rat nest had been destroyed, the centipedes had all been killed and the location, as Sasha would have put it, had been 'saved'.

I could use the opportunity to get back to reality! My character would simply disappear after a couple of minutes.

That's what I did.

An unpleasant surprise was waiting for me in the real world.

The wings of the VR capsules opened and the firm bed shifted up.

I felt dirty and exhausted. I was desperate to have a shower, wash away the remaining sensory gel and collapse into bed but it was not to be. An unfamiliar man with a gloomy expression sat in the armchair.

"Hell, that's a bit presumptuous!" I wrapped a towel around my waist.

"Sorry, don't crack it. There's a matter that needs to be resolved quickly."

"Where's Max?"

"In the capsule. Our castle is currently under siege."

"Fine. What's the problem?"

"My name's Igor," the mysterious visitor finally introduced himself. "I'm responsible for finding and studying artifacts in the Clan. We have a business proposition for you."

"Go on," I put on a dressing gown and sat down in another chair.

"You're not going to make it through the dungeon," Igor began.

"Wait, why not?"

"We analyzed the latest logs. No matter where you go, you'll run into Abyss-altered beings that you can't handle. You'll waste the character and we're desperate to get our hands on the items in your inventory. Especially the Soul Crystal and the Thread of Time Amulet. We managed to find several mentions of the latter. It's a very powerful invocation artifact."

"It'd be better if you had a strong word with that trio of assholes and opened the portal," I interrupted. "I wouldn't mind some help."

"We've done that already," Igor replied coolly. "We found them in the real world and had a heart-to-heart but didn't get anywhere. Nobody has figured out the secret of the Abyss portals."

"They're lying."

"No, they're not. Believe me, we really needed that information. We had to apply pressure."

"But Wang opened the portal in front of me!"

"Wang has no idea how he did it. The ritual is known, officially, but nothing normally happens. Wang didn't want to argue with Savage because he's afraid of him."

"Oh, so it was an accident, huh?"

"We checked. In the same place. The portal didn't open. We found another mark of the Abyss invasion with the same result. Wang gave us the video recording of the event and we followed his moves to the letter."

"So, what's the conclusion?"

"There's only one logical explanation. There's an item in your inventory that is the missing component, a sort of key to open any portal."

"The Soul Crystal?" I guessed.

"I can't say for sure. Either that or the Guardian's Amulet."

"Can't you find similar ones?"

"*This item does not exist*," Igor quoted the results of the search systems.

"Bullshit!"

"We think so too. Perhaps there are plenty of such items in the Dark Frontier, but this is the first time that they've been found by a player. Or people possessing similar artifacts are concealing information about them."

"That's logical. I have a personal quest and the item is personal too."

"Andrey, try to understand, you're in cyberspace by accident. You don't have the motivation or the gaming experience, and your health's not the best. The portal key and the related quest are a unique find."

"There are options?"

"Yes. One."

"Let's hear it then."

"You don't log into the Edge of the Abyss through that account again. We'll create a new character for you. You'll become a rich man and be able to enjoy life on our lands, under the protection of the Clan."

"Wait," I was shocked, "What about my Dan?"

"You'll leave him in the dungeons. Ideally, in the tunnel with the carnivorous moss."

"What happens then?"

"It's a dangerous place so the character won't disappear. He'll die, and considering the circumstances, his remains will become part of the level since you'll never log in as Dan again. We'll eventually make our way to the dungeon once we figure out which corner of the map it's in and collect the artifacts."

"Off my dead body?"

"Yes. This solves all our problems. The personal quest will be transferred to a player especially prepared for the mission when they obtain the quest items."

"And for that I'll get a comfortable life in a safe area? I'll be able to wander through the forest, pick mushrooms and catch fish?"

"That's right," he perked up.

"Igor, what will happen to Jeb?"

He simply shrugged. "I won't lie to you. I doubt that he'll get out of there. It's bad to mess around with realism levels. He's lost his mind and doesn't leave the VR capsule. He was probably a successful player but couldn't handle the Dark Frontier. Even if he has a fancy VR capsule, he might last another month, no more."

"And then he'll die?"

"If nobody interferes in the real world and doesn't get him out, then yes, he'll die."

"This is also the price of my artifacts?"

"Don't exaggerate."

"I'm not. Since when have virtual items that you can't even touch become more valuable than a human life?"

Igor looked at me coldly and dispassionately. "It is your decision, Andrey Dmitrievich," he switched to an overly formal tone. "Don't rush, think it through. Complete safety, the opportunity to live in a perfect virtual world and have everything at your fingertips. This is our offer."

"Why can't I get out of there by myself?"

"We don't want to count on luck and I doubt it'll be on your side, anyway. You're in a godforsaken place. An attempt to clamber out on your own will likely land Dan in a hole that even the most well-prepared team won't be able to reach to collect the artifacts. We're being realistic. You should agree while you can still leave the character in a low-level location. You won't get a better offer."

I didn't like the way he was looking at me. "Here is my counteroffer. I'm going to rest and then explore the remaining two tunnels. Let's speak again after that."

He agreed surprisingly easily. "Good luck."

I didn't get the rest that I needed. I had barely fallen asleep when a beep sounded at the door.

"Open," I grumbled.

Two technicians entered the room. "Sorry, we have to take an urgent look at the VR capsule."

I gestured for them to go for it, took a glass of juice and sat at the table.

One of the technicians opened the front of the

capsule, the other one touched the access panel and checked something. Then he glanced at the video camera mounted just below the ceiling, roughly placed his instrument case on the table and took out an electronic device while surreptitiously dropping a folded scrap of paper and shooting me a meaningful look.

They left five minutes later.

I calmly finished my juice, threw the disposable cup into the recycler and went into the hygiene module. The paper contained the access chip to my account. Max had hurriedly written a couple of lines on the scrap of paper.

Don't approach the VR capsule. Don't log in from here. Go to the rec zone, you'll understand everything there. Then head to the address: Shebnev 10, Apartment 502. The access code is the number of our unit. Don't delay. Max

I understood that we were up the creek. It seemed that the artifacts in my possession were indeed more important to the clan than human life, for how else could one explain the technicians' visit, the note and the chip? I didn't put on my coat, just headed straight to the bar and ordered a drink. I sat at the bar for a little while until people started gathering around me. From their conversations, I understood that a combat shift had finished. The castle was indeed under siege but the Mongooses were doing fine.

Sasha sat down beside me and jostled me slightly,

indicating a fire escape door with his eyes.

"The video cameras and security systems along the way have been switched off. You've only got a couple of minutes," he whispered.

It was drizzling outside and the gloomy autumn clouds hung low overhead. Two flights along the fire escape brought me to the backyard of the entertainment center, next to the ramps where cars bringing consumables for the VR capsules were unloaded. I crossed it quickly, turned onto the avenue, waved over a passing taxi and told the driver the first address I could think of.

About twenty minutes later, I paid and got out, went down to the metro, traveled for several stops, went back up to the surface and caught another taxi. "Shebnev 10."

The access code worked.

I found myself in a standard apartment with 'transformable space' and a VR capsule in the center. A comms device lay on top of the control panel. I snorted and touched the activation sensor.

'You have one unread message'.

I touched the envelope symbol. As I expected, the message was from Max.

Andrey, I'm sorry, I didn't think that it would turn

out this way. A war has begun among the clans and they're ready to kill for artifacts, and I mean that literally. While you have a trial account, we can fake your social media and replace you, like you replaced Denis. Nobody knows about this place. The communicator is clean and the apartment is secure. This is my back-up place, just in case. You decide what to do next. I can't get away right now or I'll arouse suspicion and implicate Sasha.

I sank into an armchair, deep in thought.

No. I wouldn't abandon Jeb. I'd keep leveling up. I certainly had plenty of stubbornness and patience.

I didn't feel sleepy any longer and the fatigue was gone.

I'd have to set up the VR capsule again and go through the metabolic correction process, so there was no point in delaying.

The Edge of Abyss welcomed me with the dimness of its dungeon. The fire was almost out. I couldn't see Jeb anywhere. A little daylight seeped through the crack overhead.

After quickly dispatching the nearby centipedes, I returned to the resurrection circle, opened the character panel and found to the tariff plan tab, clicking on the 'Change account status' link.

I had some savings so I wouldn't starve. Payment could be made only from a statcard, to link the account to a person's biometrics. This meant that Dan_23214 was now my character.

Congratulations!
You have set up a permanent account. Activate auto-payment?
...

Gee, they were quick. I'd think about it. I had a whole month.

Over the next day, I farmed the rats with the persistence of a maniac, getting my character to Level 21. I continued to invest all available points into Adaptability, which gave me a noticeable increase in resistance to various kinds of negative effects. This was important if I ever wanted to escape the underground.

The Edge of the Abyss was drawing me in more and more, my mind seeming to dissolve in cyberspace and become a part of it. I was unwittingly starting to believe that everything around me was real.

Alarm bells were ringing but I couldn't go back to my old life. I understood that clearly.

In between farming, as I waited for the mobs to respawn, I explored the central sewer hall again. There was nothing new or worthy of my attention. The underground was populated by insects and rats.

I tried to establish contact with Jeber_Arium. The guy's mind was severely affected. He continued to shy away from me so I had to be cautious. The only thing that drew him was the fire. I regularly started one but he wouldn't approach for some reason, staring at it from a distance. Eventually, I thought to walk away, pretending that I was looking for wood among the piles of garbage.

I saw him draw closer and then sit down by the fire, warming his cold hands and being mesmerized by the flames.

I indeed found another tree branch in the trash, but I was struggling to pull it out. Jeber_Arium heard the noise and glanced in my direction. The stupid branch wouldn't budge.

"Jeb, help me, will you? Can't you see that I can't manage by myself?"

He didn't even twitch and then, annoyingly, my timer went off.

The mobs were respawning!

An angry squeak came from the nearest nest. A large rat climbed out, spotted me, immediately went hostile and leaped for my throat.

I instinctively threw out my arm to protect myself and the creature sank its teeth into my wrist. My usual tactic wouldn't work now. There were a lot of rats and I had accidentally put myself between two nests.

I pulled out my broken sword to beat them back but there were too many enemies. They overwhelmed me with their numbers, biting my legs and several jumping on me at once.

The Bleeding debuff appeared. My Life bar turned

yellow and shrunk in half.

I was going to be so pissed off if I died right now!

A crooked shadow flashed past and one of the rats shrieked and died as a thrown stone smashed its skull open.

I was barely alive. The mounds of garbage shifted as rats surrounded me on all sides. They were going to overwhelm me. I couldn't even reach the poisonous fog. It was too far and I didn't have enough Stamina to cross the whole room.

Jeb threw several more rocks and rushed towards me, pulling out an object from a pile of trash as he went.

It was a roughly cobbled-together fragment of a door with an awkward handle, made out of boards that were beginning to rot around the edges.

Jeb used it as a shield and began waving a firebrand around.

Sparks flew in all directions and the smoke scared away the mobs. The rats scattered but Jeb didn't stop there. While I retreated to the respawn circle (regeneration went faster there), he managed to run back to the fire, use a fragment of pottery to scoop up some hot coals and poured them into the disturbed rat nest!

An enraged screech echoed through the space. The garbage was tossed into the air as if there had been an explosion. What was going on?

A miniboss! An enormous rat the size of a calf, its

fur singed in several places. Well done, Jeb! Did he aggravate it by accident or did he know what he was doing?

Protorat. Level 30.

Its stench washed over us.

…

Aura of Malodor. The speed of your Stamina regeneration is reduced.

Aura of Disgust. Your movement speed is reduced when you attempt to approach the Protorat.

Toxic breath. Damage 2 HP/sec.

…

"Jeb, get back!" I yelled.

He understood me and retreated to the fire.

The Protorat screeched again and launched itself at us. It's health bar dropped slightly as the burns on its skin continued to smolder, inflicting small amounts of fire damage. It was probably the only weakness of the rat miniboss.

I had absolutely no idea how to kill it. My glove wasn't much help. I'm no pyromaniac. I had to put quite a lot of effort into starting even a normal fire.

Thoughts raced through my mind. My Life bar hadn't even returned to half-full and continued to pulse a yellow color. Jeb was OK but could I count on him?

The Protorat pounced on us.

"Shield!" I screamed.

Jeber was quick on his feet in battle. He gave me

the wooden door and rolled out of the way.

Sadly, it ended quickly and painfully. The first swipe of the clawed paw smashed through the improvised shield and the next swipe ended my life.

...

YOU HAVE DIED.

1,234 Exp lost.

Chapter Eight

MAX WAS RIGHT. I was catastrophically lacking in gaming experience. Why did I stand there like a dolt, covering myself with the door? Was I hoping that the hit wouldn't get through my defense?

I could feel my nerves fraying. Wasn't it a bit early? Was my mind that weak?

That's all right. Let's try again.

The trembling wouldn't settle. The 50% of realism was making itself known.

During the war, we were all in God's hands. Only an idiot didn't fear death. What were the new technologies offering us?

The chance to die again and again. The sensations were enough to send one mad. My arm was still aching and there was a lump in my throat from the reeking breath of the beast that had killed me.

What do we need VR capsules for? Why do we need full immersion?

A hissing interrupted my thoughts and a bright light shone in my eyes.

Mandatory exit for medical reasons, flashed the message.

My health was fine. This VR capsule was more basic, one of the older models. The metabolic correction wasn't as gentle and the 50% of realism were having an effect. I looked at the system message. I was blocked for 4 hours from going back into VR.

How annoying. I was worried about Jeb. How was he doing in there? Had he been sent into respawn as well or had he survived and was hiding somewhere the miniboss couldn't reach him?

I clambered out of the VR capsule, spent a long time in the shower, then ordered dinner and went online.

I probably looked quite weird. A grown-up man staring into space. Only my pupils were moving from time to time.

Well, how else to do it? All the information was displayed through the contact lenses. Reading off a holographic monitor no longer seemed convenient. One got used to good things quickly.

What did experienced players say about realism levels? It was an important question. I needed more information about all aspects of virtual life, as long as the information was trustworthy since the internet was full of flooding and trolling. It could be difficult to separate fact from fiction.

'If you haven't been to the Edge of the Abyss, you haven't lived...'

'We have been asked to cast off our moral bonds and show our true nature...'

'Let the strongest survive. The Abyss forever! All the trappings of civilization disappear like chaff in less than a day. You will do things that you would have never thought possible. Seriously. This isn't an ad. We're animals.'

'Restricted to 18+. What a joke. What about the children whose parents rent VR capsules in entertainment centers and are away from home for days at a time?'

Those were the most sensible posts taken from a mass of swearing, confusion, exalted excitement, fear and madness.

The situation appeared to be in freefall. The Edge of the Abyss couldn't be shut down since the servers were scattered all over the world and many countries, such as India, refused to do so. They had no intention of switching off millions of VR capsules. On the contrary, they were building skyscrapers filled with equipment designed for full immersion.

After this trip through the World Wide Web, I was left with the persistent feeling that someone had poured a bucket of ice water and kitchen scraps over my head.

All right. I had nothing to lose. I'd keep digging.

OK, what could I find out about the gameplay?

I searched for 'level of realism and leveling up a character'.

To my surprise, I found an intelligent answer quite quickly. It turned out that there were plenty of sensible players, who published genuinely useful information. This is what I found:

The 10% of realism recommended by the developers is a dead end. The character needs to be leveled up at 50% at least. I'll explain why.

First, weak pain sensations (when a wound feels like a scratch) lead to a dismissive attitude. You don't develop your fighting skills. You act carelessly while your opponent, who has at least 50% of realism, knows the price of pain and has practiced every move, trains hard and is motivated.

Second, the fear of pain can be overcome. You will be rewarded with an intensity of other sensations, plus, pain can be reduced to a minimum. Don't let yourself get hit. Don't start fights that you can't win. Don't neglect the abilities of a multiclass character if you're traveling solo or gather experienced healers into your party. Healing during battle removes all the painful effects — I've experienced this in practice. Some buffs significantly reduce negative sensations, plus, your defense and resistance increase with time (as you level up).

Most importantly, remain in control. Pick the regions and locations that match your level. Pay more attention to daily training and then the Edge of the Abyss will show you its best side.

Weigh up your strength and stay calm when you confront your enemies...

The return to the Edge of the Abyss went as normal.

First came the intro and then I found myself standing in the resurrection circle.

Nothing had changed. The same muted light came from the fissure and the hunched figure of Jeber_Arium could be barely seen through the fumes.

"Hello!" I waved to him.

He started in surprise, stood up and raised his spear to attack but then recognized me. The tip of the weapon dropped back down and then an incredible thing happened. He hurried towards me, stumbling, grabbed my elbow, squeezed it tightly and stared intently into my eyes.

"I thought you weren't coming back," he said, his voice gruff and hesitant.

The long isolation had disturbed his psyche. Alone among the mobs, in a completely hopeless situation, he had gradually lost all hope and remained alive only thanks to his instincts. His hopes and dreams had all faded away and his desires had grown simple, limited to a gulp of water, a bite of food and the search for a safe corner where he could fall into a restless sleep. But now I could see a glimmer of awareness in his eyes.

It was worth coming back just for this. The important thing now was not to let him sink back into himself and become apathetic.

"What happened to the miniboss?"

"I ran away and it buried itself back in the garbage."

"How are we going to get out of here? Have you thought about it?"

"We're too weak," he shrugged hopelessly.

"That's true. Yet you used to be much stronger, right?"

I couldn't even imagine what this guy had gone through. I could see the internal struggle reflected on his gaunt and haggard face. Paleness spreads over his cheeks like gray spots.

"Yes," he said hollowly.

"Can you remember and teach me?"

"I can barely remember that power," Jeb admitted. "I lost it..."

"What was your level?"

Jeb wrinkled his forehead in thought. His thinness made him look like an old man. "Seventy-three, I think."

"Cool... what did you specialize in?"

"Battle magic," he said, sounding uncertain.

"Could you teach me?"

Jeb hesitated. The guides that I had read insisted that two multiclass players could train each other and level up.

"I've forgotten everything,"

"No, you haven't. It's just that the game penalized you by reducing your highest characteristic. Which is Intellect, right?"

He shrugged and seemed to shrink into himself.

"Come on, don't give up already! Do you remember how to use the interface?"

He nodded.

"Open the characteristics tab. How high is your Adaptability?"

"Ten," Jeb replied after a pause.

"Excellent. Let's get you up two more levels. Then we'll start teaching each other all sorts of tricks. Combat and magic ones. Got it? Excellent. Go and gather some rocks. Let's piss off those rats and drag them into the fumes."

We raced back and forth through the tunnels until evening, disturbing nests, annoying the rodents and killing them in the dead end beyond the toxic cloud.

We had completely exhausted ourselves out but also advanced Jeb up three levels. We barely spoke during the monotonous farming, and even now, sitting by the fire, we continued to breathe heavily. We were both very drowsy but had to eat something first. I had already received two warning messages about the upcoming debuffs.

I found an old, crumpled metal helmet and attached a clumsy handle, turning it into an impromptu cooking pot, which I filled with water and hung over the fire. Our ability to survive in terrible conditions was the result of our minds and not brute force.

Once the water had boiled, I took the rat meat out of my inventory, which the mobs often dropped as loot, and added two pieces to the pot. At least I didn't have to gut the rats first.

The night passed calmly.

By sleeping in shifts and keeping the fire going, we both got a good night's rest and received the Vigor buff.

Jeb continued to act like a wild thing, at times peering at me worryingly or growing melancholic and withdrawn, but this was tolerable.

The mobs had long respawned and were darting about among the garbage but not coming close to the fire and the respawn circle.

I hung the pot over the fire again and warmed up yesterday's stew, making myself eat a little. Jeb wasn't too picky in that sense, chowing it down merrily.

While he finished breakfast, I found the remainder of the hapless door. The handle was still attached to it. It would do for now. I had none of the necessary instruments in my possession, only a dagger. I used it to sharpen two sticks. I gave the long one to Jeb and kept the short one for myself.

"Let's go," I indicated a small open area on the other side of the creek.

"There's nothing to farm there," my companion noted.

"Today's training," I replied. "Attack and defend!"

Jeb didn't understand what I meant at first, staring at me with distrust. I had to poke him with my stick, which imitated the length of the broken sword. The wooden stick inflicted 1-2 points of damage. It had laid in the water for a long time and was swollen with moisture, weighing about as much as the sword.

Jeb got annoyed and struck me with his 'spear' but I managed to throw up my makeshift shield in time and block his attack, and immediately tried to perform a somersault towards my opponent.

Incredibly, it worked! To be honest, I was worried about snapping my neck. However, cyberspace is lenient towards certain things, despite the level of realism, so combat acrobatics were possible in principle. Rolling over stones (most of them pointy) didn't inflict any injuries. I became slightly disorientated, which meant that I couldn't perform my finishing move but it was decent for a first try.

Jeb jumped back and jabbed at me with the spear, managing to wound me. A creepy smile lit up his face. There we go! I received 3 points of damage and a small scratch.

I got back to my feet and covered myself with the

shield.

Jeb had decided to test how tough I was. He performed a series of quick thrusts that almost pushed me into the wall and then I used a simple but effective move, batting his spear aside with my shield and immediately making a thrust into his chest.

It went very well! Jeb was knocked off his feet. If I had been holding a real sword, the scuffle would have been over.

I gave him my hand and helped him back up.

Was Jeb angry? I couldn't tell. The smile on his narrow face looked more like a scowl.

"Why fight if we don't get any experience points?" he asked huskily.

"You'll see soon. Attack me," I encouraged him.

By noon we were both swaying on our feet.

"That's it. That's enough."

Jeb lowered his spear, breathing heavily.

"Let's head back to the fire."

I opened the character tab back at the respawn circle. Not bad. Dexterity, Stamina and Strength had all increased by 12-13%. More importantly, I had learned how to do rolls and no longer responded to them with intense dizziness.

"Jeb, do you remember any simple spells from your past arsenal?"

He thought for a long time, then slowly raised his arm and made a clumsy pass. Several runes glowed and faded in the air between us.

"What is it?"

"Phantom Shield... It didn't work."

"Try again!"

Jeb hung his head. "It won't work." he whispered.

"You ought to try again!"

"Alright," he tried to draw a rather complicated (in my opinion) symbol in the air again. He was whispering something inaudibly. The piercing golden runes appeared in the air again, this time taking the shape of concentric circles that remained glowing for several seconds.

Too slow for battle. However, the most important thing was to make Jeb believe in his abilities again. If I wasn't mistaken, spell casting speed depended on Intellect and Dexterity scores. I had watched several video guides the previous night so knew what I was talking about.

"We're going to train. We'll develop our skills and teach each other."

Jeb was pessimistic despite his success. "What for?"

"To get out of here."

"What for?"

"I don't understand the question."

"It's not so bad here," Jeber_Arium spoke quietly.

"Come on, man, that won't do. Rustling through the refuse is no way to live, trust me!"

He drew his head into his shoulders. "I am afraid! I was killed... A lot... I don't want to die anymore!"

After a rest and recovering our Life and Stamina points, we returned to the other side of the creek. I decided to make the task more difficult to stop Jeb from becoming listless. A person didn't have time to mope when he was busy. It's been proven.

"Right. Look what I've got," I showed him the salamander skin glove. "Can you make a fireball using this?"

"Will you give it to me?"

"Temporarily. Then you'll give it back to me. Agreed?"

Item exchanges between players were a common thing. I could see my companion brighten up. He was clearly eager to try the glove. It was a catalyst and would speed up a cast, as well as reducing the mental energy required. Plus, he was familiar with pyromancy.

The most primitive fireballs fly in a straight line and inflict a small amount of damage. Jeb needed about ten minutes to remember the spell and get the skill back. Soon he was confidently flinging lumps of flame at me while I evaded them by practicing my rolls, hiding behind cover and even trying to attack this 'enemy mage'.

Phew...

At the end of the day, I didn't have that much Stamina. Jeb had utterly exhausted me. The leather armor was singed in a number of places and looked ready to fall apart, but I had nothing to replace it with. I would have to use the remaining rags during training instead.

I was desperate to get out of here but I still had no idea how to make it happen. The path to the portal was too dangerous. We wouldn't be able to handle the mobs living in the cave. The way to the town above had now been sealed shut. I had two unexplored tunnels but in my opinion, it was too early to explore them. We needed to train for a few more days at least, then farm the rats again to level up Jeb.

I received the following system messages today:

*You have failed to complete the quest **Rural Days. Monsters' Lair**. You have missed the full moon.*

*You have failed to complete the quest **Survival Environment**.*

*You have failed the complete the quest **Terra Incognita**.*

It was a shame, of course. It was a shame that I couldn't level up quickly enough. I was on Level 24 now but needed to reach Level 30 according to the quest and uncover the map. Nevertheless, I had learned a lot.

In the evening, I asked Jeb as we sat by the fire, "How much Intellect do you need to use the Phantom Shield?"

"Seven," he responded.

I had five but after today's farming, I also had two unused characteristic points that I received when I went up the levels. I spent them on Intellect.

"Jeb, I want to learn some simple magic."

"It's hard. Do you know the language of the ancients?"

"No, but surely I can remember how to correctly pronounce a few phrases!"

He thought it over. "What do you need it for?"

"We're in a bad spot. You can't use strong spells and I lack a decent weapon. Take shields, for example. They provide a defense bonus when they're used, but look at this," I took a screenshot and showed it to Jeb. "See how the system identifies my shield? As a 'door fragment'. My weapon is no better. Minimal damage."

My companion had noticeably perked up after our session with the fireballs.

"Fine. Let's try it. I will say the spell aloud and you will memorize it. We don't have any paper to write it down."

So that's what we did. I spent the rest of the day and evening learning a few phrases. They could be pronounced silently. When a mage learned the essence of things, they could simply think 'Fireball!' and indicate the direction with their gaze. It took a fraction of a second. It was even easier with staffs and other catalysts. Many of them were charged for a specific spell. For example, an Ice Arrow Staff or a Fireball Glove. These items could be used by any character class but required a high level of Intellect. According to the guides, this problem could be solved using various rings, amulets and other accessories (usually enchanted ones) that added extra points to a specific characteristic.

All these were pricey items. We had neither money nor the ability to visit a shop and buy enchanted objects.

Our only hope was Adaptability, continuous training and the knowledge that still remained in my companion's head.

The burning fire illuminated our haggard faces.

"Shall we try?" Jeb seemed nervous.

"Let's do it."

"Okay. Get up. Stretch your arm out as if you're holding a shield. Ready? Now say the spell aloud!"

I uttered the short casting spell without stumbling... but nothing happened. A total failure.

"How much Intellect do I need?" I asked again.

"Seven points. This is ancient battle magic," Jeb replied. "Even the wild wandering tribes that live far to the south use it."

"Are you trying to say that I'm dumber than the wild NPCs?"

He shrugged. "Try one more time."

Nothing happened again.

"It shouldn't be like this. We're doing everything right!"

"Then what's the problem? Am I supposed to be holding something in my hand? Something that looks even slightly like a shield?"

"No, the magical shield is incorporeal. It is made up of energy and wraps around the hand..." Jeb suddenly stopped and smacked himself on the forehead. "Of course! I remember! They have tattoos! I remember that I was surprised when I saw what looked like mindless squiggles. But... make a fist!"

He grabbed a piece of coal from the embers and drew a fancy symbol on the knuckles of my left hand. "Try it now, but keep your fist clenched!"

I spoke the words of the spell.

My fist was suddenly enveloped in a glow with pale yellow runes flaring into life. The air seemed to thicken and assumed the shape of a shield.

"Hit me!"

Jeb leaped up, grabbed a nearby rock and flung it at me.

I reflected the attack. There was a dull thud as if the stone had struck wood. The glow died down a moment later.

"Twenty-one seconds!"

"Three seconds for each level of Intellect?"

"Right. What about Adaptability?"

I opened my interface and had a look. The Intellect scale had filled up by a third! If I learned a few more simple spells and used them frequently, I could go up another Level!

"Jeb, how's your development going?"

"Today has half-filled up my Dexterity, Stamina and Strength bars. Plus, a new characteristic has appeared."

"Which one?"

"Faith. But I don't really know what it means yet."

"Hey, I have it too!" I said in surprise. "Just before the Influence of the Abyss, right?"

"Yup. But instead of a hint, all I get are question marks."

After such a busy and difficult day, Jeb's interest waned rapidly. He muttered something, lay down by the fire and was asleep almost immediately.

Let him rest. I'd achieved what I had set out to do, snapping the guy out of his melancholia.

I hadn't returned to the real world for a full day.

It was a restless night. I woke up frequently but then drifted back into an uneasy sleep.

In the morning, while Jeb caught some dubious-looking fish in the murky water and made breakfast, I read the guides.

It was time to decide on my character's future development once and for all. Yesterday's experiments had clearly demonstrated that even the simplest magic would be helpful in battle, especially since I wasn't using my mana at all. Even a few points of inflicted or, on the contrary, absorbed damage could play a deciding role in a critical situation.

That's a plus. What are the negatives of a multiclass character?

According to experienced players, stretching yourself too thin wasn't worth it. They recommended sticking to your class until at least Level 50 and then using rings with Intellect bonuses, which enabled you to cast a few strong spells, such as healing and various buffs to resist damage.

That wasn't for me. I had to survive in the here and now.

I found some interesting information on one of the in-game forums.

Invincible_Orus:

Today I came across a Warrior of the Abyss, level 93, at the edge of the Wild Lands. He didn't look any different at first glance. I'd seen such armor before and he had pretty average characteristics. He was armed with a great sword.

My level is 95. My outfit has bonuses for Strength, Dexterity and Stamina. I don't usually lose in single combat.

This punk buffed himself with some kind of spell and managed to coat his blade in darkness while we were nearing each other. I attacked first and the damage was minimal. I noticed that during the attack, his armor glowed with unfamiliar symbols. Then he just one-shotted me without batting an eyelid.

I looked at the logs after respawning. My attack was absorbed by Steel Flesh. I've never heard of such a buff before. Then his sword inflicted 270 points of physical damage and 470(!) was caused by the darkness. And the blade ignored my armor!

A cheater?

If anyone has come across something similar, let me know.

...

Wise_Zheka:

Not a cheater. You've met a classic example of a leveled up multiclass character. Very hard to develop at the start, like pulling teeth, but later it's best to avoid such types. Steel Flesh can be cast from Level 40 Intellect. Dark Blade requires 35 points of Intellect and 30 points of Adaptability. It does indeed ignore normal armor but fails before Light benedictions. My advice is to change your bling. Get Intellect and Faith rings, and use the Blessed Shield, which will deflect 50% of the incoming damage no matter if it's physical or elemental.

...

Well, that was something to think about. I could understand the warrior's bewilderment. A strong mage wearing armor and carrying a great sword is a killer combination of Intellect, Dexterity, Adaptability and Strength.

But the impressive result was due to persistent effort, constant physical training, intellectual exercises and careful selection of each piece of apparel.

Would I be able to develop along the same path? For example, what should I do with my one free characteristics point? Spend it on Stamina? Increase the number of HP or raise my Intellect to get three more seconds of the Phantom Shield?

To be honest, magic looked like a dubious asset for me at present. The Phantom Shield didn't last long. I could cast it a couple of times and then would have to wait for my mental energy to regenerate, or have a store of potions that refilled it instantly. But the defense that I gained from increasing my Strength remained with me forever. How could I make the right choice?

An unexpected event answered my questions.

Jeb called me to breakfast. Forcing down the tasteless broth, I didn't ask him what it was made from because I knew that we had a hard day ahead of us. We need to level up at least a couple more times before we ventured into the unexplored tunnels.

The amulet on my chest suddenly started vibrating.

I hadn't really figured out who the Guardians actually were. I tried to search for information in my free time but had found only a vague description.

The ancient legend of the Guardians states that those who are in desperate need of help will always receive it.

I started and touched my chest. As soon as my fingers made contact with the amulet, everything went dark and there was a sudden feeling of vertigo.

...The sunlight was blinding. After the dimness of the underground, I couldn't see my surroundings straight away.

What was going on?! Where was I?!

The clatter of weaponry. Heavy footsteps. The feeling of a warm, rough stone surface beneath my palm.

A respawn circle?

Had I managed to escape the cursed tunnels? But how? And what would happen to Jeb now?

...

You have discovered a new location: The Abandoned Fort.

...

I leaped to my feet and looked around. An eroded limestone staircase ran down from a platform on an old fortification standing by the river's edge.

At its base, a young fellow in awkward, blood-spattered armor struggled to stand back up after being knocked off his feet. His opponent, a tall, muscular and tough-looking barbarian, armed with a frightening great sword, smirked and squatted down beside him. He dropped the sword into the grass and took out a dagger.

I read their frames:

Sir_Lans, Knight, Level 12.

Your_Death, Dark Barbarian, Level 31.

Not what I would call a fair fight. There was an

obvious discrepancy in the levels. The shield cleaved in two, the dents on Lans' armor, the smoking fire and helmet with broken straps lying nearby — everything spoke of an unexpected attack.

"I will cut out your heart," the barbarian chuckled hoarsely. "It will be still bleeding. I am sure I will get an advanced aura for such a trophy."

The beginner knight was doomed. I only had a few seconds. Why did I need to help him? I had no idea. It was what my conscience was telling me. Even if I had to respawn after this, I wouldn't be able to hide and watch as the Dark player cut out the guy's heart.

The dagger sliced through the straps holding the breastplate in place.

I rushed to the platform and stood at the very edge of the pitted stone.

It was a hunch. I had read enough guides over the last few days about balance in the digital world and the patterns and variations in character developments to be certain that to use the heavy great sword, the barbarian would have had to invest heavily in Strength and Stamina. He was thus unevenly developed. He hadn't developed his Life Force and so wouldn't have that many HP.

I jumped down, clutching the sword fragment with both hands.

...

You have studied Falling Strike. Critical damage 200%.

The barbarian's Life bar was almost completely wiped out and he was flung to the ground but not killed.

Swearing incoherently, he managed to get back on his feet, grab his daunting sword and swing it overhead. Where did he even find the strength?

I would have normally panicked but no longer. The training with Jeb hadn't been wasted. I rolled away from the slashing blow and jumped back up, noting as I did that Falling Strike had a price — my own Life bar had shrunk by a third.

This was bad. The barbarian wouldn't let me get closer.

The stump of a rusty sword was no match for a great sword. I doubted that I would have the Stamina to exhaust my opponent and catch a good moment to repeat my attack.

I shifted the broken sword to my right hand, automatically made a fist with my left and the ancient phrases that I had studied so intently last night raced through my head.

It worked!

The Phantom Shield enveloped my left arm. But how did I manage to cast it when the rune written in charcoal must have rubbed off by now?

That wasn't the case. Jeb had pressed too hard. My skin was still covered in scratches that formed the ancient symbol when I clenched my fingers.

Twenty seconds.

I rushed forward, the transparent energy shield doing what it was meant to do by absorbing the damage and then shattering into gold fragments.

The sword fragment crunched through the barbarian's Adam's apple and wiped out his remaining Life points.

The Dark one's legs collapsed under him. He tried to say something but choked on his own blood, fell to the side, twitched and lay still.

I was shaking from the adrenaline rush.

...

You have defeated an enemy.

You have saved Sir_Lans from death.

The quest Secret of Forest Hill has been updated. Find out who the Guardians are. Unlimited time to complete. The reward varies.

You have reached a new Level.

...

The world around me faded to black again. The last thing I noticed before disappearing was the shocked face of the young knight. "I thought the Guardians were just a legend!" came his words and then the dark claimed me and the stench of refuse returned.

Jeb was backing away from me as if he was seeing a ghost.

"What?"

"You disappeared! You were gone for several minutes." He was completely taken aback, unsure of how to react.

"I don't know what's happening myself. Calm down and I'll tell you what I saw."

Chapter Nine

THE FARMING HAD to be postponed. Jeb was really puzzled and intrigued, and I was baffled as well. The place where I had just been wasn't marked on the world map at all, but a sketch had appeared in my traveler's diary: the ruins of an old fort, the riverbank, Lans and the barbarian. It was made to look like a stylized pencil sketch done by the firm hand of an experienced artist.

We examined it.

"It's our time zone," Jeb noted, pointing to the position of the sun.

After yesterday's experiments with magical abilities, he had finally remembered himself and was speaking coherently and to the point.

"I didn't see a portal anywhere in the vicinity!"

"It was a summoning," Jeb replied confidently.

"High-level magic. It requires Level 50 Intellect, at least."

"So, Sir_Lans couldn't have called me?"

"With his Level 12? No, of course not!" he laughed and then added more seriously, "A 'third power' must have been involved, mighty enough to manipulate cyberspace. I doubt that we'll find out who had summoned you and how, unless you receive a relevant quest."

"I received one ages ago," I responded, briefly telling him about the Secret of Forest Hill. "But I have to get out of here to complete it."

"True," he sighed.

Taking advantage of his interest and good mood, I decided to bring up an issue that had been bothering me. "Jeb, I've got something serious to discuss with you."

"Yeah?" he squatted down, keeping his spear ready and not looking at me, but rather monitoring our surroundings.

"You haven't left the VR capsule in a long time. Jeb, you need to exit into the real world."

"No," he snapped.

"Why?"

"I can barely remember anything."

"Don't avoid the question!"

Jeb was silent for a long time, then sighed and quietly confessed, "My logout doesn't work. It's blocked 'due to medical indications'," predicting my next question, he added. "I've drowned in the digital world, and there's nothing I can do about it."

"I don't see how exiting the game could harm you. Do you remember anything about yourself? Where you live, for example? I could find your relatives and get you help. The capsule can be pried opened, after all, even if the tech has blocked the exit, believing that it'd be better for you to remain under the care of the life support!"

"It's not an option," Jeb replied with a frown. "I'm afraid that I don't have anybody. Plus, my past is a fog. Let's drop it, OK? I can't tell you my address or my real name. I simply don't remember them."

"The VR capsule's resources aren't infinite!"

"I know. I just don't want to think about it! I become scared, don't you see?" his fingers whitened around his spear.

"All right. Calm down."

We sat by the fire for a while. I told Jeb my story and he listened, staring intently into the flames.

"I've heard about portal keys," he said. "But not about Soul Crystals. Still, I think Igor from the Mongooses is right. The artifact has something to do with teleportation, just like your Guardian's Amulet. Do you want to try getting out of here using them?"

"I'd be curious to know how."

"Come, I'll show you," he stood up, picked up his weapon, and with no further explanation, walked towards one of the two unexplored tunnels.

We didn't have to go far. Thirty paces in, we saw an old, partially destroyed brick wall. Someone had bricked up a side branch of the collector but prospectors had been here at a later time, for we could see the evidence of pickaxe blows in the light of the torch.

Jeb clambered into the break. "Dan, over here!"

The hole was quite long and narrow. I followed Jeb with a grunt. The musty smell and the cobwebs touching my face made me grimace.

A familiar iridescent glow appeared up ahead.

A portal, really?

Another push and I clambered out into a more or less spacious room. The walls contained archways, collapsed and filled with mountains of rubble. In the center, outlined by barely smoldering runes, trembled a black and purple clump of magical energy.

"Did the Abyss break through here?"

"Yep," Jeb confirmed and added, "This actually used to be a normal portal, but then something happened to it and the room was bricked up."

"How do you know?"

"I can read the ancient runes," Jeb squatted down and ran his hand over the dully glowing symbols, some of them flaring a little brighter in response. "See?"

"You tried to activate the portal just now?"

"Yes, but it is blocked by another order, prohibiting

177

teleportation. A powerful mage created it. There's an explanation. A symbol that means danger."

"To put it simply, someone has blocked the portal and wrote, 'Don't climb in, it'll kill you?'"

Jeb laughed. "I didn't think of such an interpretation but yeah, that's the right meaning!"

"How do we get past the block? Do we need to remove some of the runes? For example, smash the stones upon which they are carved?"

"I'm sure the runes are protected. Still, if one of your artifacts is really a portal key, the passage will open. Try it yourself."

"Okay," I gently and slowly began to move my hand over the portal stone, and one of the characters suddenly shone brightly. As if bright, golden rays had cut through the stone surface.

"Stop!" Jeb grabbed my arm. "That's enough!"

"But it's working!"

"We don't know what's over there. We have to prepare ourselves..." he seemed to be overwhelmed with panic.

I moved my hand reluctantly away and the glow faded.

Jeb scanned his surroundings. His pupils were dilated and his face frozen in an expression of inexplicable horror. I understood his sudden state. He'd been exposed to way too much realism. It was better not to push him, forcing him to go against the surge of fear. I could easily drive him back into his

178

shell.

"Let's go back to the fire."

We returned to the central hall. Jeb was silent yet I could see a fierce internal fight taking place.

"I've got the Cooking skill. I'll prepare some meat for our journey." he promised, sounding lost.

I nodded, sank down by the fire and started looking for information on portals.

I had landed in the Edge of the Abyss by accident and I simply didn't know many aspects of the virtual world, so I had to catch up as questions arose.

So, portals. As it turned out, each location was equipped with its own teleportation stone, usually not far from the respawn point. Anyone could use the instant transport system without any special abilities. In addition to the stationary teleportation network, there were also scrolls, which could send a player to a known location. Moreover, a powerful mage, a sorcerer or a druid could create a temporary portal.

The instant transport system had failed when the Abyss appeared. A large part of the cyberspace had been visibly altered. Portal stones in the Wild Lands changed their location, lost their links to known coordinates, but didn't lose their properties. Travelers could find them and put them on the map and then the discovered portal became accessible again. It was harder in the Dark Frontier. The few who had been here noted that the stones they found were protected by additional runes. To activate the portal, one needed to know the correct touch sequence. There was a note online stating that trying random combinations through trial and error could easily send one into respawn.

As far as I could understand, the ill-fated Abyss portals (through which the invasion had taken place) had been mostly shut down or destroyed, while the remaining ones spread negative effects around them (i.e., Abyss mutations).

Did that mean that the teleportation stones located in the collector and in the former dwarf settlement could take us to safe regions to which they'd once been connected?

Not a given, since we couldn't accurately predict where we'd be sent because of the past catastrophe. It was possible that the receiving devices now lay at the bottom of the ocean or at the top of snow-capped mountains. There was a reason why someone had blocked the portal and drew a symbol indicating danger.

Right, what about my newfound (but completely undocumented) ability?

It was definitely being generated by one of the items in my inventory. It was likely that Igor from the Mongooses was right, and the Soul Crystal was a master key to the teleportation system. It allowed me to ignore bans and even use 'destroyed' portals, as had happened in the ransacked estate.

It all made sense in general, but there was still

plenty to figure out...

I opened my character panel. Thanks to the unexpected summoning, I had reached Level 25 today, and with it, a significant and long-awaited event.

Choose your first ability from the three options:

Rage — you become completely immersed in the element of battle. Effect: sustained damage is reduced by 5% while the damage you inflict is increased by 5%, duration 30 seconds, cooldown/reload 5 minutes. With each new ability level, your damage absorption increases by 5% and your inflicted damage increases by 5%. The cooldown/reload time is reduced by 30 seconds. Maximum ability level — 5.

...

Resilience: you are cold-blooded and calculating in battle. Permanent effect: use of Stamina when blocking attacks is reduced by 5%. With each new ability level, Stamina expenditure will decrease by 5%. Maximum ability level — 5.

...

Purist: you are used to relying on your physical abilities without being distracted by various magical 'tricks' in battle. Effect: mana is spent instead of health points at critical moments in battle (HP <5%)

...

Purist clearly didn't suit me if I was planning to develop a multiclass character. I was left to choose between Rage and Resilience.

I make a quick calculation: if I developed Rage to

the maximum level, I would gain a temporary +25% to my defense, +25% to damage, and the ability cooldown would drop down to two and a half minutes. Given that the bonuses were expressed as a percentage, their values would grow, or, as they say, 'scale up' as I developed.

It was decided. I chose Rage.

Now I had to distribute several free characteristic points. This was what I got in the end:

Dan, Level 25
Race: Human
Class: Warrior
Life Force 12
Strength 12
Dexterity 5
Stamina 13
Intellect 7
Adaptability 15
Luck 5
Charisma 5
Damage (fists) 24
Faith (undetermined)
Effect of the Abyss 0
Mutations 0

Primary skills:
Race bonus +2 to Adaptability
Class bonus +1 to Strength, +2 to Stamina

HP 240/240

Maximum load 60 kg

Dodge Chance 5%

Physical Energy 65

Mental Energy 35

Resistance 15%

Chance of Successful Hit 2.5%

Attractiveness 5

Damage (magic) 0 (no spells)

Physical Defense 12+20.3

Agility 5

Faster Regeneration 6.5%

Learning Ability 7, Mental Defense 17.5

Adaptive Leveling (active)

Ability to Create Multiclass - available

Chance of Finding Items 2.5%

Possible number of NPC companions 1

Damage (broken sword) 48-60

Secondary skills:

Battle technique + 5% to physical defense when using light and medium shields

Abilities:

Rage (level 1)

Fame 2 (Normal Wanderer

Required to reach next level: 5500 Exp (0 Exp available)

While I mused about all this, Jeb had calmed down a little and recovered from his panic attack. He was preparing the meat and casting occasional guilty glances in my direction.

I had to cheer him up. Yes, I was also afraid to plunge into the unknown, but we couldn't remain here, eternal prisoners of the musty dungeon.

"Jeb?"

"Yeah?" he turned around.

"I suggest we form a party."

"Sure, I don't mind." he said and a message icon blinked in my interface.

I opened it and read,

Jeber_Arium invites you to join a group.

Many of our dilemmas were solved by chance again.

It felt like events were forming a slowly spinning whirlwind with Jeber_Arium and I in the epicenter.

The distant light of a torch flickered through a gap in the wall and a muted echo carried the sound of voices muffled by distance.

Jeb was immediately on edge, "Someone's coming!"

"I can hear it. Go and hide!"

"What about you?"

"I won't stick my head out either, for now. We'll observe first."

The Dark Frontier was a dangerous place. It would be naive to think that its inhabitants, whoever they were, would be friendly.

I rushed over to the creek, scooped up some water, put out the fire and hid behind a pile of stones that had accumulated under the fissure in the vault.

"Check it out, amber resin! A lot of it!"

"Mark the place on the map. We'll come back here later." replied a second voice.

"Have you decided to become a crab[4]?" a third voice chuckled.

"What's it to you?"

The uneven light of a torch lit up the jagged break.

"I think we're here. He should be somewhere nearby. See the respawn point?"

"Yep, behind the mounds of garbage. It's activated."

"Dan must be here! Hey, come on out or we'll find you anyway!" hollered the large Dark Warrior.

I wondered what they needed me for and how the heck they had found me in the first place.

"Hey, kiddo, there's no point in hiding from us! The Shadows want to talk to you."

I was all for having a chat, especially as I had plenty of questions. It was the players' smoky auras that concerned me. Someone had sent three Dark players after me. A Warrior, a Mage and an Archer, all Level 35. The mysterious Shadows were aware of my progress

---

[4] Crab (slang) - a player engaged in collecting resources.

and were operating within the PvP range, without the risk of subjecting their minions to penalties, even if they decided to send me into a series of respawns.

Well, what were my chances in a fair fight? In my worn-out outfit and with a broken sword in hand, I wouldn't last a minute against any of them.

"Listen, Dan, don't be a newb and get yourself in trouble. There's three of us. You've got nowhere to go, so come on out! Otherwise, we'll get very upset and may keep you in reskill for a little bit, which is painful and unpleasant, as you surely know!"

He was clearly mocking me, aware of his superiority.

I sent Jeb a quick message,

Stay hidden. This is my problem.

I didn't want him to get killed.

It was relatively quiet underground. I could hear the gurgle of the reeking creek and the squeaking of the rats.

"Well, well, well," the Dark Warrior interpreted my silence in his own way. "You asked for it, so don't complain later."

I could see that Jeb hadn't obeyed my warning and was plotting something. He was silently and stealthily making his way to the center of the hall, between compacted piles of refuse. He had the salamander glove on his hand!

"What do you want with me?" I asked and rapidly rounded a mound of stones, changing my location.

"Ha! There you are!" the Dark Warrior smiled condescendingly but answered nevertheless, "We're on a mission to capture you. You shouldn't have revealed yourself as a Guardian. The Shadows are furious. They hate people like you so they've given us an assignment."

"What will happen to me now?" I asked, playing for time. I thought that I had figured out what Jeb was planning.

"That's not for us to decide. You can ask the Shadows yourself," the Dark Warrior headed in my direction decisively, having determined it from my voice. The Mage and Archer also came through the break in the wall, grimacing at the smell of sewage and toxic fumes.

Jeb grinned creepily and sent a fireball into the Protorat's lair.

The garbage was thrown up in all directions. The surviving miniboss flew into a rage at once, his aggro zone covering the whole central hall. The Dark players found themselves cut off from the gap that they had come through but I had to give it to them, they kept their cool. The Warrior covered himself with his shield, the Mage instantly cast some kind of buff on him, while the Archer raised his weapon, pulled back the string and released five burning arrows, one after another, which struck the Protorat's snout.

The creature screeched terribly.

Stun 5 seconds.

Horror 20 seconds. Effect: -5 to Stamina, -5 to Dexterity.

Aura of Malodor. Your Stamina regeneration rate is reduced.

Aura of Disgust. Your movement speed is reduced when you attempt to approach the Protorat.

Toxic Breath. Damage 2 HP/sec

...

Jeb rolled away, shaking his head. My legs gave out from under me and I could barely move but the Protorat ignored us, focusing on the Dark players instead. They had made a mistake in injuring him and thus attracting his attention.

However, Jeb and I weren't faring much better. The screech of the miniboss had drawn all the other rats to the fray. I had never had to deal with so many of the smaller creatures at once. They came from everywhere, trickling in like gray streams.

Jeb deftly dodged several attacks and with a wave of his spear, pointed in the direction of the tunnel where we had found the portal.

He was right. It was the only way out now!

I rolled over the piles of garbage, noticing out of the corner of my eye how confident and well-coordinated the Dark players were. The Warrior was bravely taking the damage, blocking attacks with his shield, the Mage was constantly buffing and healing him, while the Archer dealt damage. The Protorat's HP bar had already decreased by a third!

We were breathing heavily.

We had escaped the central hall with hardly any Life points remaining — there had been too many rats in our way.

"Hurry! Activate the portal!" Jeber_Arium switched from his spear to a curved handmade staff, and we were enveloped in a pale golden aura that slowly restored our Life points.

The guides weren't lying! The pain from the bites immediately became bearable and the numerous wounds stopped bleeding.

"Watch the tunnel!" I stretched out my arm. A roar came from some distance away. It seemed like things weren't going well for the Protorat, so the miniboss had moved to the next fighting phase, showing the Dark players a new set of abilities.

My fingers were shaking. The hand hovering over the runes began to rapidly go numb yet nothing was happening.

"Concentrate!" Jeb screamed. His words were louder than the Protorat's squeal.

"I'm trying!"

Smaller creatures crept into the tunnel after us as the mobs also tried to avoid the enraged miniboss. The walls were plastered in centipedes and poisonous spiders that had appeared from somewhere. I'd never come across them before in this dungeon,.

The first symbol finally flashed brightly. I was bathed in sweat. My mental energy decreased and the blue bar grew rapidly shorter.

The second rune lit up with brilliant rays.

Jeb was fighting off the spiders and centipedes as he gradually stepped closer to me.

Four... Five...

The portal turned into a humming, almond-shaped eye.

"Quick!" I stepped first into the unknown, desperately hoping that Jeber_Arium would follow me.

Unbearable heat licked my face.

My hair crackled, coiling into stinking balls. The portal shimmered behind me while an endless starry sky spread out overhead. A green moon, half-enveloped by clouds, hung in the zenith, while a fissured and flaming plain stretched out before me, fiery tornadoes swirling among the building ruins.

...

You have unlocked a portal!

+10 to Fame if you place its coordinates on the public maps.

...

You have discovered a new region, the Scorched Lands.

+10 to Fame if you publish the information in the Game Encyclopedia.

The mage who had sealed the teleportation stone and left a warning had been farsighted, while we were stupid and arrogant.

The flames were erupting everywhere!

Jeb screeched, his eyes bulging, but it was impossible to predict when the next pillar of fire would appear. They flared up chaotically and lasted bare moments, managing to burn but not to kill...

"Retreat!" I croaked, but my limbs were paralyzed by pain, the skin blistering and bursting, causing suffering and yet making the Life bar drop only little by little. Respawn was still far off but madness hovered close.

An ash cloud with a crimson glow was coming at us, shaggy, smoky emissions shooting out from it, flowing around obstacles and momentarily assuming the shapes of fantastical creatures. Or was I going crazy?

Jeb swung his crooked staff as if in slow motion, and a bubble of cool air formed around us.

I looked around. Curiosity was stronger than the instinct to flee. Clusters of ruby crystals lay underfoot, smoldering like coals. There was no time to identify them since the effect of the buff wouldn't last long so I simply scooped them up into my inventory. I didn't want to leave empty-handed!

The ash cloud was getting closer, Jeb was shouting something and trying to pull me away but I was glued to the spot by the sinister beauty of this place. I couldn't have imagined it or seen it in my dreams, but the sensations were so realistic that it sent shivers down my spine.

"Let's go, let's go!" Jeber_Arium dragged me back to the portal's iridescent film before the air bubble dissipated, the only thing saving us from a painful death.

A fire devil split off from the cloud and rushed towards us.

...

Ifrit Level 50, reported the interface.

...

I think I screamed. I could barely remember any details, everything merged into a single shocking impression.

Jeb managed to pull me back into the portal.

The burning plain, ash cloud and velvety green moon all disappeared. We were back in the reeking, dimly lit cavern.

"Dan, turn off the teleport!"

I obeyed automatically and raised my hand, intending to extinguish the runes. In that moment, the Ifrit burst through the rainbow film. A wall of heat washed over us and we were scattered aside as if there had been an explosion.

The portal died. The fiery beast raced further into the tunnel, burning everything in its path.

Jeb and I barely survived. We coughed convulsively. The Protorat's roar could no longer be heard and the underground was rapidly filling with suffocating smoke. It wasn't clear what had happened to the Dark ones, but right now, we had other things to worry about.

"Jeb, we need another air bubble!"

"I can't! My mana's at zero."

"What do we do?"

"The other tunnel." he croaked. "There's another portal!"

"A sealed one, too?" I asked, horrified.

"Yes! Over here, quick. It's not far."

Chapter Ten

JEB AND I MADE our way in the dark through a crevice of some kind. We moved almost exclusively by touch but Jeb knew the way and led me forward confidently. The Ifrit was rampaging in the central hall, beside the respawn point. Acrid smoke drifted into the fissure.

Jeb stopped.

"What's the matter?" I asked worriedly.

"I've accumulated some mana... Here..."

A pale light source appeared over our heads, looking like a tiny clump of milky white radiance. Now I could see the walls and uneven vault of this narrow tunnel. It looked like it had been made by dwarves.

"This way," Jeb forced aside a heavy boulder.

I followed him through the opening.

We were in a dark square hall with the entrance

blocked off. A stone circle stood in the middle of the floor, segments carved into its surface. A magical symbol shone dully on each one. I was already familiar with some of them.

"Can you activate it? Have you got enough strength?"

"I'll try."

The walls were trembling and small stones occasionally clattered down from the ceiling. The fiery monster continued its rampage.

The smoke was reaching us even here. My mind began to drift and my eyes stung.

...

You have received carbon monoxide poisoning.
You are finding it hard to breathe.
You're suffering from a lack of oxygen.
Your Intellect has been reduced by 1 point.

...

This was bad. My mental energy was running low anyway!

"Dan, focus! Quickly, activate it."

My only hope was the mysterious artifact. I moved my hand over the symbols. Some of them flared up brighter than the others but I was struggling to keep a grip of reality. My dizziness intensified and it wouldn't be long before I lost consciousness.

The portal flared purple.

Jeb slumped to the floor. With the last of my strength, I picked him up and pushed him into the sinister glow, then stepped in myself.

It was cold.

The air was thin but clear. Were we in the highlands?

The mental question finally brought me to my senses. Jeb and I had been very lucky. We had barely made it. A little longer and we would have remained underground as amusement for the Ifrit, who would have sent us into respawn time and time again.

...

You have discovered the Deadly Crag.

...

I stood up with a groan, picked up the broken sword and peered around me. What a strange place.

Where was the portal? And what the hell had happened to Jeber_Arium?

There was no vegetation around me, only bare, cracked and weathered cliffs. A small stone ledge extended over the precipice. The respawn circle flickered unevenly at the edge of the platform, and further out... honestly, the imagination of the game designers! I couldn't believe my eyes at the start. Everything below the precipice was covered in a thick, greenish fog that swirled and twisted in fleeting knots, forming currents, but this wasn't the most remarkable thing. In the gloom, I could see a lifeless planetoid covered with craters!

How was this possible?

Man, I kept forgetting that I was in cyberspace. All right. I'd take that as a given. So what if a small moon was hanging right under the cliff? Someone had obviously been in a surreal mood when they had sketched the location, that's all.

I suspected that the bizarre designs would soon stop surprising me altogether. Right now, I had to think about the most pressing issue. Where had Jeber_Arium gone?

Oh, there he was, cautiously peeking out from behind a sharp fragment of rock.

"Jeb, where's the portal?"

"I have no idea! Maybe it's higher up? We seem to have rolled down a scree but it's very steep so we won't be able to climb back up. Dan, come over here, I've found something!"

"Coming. Did you see what's happening below the cliff?"

"Fog and some kind of planet."

"Is that normal, in your mind?"

"I don't know. I don't care. If someone wanted it like this, it may have been created as a special order."

"Do you mean the location?"

"Of course."

I shrugged, involuntarily glancing toward the roiling, ghostly haze, then walked over to Jeb.

"Look!" he pointed to a pile of mixed bones. You

couldn't tell whom they had belonged to but among them lay familiar outfit items.

I picked up a shield with a faint pattern on its scratched surface. It turned out to be surprisingly light and probably very durable. There was not a single dent on it even though its previous owner must have been in hundreds of fierce fights, for what else could have almost completely erased the intricate coat of arms?

"Cool, huh? It fits your arm perfectly!"

Yes, the grip was comfortable.

"And this!" Jeb pulled out a one-handed sword with a sharp but tarnished blade from under the remains.

I examined it, reading the properties.

...

Long sword. A typical weapon for a knight, convenient, reliable, but not possessing any outstanding qualities. Damage 8-10 with scaling depending on Strength. With a high Adaptability score (15 and above), the damage can be increased using various temporary effects (magical or alchemical).

...

I rejoiced like a child. What a find! My Strength was currently 12, so the sword's base damage was 96-120! What if I buffed the blade with magic, or at least the amber resin that I had found in the cave?

I would have to try it later, but meanwhile, I examined the second item.

...

An ancient shield with a coat of arms. Creator

unknown.

Material undefined.

Protection from physical damage: 70%. Affix: Stamina consumption reduced by 10% when blocking attacks.

...

I put the rusty sword fragment away in my inventory. I couldn't throw it out. It was dear to me as a reminder of my first days spent in cyberspace.

I placed the shield on my left arm. It fit perfectly.

A paradox. A week ago, I had been whiling away my time in front of the spherovision, believing that old age had come for me and now...

"Dan, what are we going to do?" Jeb stared at me questioningly.

"Have you found the portal?"

"Not even a hint of a teleportation stone."

"Then look for any evidence of the invasion of the Abyss. Any kind of dip or scorched area. I'll examine the respawn circle. I wasn't even offered the option to change my anchor point!"

"Strange, neither was I. Nor did I receive the message that I've found a new area. There have obviously been players here, long before us. Dan, just be careful, okay? See all the bones? It's no accident."

It was a very odd place. Somehow, I wasn't surprised when I discovered that the respawn circle (roughly hewn at the edge of the cliff) was cracked and parts of it had crumbled away into the abyss. This was a problem. Some of the magical symbols were missing. HP regeneration was proceeding at a normal pace, even though natural recovery was supposed to be twice as fast at a respawn point.

The greenish gloom looked ominous. It twisted in lazy currents, streaks of fog floating above, and occasionally the ghostly substance swelled as slow flares rose to dozens of meters.

The small, lifeless planetoid drowned in the murk. I could only see the large landforms on its surface.

Meanwhile, one of the flares headed in my direction. I threw up my shield instinctively, defending myself from a possible strike.

"Jeb, have you found anything?" I shouted without turning around.

"Not yet," his voice came from afar. "There's a crumbling stone staircase. I can't climb it."

"Come back here."

The flare suddenly split up into many foggy streaks. I thought I could see ghostly figures followed by plumes of darkness.

My guess was instantly confirmed by the system

message,

Wild (mad) Shadow, Level 43.

This was once a living, sentient being, but all that remains is a clump of mental energy in an ectoplasmic shell.

Shadows of the creatures devoured by the Abyss are very aggressive and dangerous. Normal armor can't protect you from their mental attacks.

...

"Jeb, get back!"

The ephemeral figures were rapidly approaching. They were distorted beyond recognition. They moved in a zigzag, sometimes randomly rushing from side to side or ascending in a spiral.

"Are those Shadows?" Jeber_Arium took up a position behind me, cautiously peering from behind an outcrop of rock.

"Yes!"

"That's why there are so many bones here!"

"The respawn is buggy. Several ruins are missing."

"That's for the best," my companion muttered. "I wouldn't want to get stuck here."

"No sign of the portal?"

"I couldn't find anything. It must be higher up! Shall we try and climb up?"

It was a good idea. Shame that we ran out of time to carry it out.

The clot of ectoplasm crashed into my shield. I sustained no physical damage from the blow but an otherworldly chill washed over my mind and the distorted ephemeral creature pierced me with its cold.

I took a step back. The Shadow spiraled upwards. I could hear an insinuating whisper coming from all around me.

Another phantom tried to attack me. I dodged and slashed at it with my sword, but the steel passed through the disembodied figure without encountering any resistance.

"Dan, it's useless! We have to get out of here. Follow me!" Jeb shouted.

The greenish murk stirred. Hundreds of flares shot up into the sky. It had probably been a mistake to try and attack the ghost.

"Run!"

We went as fast as we could. The platform was getting narrower and narrower, passing over the rocky spurs as a treacherous, cracked cornice.

Shadows chased us. The mad clusters of mental energy drew intricate patterns in the air, slowly fading plumes trailing behind them.

We finally reached the collapsed stone stairs. We pressed ourselves close to the cliffs because the path was so narrow. We were basically balancing over the precipice.

The stone steps were crumbling. We couldn't climb up them but what else was there to do? A little longer and we would be caught and cast down into that creepy darkness.

"Dan!" Jeb lifted his spear. "I don't want to turn into a crazed Shadow!"

"What do we do? We can't go any higher. This is a dead end!"

"Kill me! Please!"

There was no time left to think. I also had no desire to become part of this eerie green murk.

"Together! Crit here." I lowered my shield, exposing my neck.

He nodded jerkily. Jeb and I struck each at the same time.

...

You have died.

You have lost 2,634 Exp.

Respawn in 19:59...

I woke up in the respawn circle, among the gloom and stench of the fire.

The underground was changed beyond recognition. The rough brick walls were covered in a layer of soot. The fissure in the vault had become wider, the tree roots hanging down having burned away, and the pile of rocks was higher. Part of the ceiling had obviously collapsed.

Jeb appeared beside me.

"How are you?"

"OK," he was staring around him as well. "The Ifrit burned down everything in here!"

"I wonder where he went? And where are the Dark players?"

Distant screams were the answer to my question. It sounded like they were coming from the gap in the ceiling. A large city previously lay on the surface. After the invasion of the Abyss, only a small settlement had remained and now it had also been destroyed, as the interface immediately informed me,

You have gained the achievement 'Culprit of the Disaster'.

Thanks to your actions, the above area has been turned to ashes and has become a home for the Ifrit. Achievement effect: +10 to Fame (a penalty of -10 to the attitude of small town inhabitants in the Dark Frontier).

...

You have received 13,750 Exp 1,375x10 (Fame).

...

You have gone up a level.

...

You have gone up a level.

...

You have received a new quest, Correcting Mistakes. Find a way to banish the fiery monster. Time to complete: unlimited.

Reward: experience, random item, improved relations with the inhabitants of small (up to 1,000 NPCs) settlements in the Dark Frontier.

"We're not ready to take on the Ifrit just yet," Jeb's shoulders slumped when I told him about the so-called achievement and the related quest. "Dan, we have to get out of here, the Dark ones will come back for sure!"

"I have an idea," I tried to cheer him up. "Can you keep an eye on the situation? I need to check the forums."

Jeb nodded. I unfocused and the digital reality faded into the background.

I entered a search query: Portals, portal projections, secret paths, portal keys.

As I expected, there wasn't much information. Most players noted that after the invasion of the Abyss, additional magical symbols had appeared on many of the teleportation stones, but nobody had yet figured out in what order they should be activated and what this would lead to. Those who had unraveled the mystery of the sequences either remained silent or had been killed. My personal experience had showed me that the latter could not be excluded. Jeb and I had been very lucky. We had managed to escape the Scorched Lands and the respawn circle had been damaged in the Deadly Crag so our anchor point hadn't changed.

Portal keys were described only hypothetically on the forums, with a promise of large sums of money for credible information about these kinds of artifacts. There was an opinion that portals could now be used both in normal mode and in the Abyss Trail mode. The additional symbols were needed to open them.

Well, although indirectly, I had nevertheless confirmed my guesses.

"Jeb!" I called, returning to the underground.

Wait, where did my companion go?

"Jeb, where are you?"

"Over here!" his voice echoed off the stone walls and vault. "Look what I found!" He emerged from the shadows grimy, covered in soot and ashes but proudly showing me a few silver and copper coins. "The Ifrit has burned away all the garbage! Do you know how much good stuff was left behind? I even found a ring!"

"Show me." My interest in the nondescript, oxidized metal ring was genuine.

"Plus 2 to Charisma. Pointless in our situation. Why did you call me?" he glanced greedily at the piles of ash.

"I need the original rune sequence found on a normal teleport."

"How would I know that?"

"You used to be Level 73. Try to remember, you probably started back on the Land of Chosen, right?"

He thought for a while, wrinkling his forehead. "Yeah, I think so."

"You don't have any records or pictures from that time?"

"I'll have a look, maybe I still have something."

Jeb soon sent me a picture of a teleportation stone before it had been altered.

How curious. I immediately began to compare it to the images obtained during the recent portal activation.

There they were, the Abyss runes! The magic symbols that opened the way to uncharted territories!

So, if we excluded them from the sequence, would the original script for instant transport work?

"Jeb, how do we switch off the extra runes?"

"I have no idea!" he responded, eagerly stirring the piles of ash with his spear.

I thought about it. I'd have to experiment a bit. What a puzzle... I suspected that my artifact simply gave me access to the last active route. At least, the system had never given me a choice.

"Jeb, let's go."

"Where and what for?"

"To the teleportation stone."

"You want to release another Ifrit?"

"No. We need to activate the original sequence and then we'll be able to get out of here!"

"Can you go over there by yourself?"

"What about you?"

"There's a lot of interesting and valuable stuff here! The items didn't perish in the fire since they're content and not garbage. Look at this!" he showed me a usable, albeit torn in several places, chainmail shirt.

"What if the Dark ones come back?"

"I'll hide. Just don't teleport without me, okay?"

I could see that arguing with him was pointless.

Jeb was overcome with gold fever. Quite understandable, given how much he'd had to endure. He knew the true value of every little trifle, even if it looked like nothing but could save a life. So, I went to the portal alone.

I made my way through the narrow passage and was back in the immured room. I stuck a torch into a rusty bracket, took the Soul Crystal out of my inventory and squeezed it in my palm.

The portal stone had melted and the symbols on it were dark.

I passed my hand over the runes but to no avail.

Maybe the key was the Guardian's Amulet? Because I didn't have the Thread of Time medallion when Wang had opened the teleport.

Okay, what if I did this? I clutched both artifacts in my sweaty palms.

Nothing.

I slowly moved my hand over the symbols. Got it! Suddenly, piercing crimson rays erupted from the stone surface.

I was recording what was happening. The runes were barely smoldering after activation. There were eight in total.

I compared them with the image that Jeb had given me.

These three were extras. I needed to 'switch them off' and then the teleport would start to work in normal mode. At least, I really hoped so!

I concentrated on the runes. I imagined them going out.

The Soul Crystal and Guardian Amulet vibrated perceptibly in my sweaty hands. Something was happening!

At last, my efforts were successful. The three 'extra' symbols went dark and the others remained glowing faintly.

Messages suddenly appeared before my inner gaze,

The local teleportation network is unavailable. To activate interregional mode, enter the missing symbols.

...

The portal obelisk is damaged. You don't have enough mental energy to open the passage.

...

I returned to the respawn point, feeling absolutely exhausted.

Jeb was happy to see me.

"Check out all the stuff that I've found!" he turned on the Exchange option, allowing me to look at his inventory.

Two gold, fifteen silver and about fifty copper coins. Arrowheads, several daggers, a long sword, various pieces of armor, the latter highlighted in red since neither Jeb nor I have enough Strength to wear them.

"The Dark ones didn't drop anything?"

"Here," he pointed to one of the daggers. "It has a smoky aura but you need to obtain some kind of achievement to use it."

"What does that mean?"

"It doesn't say. I can only see question marks."

"Anything useful among the jewelry?"

"The rings. They provide +1 to Intellect and +2 to Dexterity. What about you?"

"The Ifrit managed to damage the portal stone."

"And?" Jeb raised an eyebrow.

"I don't have enough mana. I managed to activate eight runes and even extinguished the extra ones but then ran out of steam. There's another snag." I told him about the local and the interregional transport systems.

Jeb's shoulders slumped, "A short teleport is not an option. The portal in the dwarves' cave would have suited us too, but it has already been used after you appeared here. We need to know the exact sequence that sent you to the Dark Frontier. It's a shame that you don't remember it."

"But I know whom I can ask. Jeb, I'll have to go out into the real world. Will you manage here without me?"

"I'll hide. It won't be the first time."

"All right. Wait for me, I won't be long," I promised.

Chapter Eleven

T HE EDGE OF THE ABYSS erased any sense of time.

You have played for 20 hours and 32 minutes.

Holy crap! That's nearly a day in the VR capsule. A personal record, if I could call it that.

I felt utterly exhausted. The sensation of hunger was sharp and unpleasant. I approached the inbuilt screen, which automatically switched on, showing me a panorama of the night city. Obeying a command sent through the neural interface, the pneumatics hissed and a plastic bottle with cold mineral water rolled onto the opened tray.

I took a long drink, quenching my thirst and dulling my hunger. Rivers of lights flowed beyond the electronic window. From the height of the 110th floor, the metropolis looked like a flaming octopus.

The news information module suddenly switched on. I'd been here since yesterday but I had no idea which settings Maxim had set for the home cybernetic system. It was clear that the apartment was protected in terms of information security, so this had to be something really important...

I turned up the volume and allowed video.

"A large fire has occurred tonight in the South Megasuburb. The Mainstream Entertainment Center has completely burned down. According to unofficial data, hundreds are dead and even more are injured. The club's VR capsules could not withstand the high temperatures. The fire safety system failed to activate..."

My mouth went dry.

Forgetting about secrecy, I dialed Max' number.

We apologize but the call recipient's device is currently switched off.

Damn it... Sasha had mentioned that Mongoose Castle was currently under siege by one of the Shadow clans. Could this confrontation have spilled over into the real world?

The idea that this was an accident seemed ridiculous. Mainstream's security system was top notch. If not for the help of Sasha and Max, I would have never gotten out of the club. Arson, then. With so many fatalities, it must have been planned and carefully executed.

I dressed quickly and called a taxi. It was drizzling

outside. The car arrived quickly.

"Mainstream Club!"

"Apologies, that district has been temporarily shut down," replied the smooth voice of the autopilot.

"Any closest point."

"Incorrect search criteria. Please specify the address."

Oh, you electronic moron!

I climbed out of the automated taxi with irritation, went to the edge of the sidewalk and raised my arm.

After a couple of minutes, the driver of a silver SUV responded to my gesture.

"Where to?" he asked, stopping and lowering the side window.

"Mainstream Club! Where the fire happened today, if you've heard about it?"

"Get in."

Sirens howled in the cold morning air.

The flashing lights danced across the building walls. Despite the drizzle, a persistent burning smell hovered over the streets.

There were cars everywhere, firefighters, ambulances, emergency vehicles. The police patrol service was trying in vain to restrain the crowd. I could see fear, confusion, bewilderment and pain on people's faces.

The cordon kept breaking and coming back together. Someone was screaming desperately.

The news had spread quickly and the crowd consisted mainly of the relatives of the victims. I pushed my way through with difficulty. The fire had been extinguished, but the five-story building complex had burned right down to the ground. Even the roof of the club had collapsed, leaving only the blackened walls.

Emergency medical tents were being erected right in the street. Clusters of spotlights switched on. I could hear screams coming from all directions, it was still chaotic, the cold wind pushing acrid plumes of smoke into the ground.

"The capsules were set alight from the inside... The servers were exploding..."

"Ilya! My God! Ilya!" A woman broke through the cordon, ran to the ambulances, tripped and fell.

"Help, damn it! North exit, we need medics!"

I was pushed aside and almost knocked down.

Coughing and swaying people were coming towards me — another group who had been saved. They were completely disoriented. Their clothes were stained, burned and torn, and horror was written on their faces. Some of them were helped into the tents, where the doctors met them.

The surrounding skyscrapers were as dark as the night. Not a single window was glowing in the radius of several blocks. The network was down. The communicators weren't working. Emergency services were using radios.

I'd seen this sort of thing before. Mainstream was attacked using an electromagnetic pulse generator. An army sample, turned to maximum power. The VR capsules were stuffed full of electronics and much less protected than military machines. Cybernetic components didn't just fail from an EMP, many parts heated up to critical temperatures, then caught alight and exploded. That's why there were multiple fires on all the floors of the club!

It was a terrorist attack. Whoever did this knew that the VR capsules wouldn't hold.

I gazed around me with no idea of what to do or how to help. Suddenly, I noticed a familiar face in the crowd parting to let an ambulance through.

"Avicenna! Wait!"

He turned around, stared at me for a few seconds and then remembered, "You're Max' friend."

"Yes! Is this because of VR?"

"It's the Dark ones!" Avicenna nodded, sitting down on the wet curb. "I'm sure it's them. Today we repulsed their assault on the castle and drove them from our lands. The Shadow clans had nothing going for them... Bastards..." he spat on the ground and asked, "How did you get out?"

"I wasn't here."

"I finished my shift an hour ago, too. I hadn't even

reached home..."

"Max and Sasha. Have you heard anything about them?"

"I have no idea about Max. Sasha was taken away with severe burns to Clinical Hospital No. 3."

"What's his surname?"

"I don't know. His nickname's the Analyst, but I don't know his surname."

He stood up and walked away, becoming instantly lost in the crowd and leaving me on my own again.

I spent the morning in Clinical Hospital No. 3. Max seemed to have disappeared into thin air but I had managed to find Sasha.

They didn't let me into the ICU. I left my communicator number with the doctors and asked them to call me when Sasha's condition changed as they were keeping him in an induced coma. No relatives turned up even though the main channels on the spherovision were constantly reporting about the tragedy in Mainstream Club and scrolling through the victim names.

I returned to Max' apartment with a heavy heart. Many things weren't making sense. Why did we need virtual reality, where rampaging assholes could do whatever they wanted, and if they suddenly started losing online, they eliminated their opponents in the real world?

Yes, I knew that huge amounts of money were involved in the Edge of the Abyss, but I still couldn't accept what had happened.

Nevertheless, I had to go back. Jeb was waiting for me. Another life broken by VR. I couldn't understand how we'd come to this — knowing each other only by nicknames, hiding behind avatars, loving and hating in cyberspace while living and dying alone in the real world...

The VR panels slid open and the rigid bed rose obligingly.

While the neural interface was being set up, I glanced through the news of the virtual world.

...

A sensational twist in the battle for the Mongoose Citadel.

For the first time in the Edge of the Abyss' recent history, the alliance of Shadow Clans has managed to gain a foothold away from the Dark Frontier. Having simulated a panicked retreat after failing to storm the castle, the Shadow Clan forces switched to an unexpected counterattack, found a breach in the defense and broke into the Clan Hall, holding it for an hour.

The Mongooses have lost control of the citadel. According to unconfirmed reports, the strongest combat clan in the Russian cluster is now on the verge of collapse.

...

This was terrible news. Now the whole region would fall under Dark rule. Another safe area, where many players of peaceful professions had already settled, would disappear off the map. They wouldn't be killed, of course, but they would be seriously oppressed.

The game finished loading.

...

Welcome to the Edge of the Abyss.

...

The cavern reeked of burning. Enough daylight penetrated through the overhead fissure for me to see the motes of ash swirling in the air.

Jeb poked his head up from behind a mound of stones.

"What took you so long?"

"I had to stay longer. There were some unforeseen problems. Did the Dark players turn up?"

"It's been quiet so far. Did you find out the sequence?"

"No. We'll have to figure this out on our own."

"Forget it," Jeb waved his hand. "We can't get through the dwarf cave anyway."

"But you're a mage! Haven't you got any invisibility spells or something in your collection?"

"I do but I can't use them. My Intellect's too low. And we can no longer level up here. I think there's been some kind of glitch. The rats haven't respawned. The centipedes and spiders have all fled, too. The experience points we got for them were miniscule anyway."

He was right. The situation was dire.

"What did the miniboss drop? Did you find it?"

"A shield covered with the Protorat's skin."

"Nothing else?" I was starting to cling to fragile hopes, but we weren't going to be saved by a happy accident. As I understood it, miracles rarely happened here. At least, good fortune was carefully avoiding Jeb and I. "Well, I can level my Fame up to 50. Then I'll have an aura. Here's the link, take a look."

Jeb briefly studied the description of the Aura of Fame, then shook his head, "Dwarves are intelligent beings, I agree, but what about the current inhabitants of the cave?" he asked. "Plus, how long are they going to examine you for, anyway? No, Dan, this isn't an option. We'll have better luck trying the Deadly Crag portal," he suggested. "If you extinguish the extra runes, the teleport will switch to local mode and we'll move a short distance. Here," he gave me the ring that awarded +1 to Intellect. "I took the Dexterity one for myself."

I put the ring on and said resolutely, "Let's go!"

Jeb caught my sleeve. "Dan, wait, you don't seem yourself tonight, you're all nerves."

I said nothing.

"Tell me what happened."

"People died last night."

"In the real world?"

"Yeah," I sat on the edge of the respawn circle, briefly described the situation and asked, "Tell me, Jeb, is virtual reality worth it? Everything here is fake! Why would people kill for it?!"

"It's all real here," he said seriously. "Pain, joy, madness, hatred, friendship. Don't you agree?"

"I don't know... I don't understand it."

"Then why didn't you off me when you leveled up a bit? Why did you save that girl, even though she was an NPC? You didn't even need the experience back then."

"Jeb, stop trying to 'fix' me!"

"Well, you should stop getting aggro. Just think about it."

Is that how he was talking now? Just like Max had done? I remembered his words, 'The world turned out to be harsh, but it is the result of our actions.'

Much remained unclear. The Edge of the Abyss seemed less and less like a game.

"All right. Let's head to the portal." I decided to end this unexpected and strangely painful conversation.

We made our way through the narrow and reeking passage. Soot coated the walls. The torchlight illuminated long, horizontal burn marks. It appeared that the Ifrit had passed this way in its search for a way out.

The boulder that Jeb had previously rolled aside had split into several fragments, and we had to pause to remove them from our path.

The hall with the teleport, fortunately, had not been damaged. The runes glowed dimly in the dark.

"Wait, let me catch my breath."

I'd been on my feet for more than a day with no sleep. The VR capsule's system had warned me several times about the likelihood of an 'emergency exit for medical reasons' and I'd been angrily swiping these messages away with a flick of my pupils.

Right, no time to sit around. I took a sip of water from the flask and approached the stone circle.

Unlike the portal in the Scorched Lands, this one was working properly. I didn't need to waste my mana to activate it. My problem was extinguishing the extra runes. I hadn't discovered which artifact was the key so I used both.

I had a sense of foreboding. In all the time that I had spent in the Edge of the Abyss, I had only felt a momentary charm at the very beginning, and then the digital world had shown its teeth, throwing me into a series of respawns.

Driving away the unhelpful thoughts, I concentrated on the runes.

"Jeb, get ready!"

The first Abyss symbol went dark.

The Crystal and Amulet were vibrating in my hands. I wouldn't be surprised if they only worked as a pair.

The second rune faded.

Now a viscous hostility emanated from the stone, as if I had been pierced by some dark energy, not amenable to normal human understanding. My nerves were wound tighter than a guitar string. I felt rapidly hot and cold. The third magic symbol began to flicker as if it sensed my confusion and indecision.

I pulled myself together. My head was spinning and my mind went fuzzy. It was very difficult to maintain concentration.

The third rune twisted and finally faded. A golden glow appeared over the circle!

"Dan, it worked! You did it! This is a normal portal. The kind that was in use before."

Why was it that I wasn't expecting any good to come from this? Was it paranoia?

"Let's go! Together!"

Jeber_Arium and I stepped into the light together and the underground around us fragmented and faded.

"Dan!"

I went rolling head over heels down a slope.

...

You have discovered the location Sinister Forest.

You have obtained the coordinates for a lost teleportation stone.

Reward: +5 to Fame if you list the coordinates on

222

public maps.

   ...

I smashed my shoulder into a fallen tree trunk and leaped to my feet as I scanned my new environment.

I was surrounded by a dense, ancient forest growing over a mountainside. A stream gurgled nearby. There was moss everywhere, a strange one, green at the base with gray, as if faded, thin hairs at the edges.

A menacing howl came from close by.

"Jeb, where are you?"

"Here!" the voice came from somewhere below me.

There was zero visibility due to the thick undergrowth.

The clean air, filled with the scents of the forest, was intoxicating.

The beast howled again. Closer this time.

"Jeb, hold on! I'm coming to you!"

The ferns around me shook. The trembling foliage clearly showed the mob's progress. Did it seem to be ignoring me? I shouted, trying to get its attention.

Like in the case of the brown bear, a message flashed immediately,

   ...

You have used a battle cry. Your Strength and Stamina have temporarily increased by 1. The aggro radius of NPC opponents has increased by 10 meters.

You have caught the attention of the large mountain wolf.

The gray shadow stretched out in a jump but I managed to block with my shield.

The Stamina bar dropped slightly. My Life points stayed almost the same and the wolf sprang back, clearly discouraged by such a turn of events. He crouched low to the ground, growling and baring his teeth. He was about to leap again.

That's right. He bounded forward and struck with his paw but I blocked again, staggering a little yet managing to slash at him with my sword.

Blood splattered, the wolf rolled away and suddenly let out a lyrical howl.

The bushes shook.

A pack!

Rapid gray silhouettes approached from all sides, bounding towards me. A large, seasoned male with smoky fur stood out among the ordinary wolves.

...

??? A creature of the Abyss. Level 32.

...

No wonder. So close to the portal, there were probably heaps of mutated NPCs!

I fought back as hard as I could. The bloodied shreds of my leather jacket no longer gave me any protection.

Two wolves thudded down the slope as I had gotten them both with a slashing blow, but things were looking bad. My Stamina was disappearing faster than I could regenerate it. I was holding on so far, thanks to the shield found on the Deadly Crag. The sword did not disappoint either. It was quite long and well-balanced, allowing me to keep my enemies at a distance.

Here came the smoky wolf! The leader of the pack leaped from far away, instantly knocking me down like a battering ram.

I got back up at once but my Life was flowing away together with the inflicted Bleeding debuff, and everything swam before my eyes from the Stun.

How annoying would it be if I was sent into respawn again... The anchor point was still the same... I would have to wander through the underground again but this time alone.

"Dan, get away from them!"

Risking a broken neck, I began to roll down the slope.

I still couldn't see Jeb and had no idea where he was.

I was suddenly enveloped by a minor heal aura, which eased the pain and stopped the bleeding, and in the next moment, a fireball struck the smoky male right on the haunches!

The leader of the pack howled and fell back from me, turning sharply to search for the new threat.

I didn't miss the opportunity and finished off one of the wounded animals. Go Jeb! He had thought to climb a tree and was now using fireballs like a sniper with the help of the salamander skin glove.

I had to help him.

The realism was making itself known again. It was difficult to run up the slope and the Stamina consumption doubled! Having lost sight of me, the pack (the smoky wolf and four others with rather singed fur) had surrounded a sturdy pine. The mobs tore at the trunk with their claws, leaped up and gnashed their teeth, but they couldn't reach Jeb. He had climbed high enough but had unfortunately used up all of his mana.

I looked at the frames more closely. The enemies' lives were in the red zone. I had managed to seriously wound several of them as I fought back and the fire had not been to their liking either. The leader's HP had halved thanks to several hits!

Noticing me, Jeb dropped down to a lower branch and began assiduously aggravating the wolves with his spear, keeping their attention on him.

I launched myself at the leader. I had slung the shield over my shoulder and was clutching the sword in a two-handed grip, aiming for the back of the animal's neck...

"Dan, watch out!"

The smoky wolf had sensed the danger somehow and spun around sharply, showing more complex behavior than ordinary NPCs.

We struck at the same time. The tip of the sword sunk noisily into the wolf's chest, while he managed to tear my shoulder with his dying effort.

I didn't feel any pain at first. My left arm dangled

uselessly. I was overcome with dizziness and the sword dropped into the blood-splattered grass.

...

Heavy bleeding. Damage 5 HP/sec.

Painful shock. Negative effect: your Strength, Stamina and Dexterity have been reduced by 2 points.

...

I staggered but the minor healing cast by Jeb helped to keep me conscious. Everything swam before my eyes as I searched for my weapon by touch, with only one thought pulsing in my head, 'I'm surrounded, they're going to tear me apart.'

Despite my dread, the four wounded animals suddenly dropped dead where they stood.

What the hell was going on?!

A scarlet mist ran from the mobs' wounds towards the pack leader. The smoky body suddenly convulsed. His eyes opened.

My hand found the sword hilt, sticky with blood.

The pack leader convulsed again and raised himself up on unsteady paws. Death was leaving his gaze...

...

You are observing a mutation of the Abyss.

Name it and add the information to the Encyclopedia. (+5 to Fame)

You have discovered a new type of Abyss-altered creature.

...

The lines of text wavered before my eyes. Jeb used

up the crumbs of the mana that he had gathered to cast another minor healing spell on me.

I got up, leaning on my sword and croaked "Falling strike..."

He understood me at once. Holding the spear in both hands, Jeb leaped straight down, pinning the smoky wolf to the ground.

A terrible howl echoed across the forest.

...

You have gone up a level.

"Dan, we have to go!"

My HP bar was in the red. The health bar didn't recover when one gained a level at the Edge of the Abyss.

"Wait, I'm being offered to publish the new information."

"Do it later!"

"No, I have to do it now. If I have no free experience points, I'll lose my new level if I die!"

"What did you get?"

"Twenty-nine."

"Oh, I went up two levels in one go! Dan, will the publication count for me, too?"

"I think so. Let's check. We're part of one party, remember?"

"Fine." he agreed reluctantly. I had no idea what awaited us next but I didn't want to lose the level. "I'll heal you a bit in the meantime. I bet the pack didn't have any competition around here," Jeb said but nevertheless kept a wary watch around him.

I opened the field diary tab. I knew from past publications that the system would create a brief description with an accompanying illustration.

That's right. A new page had appeared in the diary. There was a sketch of the wolf, made with a few deft strokes, as it tried to get up after dying, smoky red plumes stretching toward him from all directions.

Why did I suddenly decide to publish?

The information about the wolf wasn't so valuable. I thought there were plenty of such creatures in these forests and somebody else would soon make a similar discovery. It was pointless to keep this knowledge 'up my sleeve'. I also wanted to protect myself from losing a level, and confuse the Dark ones as well. Jeb and I wouldn't stay here for long. I wouldn't mention the portal — let them try and figure out where we'd ended up. The illustration showed a forest thicket and they all looked the same.

I quickly composed a description, editing the offered option so that there was no hint of our true location.

...

Twilight Wolf. Inhabits the wooded foothills of the Dark Frontier. Obtained its mutation from the noxious

229

influence of a nearby portal that hadn't been closed after the invasion of the Abyss.

Possesses increased Stamina.

Vulnerable to fire.

Unique ability: Second Chance. Can revive itself after death by stealing the remaining lives of the other animals in the pack.

Recommendation: first kill all the regular wolves so that their leader can't use Second Chance.

...

Great! I published it. Now the Dark players wouldn't be able to find us any time soon. After reading the article, they would first prowl around the active Abyss portals, not suspecting that this one — I involuntarily glanced toward the golden glow — was now operating in normal mode.

...

Your article has been published.

You have gone up a level.

...

"Dan, I also have a note in my traveler's diary!"

"About the wolf?"

"No. When I climbed up that tree, I saw a roof. I thought that I had imagined it."

"Can you show me what's written in there?"

"Well, it's not a discovery. It's a link to a Wiki article."

"What does it say?"

"Any structure, even a dilapidated one, can serve

as a safe shelter for the traveler, providing an opportunity to rest," he read aloud.

"Do you remember the direction?"

"It's downhill. We can't miss it."

"Let's take a look. That's it. I've published the article. Did you know that we're in the foothills of the Dark Frontier?"

"In the foothills? So we got out?" Jeb looked delighted.

"Wait, we first need to find a respawn point and change our anchor point. Well, did you get any experience points?"

"Yeah! Two and a half thousand."

"Excellent! Then let's go and search for the hut."

My Life bar was back to half-full by this point. My shoulder was hurting but the wound had already closed, thanks to the frequent minor healing spells that my companion kept casting on me.

Chapter Twelve

FOR THE LAST few minutes, Jeb and I had been carefully making our way along a sloping ravine. The bottom was covered in a thick layer of rotting leaves with moss-covered branches poking out of it.

The forest rustled overhead and birds were chirping.

We didn't have to go far. Soon a picturesque view appeared before us: the outcropping of rock had formed a low cliff with water trickling from the cracks. A little further down the slope stood a cluster of long-abandoned buildings, dark with age.

...

You have discovered the location The Old Mine.

...

Another building stood level with the cliff, a primitive cage lift. The rotten decking and a winch with a rickety wheel all spoke of long abandonment.

"Jeb, I'll go first. If anything happens, you can cover me with your magic."

He nodded and made himself ready. The salamander skin glove smoldered on his left hand and in his right, my companion held his makeshift staff.

I jumped onto the top platform. The boards creaked alarmingly yet held my weight, but it was the cobbled-together ladder that tripped me up, several rungs crumbling into dust so that I just managed to grab the vertical bar and slide along it.

There was nobody around. The birds continued chirping, accompanied by the bright splashing of water on the rocks.

"All right, now you go!"

It was getting dark. The mountain slopes seemed to be covered in green velvet, while above, standing out against the sunset sky, rose the bleak and weathered cliffs of the Dark Frontier.

Jeb descended hurriedly, peering anxiously around him.

"Dan, look!" he exclaimed, pointing to a few roughly hewn slabs barely rising above the ground. "The respawn point!"

We dashed over to the sunken stone circle. Alas, we were in for a severe disappointment as one segment was missing.

"Wait," my companion looked around distractedly in search of the missing fragment but to no avail.

"Let's go into the house."

"But..."

"Jeb, do you really think that you can repair the respawn circle?"

"What do we do?" he asked dejectedly.

"Come on!" I pushed him towards the 'miner's hut' as my minimap had named the rickety structure.

It was empty inside. Rays of light penetrated through the cracks in the boards. The interior consisted of a rough table, low benches and piles of musty straw.

"We'll spend the night here and decide what to do in the morning."

I even had enough time to glance through the article, whose link Jeb had sent me. According to the rules, any structure in the Wild Lands, even such a dilapidated and abandoned one, could become a temporary safe zone for the weary traveler. I wondered if it would work in the foothills of the Dark Frontier. Let's check...

I closed the door tightly, and a faint green aura immediately appeared around the perimeter of the walls.

...

You have activated the safe rest zone.

Duration of protective aura is 6 hours. Repeat use is possible after 24 hours (absence of enemies nearby is a prerequisite for activation).

"Get comfortable. Tomorrow is another day." Jeb didn't quite understand my utterance and looked at me questioningly. "Let's go to bed."

He nodded. I could barely remain upright, the fatigue overwhelming me as soon as we found ourselves in relative safety. We had to rest. We had no idea what tomorrow would bring.

Jeber_Arium approached the task with all seriousness. When he saw how I had collapsed on the bench, he quickly went through all the straw, dragged the rotten parts away to the far corner and laid the remainder out on the ground. Yet he didn't stop there. While I was trying to get comfortable on the hard and prickly bedding, he took a strange item from his inventory. It turned out to be a ball of thread-like moss from the underground. Jeb shook it out and it unrolled like a carefully folded mist net.

He threw it over the doorway and the net clung to the cracked boards, pulsating jerkily.

All right. I hoped he knew what he was doing. Some extra protection wouldn't hurt.

I couldn't keep my eyes open and yet I didn't succumb to the staggering weakness. There was still more to do. Unfinished business. I wouldn't go out into the real world since the process took too much precious time but I'd try something different.

In the age of high tech, movement between IT environments was instantaneous. I hadn't forgotten about the chip that Max had given me but had been afraid to use it since the device had belonged to the Mongooses, and my relations with the Clan leadership were rather strained. But now I wasn't risking anything in terms of security.

The personal virtual space met me with gray murk. Several lines of text glowed against the bleak, indistinct haze.

I quickly figured out the settings and activated the 'standard background' option. There was no time to dabble in the delights of design, I needed functionality.

The haze transformed. Now I was inside an ordinary apartment. I wouldn't have been surprised if it was the same one as the apartment where the VR capsule was located. That's right. My communicator lay at the edge of the table...

Connect to the device.

...

You have two missed calls.

I frowned. Both were from the hospital. Well, that was the reason why I had gone into the personal virtual space, to find out how Sasha was doing and whether Max had turned up.

No word from Maxim. I rang the hospital back.

"Andrey Dmitrievich, I presume?"

"Yes, that's right. Sorry, doc, I couldn't get in touch earlier. How are things going? I was inquiring about Alexander, if you remember?"

"Of course. He's the reason I was calling you. His condition remains the same," the doctor said before I could ask. "However, we are facing some serious problems."

"What kind of problems?"

"Of a social nature. Are you aware that Alexander was officially listed as unemployed?"

"No."

"He has the minimum health insurance package. We haven't been able to find any relatives. It's why we called you, because there is nobody else."

"What does he need?"

"Regenerative treatment. Immediately."

"The health insurance doesn't cover such procedures?"

"No."

"I'll think of something. What kind of figure are we talking about?"

"For a full recovery, he needs at least thirty days in the bioreconstruction chamber. This includes regeneration of the respiratory system, skin, and some severely damaged muscles. We have the necessary equipment, but..."

"Doc, let's get to the point."

"It's a paid procedure and costs 1,100 credits per day."

I couldn't help but shudder. It was an impossible amount for me. Several options flashed through my mind. What could I do? Sell the house. Construction companies would transfer the money quickly and without any questions. I'd be able to get 17,000-18,000 credits out of them. Personal savings? That was another few thousands. That was it. Dead end. Denis wouldn't be able to help me.

"You can't cover that?"

"I'm going to send over copies of the documents," I replied mechanically. "Please accept them as warranty. It'll definitely be enough for two weeks."

"Sure, I'll wait. Send them over. Right, got them... Are you sure that you'll be able to make the deal?"

"Yes."

"Good. We'll start the treatment, but you must make the first payment within the next day. I'll prepare the contract and send it to you."

All I needed when dealing with the auto real estate agent was a digital signature on the documents. The metropolis had come right up to the village and offers for the urgent purchase of my house and land (which I had inherited from my parents) had been coming in regularly.

Where could I get the missing amount?

I'd have never thought that my sensible and steady life would be turned on its head in only a few days.

Right, I couldn't touch Denis' VR capsule. I needed it as a safety net. The future was now utterly uncertain.

I'd be able to get some money for teleport

coordinates. It was a shame that I had nobody to ask for advice.

Although... What about my nephew? It was time to give him a call.

Denis replied at once.

"Hi! How are you? Have you settled in?"

That's right. Less than a week has passed. In his mind, I'd been performing the simple work of a mule and admiring the beauty of the safe region.

"I have. And I've screwed up your character."

"Did you level up?" He sounded genuinely freaked out.

"I can't sum it all up. Do you have time? I need your advice."

I had to lay out everything, albeit briefly.

Denis sat in shocked silence for a while, then asked, "Listen, have you completely lost your mind? How am I going to pay off the capsule loan? And what about you? Do you realize that you're now homeless?!"

"That's not your concern. I'm trying the save a guy's life. I need advice right now, whom can I contact to sell the portal coordinates? Someone who won't screw me over and will give me a decent price."

"That's beyond my level of contacts," Denis muttered. "Once you get to Anchor, approach the Mapmakers Guild. You won't get the highest price but it'll be a safe deal. They're interested in this sort of information."

"Middlemen? Will they resell the coordinates?"

"Why do you care? Anyway, sorry, I've got to go."

"Why so glum suddenly? I know that I've ruined your character, but you can get a new one once you're back."

"Sorry," he said coldly and tersely. "People are waiting for me." Denis hung up without saying goodbye and I knew why. To avoid being rude and saying exactly what was on his mind.

I returned to the Edge of the Abyss and lay for some time, listening to Jeb's even breathing. Then the fatigue of the last few days took over and I didn't even notice falling asleep.

The morning started off surprisingly calmly.

The protective aura surrounding the miner's hut hadn't yet disappeared, but the timer in my interface was counting down its last minutes.

The net over the door was gone.

Jeb had gotten up first and had already explored the basement (the hatch in the floor was open), finding some usable pottery.

"Any meat left?" he asked when he noticed that I was awake.

"Yep, a little," I gave him the supplies and stepped outside.

After the frigid darkness of the dungeon, a typical

dawn felt incredibly special. I breathed in deeply. Despite everything, I liked this world. I wasn't regretting drowning in it.

Dewdrops glistened in the light of the rising sun. A smoky rabbit sneaked past. A squirrel pup sat on a pine branch, glancing at me and holding a bat in its paws. He was getting ready for breakfast. I winked at him. The creature hissed in response, scampered up a couple of branches and stared at me warily, wondering if I was going to steal his prey. Calm down, I don't hurt little fellows...

I didn't want to ruin this moment. I sank down on the rickety porch, thinking. Why were mobs always predators? Even the ones that should have been omnivores or vegetarians? This note of inaccuracy didn't let me fully relax.

A strange sound came from nearby, like a muffled clap. Could it be a local teleport, for example, due to someone using a scroll? I pricked up my ears, of course, but the hut's protection was still active so there was no point in leaping up and pulling out my weapon. Better to keep watch.

The squirrel pup moved even higher. He was sniffing nervously but not running away.

A gust of warm wind blew in my face, bringing the smell of the forest.

Nothing unusual... but I no longer believed in the deceptive calm of this sunny morning.

The dewdrops darkened for a moment. A shadow

was being cast over them!

Someone invisible was sneaking towards me. Someone silent and deadly. They were circling the clearing, probably trying to find a gap in the defense.

Clearly an NPC. A player would have immediately figured out what was happening. Oh, the protective aura was about to stop working. There were only seconds left...

The squirrel pup laid its prey on a fork in the branches. The wings of the bat he had caught hung down like two black tattered rags.

The animal was spooked by something so he leaped onto the cabin roof and hid among the bark, moss and twigs.

The radiant morning faded in the next moment, as if there was a sudden solar eclipse.

A puzzled Jeb came out onto the porch.

The squirrel rapidly descended, clearly fearful of something and seeking protection. He hid behind Jeb's leg but curiosity got the better of him. The creature stood up on his hind legs, the front paws clinging onto my companion's pant leg, and peeked out. All his fur stood on end. I followed the direction of his gaze and felt my breath being knocked out of me. The dead bat left on the tree branch suddenly shifted its wings, either reviving or transforming into the undead.

The darkness gathered, acquiring a smoky tint and condensing into a supernatural figure.

The eyes glowed purple and looked at me from

within a deep hood.

How could I describe his appearance? A few steps away, a creature materialized that looked vaguely human. The stranger was dressed in armor made from an unfamiliar dull alloy. He wore a tattered cloak over it, so thin in places that it resembled rags.

The face was hidden by a haze, with only the eyes burning into me.

He held a sword and a staff in his hands. Clearly a multiclass player.

The squirrel squeaked nervously and hid behind the dumbfounded Jeb. The bat didn't just come alive but grew noticeably larger. It circled around us through the darkness, as if absorbing it.

The stranger's frame was slowly revealed,

Gray_Talg. Warrior of the Abyss. Level 92.

A player, judging by the nickname!

"All the conditions have been met," he stated hollowly, looking at me like I was a bug. He ignored Jeb completely.

What conditions?

I frantically thought of what might have attracted his attention. Was it the portal activation?

"Have you come to receive a quest?" he spoke in an even, expressionless voice.

So that's what it was! I had received Level 30 a day ago. Using 50% of realism... Most of the Dark players started out in exactly the same way. They reached the necessary development threshold and made their way here, to the sinister forest in the foothills, to receive a coveted quest...

I didn't understand. How could players issue quests? He spoke strangely too, using clichéd phrases as if he was an NPC. What a bizarre situation.

"The first test," Gray_Talg interpreted my confusion in his own way and threw up the arm with the staff, pointing at Jeb, "Is to kill him!"

Yeah, sure thing... What a shame we hadn't changed the anchor point. We'd have to start all over again in the catacombs of the Dark Frontier.

"I don't need a Dark aura. My friend and I are traveling and just stopped here for the night."

"Think of what you are rejecting! Look!" Talg interrupted me angrily. The dense murk hiding his features became distorted. He abruptly raised his sword, and black flames enveloped the blade, cutting through the thicket, tree branches, bushes and moss — everything turned to ashes, creating an elongated bare patch.

The blow was aimed to the side and yet my Life bar dropped by a quarter for no obvious reason!

...

You are under the influence of the Aura of the Abyss. Random damage to all living things. The effect radius depends on the level of the aura holder.

...

The ground buckled suddenly. The yellowish skeleton of a long-dead animal shook off the adhering sandy loam, eyed me chillingly with its empty sockets, and, staggering, rose to its full height.

...

Wolf skeleton. Raised from oblivion by the Aura of the Abyss.

...

"I'm still not interested," I said with difficulty. My mouth went dry. The darkness seemed tenacious, inhibiting my movements. It wasn't hard to guess the next question...

"Why do you refuse to serve the Shadows?"

"I've been to the Deadly Crag. I saw those crazed creatures."

"Scum of past wars!" Talg spoke scornfully, expressing no surprise at my words. "The trust of real Shadows must be earned."

"By killing at their whim?"

His aura twisted again as if the Warrior of the Abyss could barely control his rage.

"Shame that I am bound by my task. Yet we will meet again," he glared at me with disdain, then turned and walked away.

The swirling plumes of darkness withdrew after him.

"Ugh," Jeb sank down on the porch of the hut in exhaustion. "He didn't touch us!"

The day grew brighter around us and the air regained its transparency but the trail left behind by the creepy visitor was clearly visible: dead leaves, a deathly silence with no birdsong, and the grass turning a strange purple shade. The morning air now chilled me to the bone.

The wolf skeleton crumbled to dust as soon as the sun's rays touched it. This wasn't new but was worth remembering.

I sat down on the porch as well and thought hard.

The mysterious Shadows clearly needed allies among the players. At first glance, it seemed that the classical battle between 'good' and 'evil', 'light' and 'dark' was taking place in the Edge of the Abyss, yet I suspected that everything was much more complicated. The high level of realism changed the essence of perception, leaving an indelible mark on the soul and mind. Darkness nestled mainly inside us. This wasn't a metaphor, given the full immersion in the game reality. It wasn't possible to play as a Dark character here just for fun and then come back the next day as a Warrior of Light. Just like in real life, every action subtly altered a person inside. Yes, you could mess up and re-create a character, but it wouldn't change your essence.

I would bet anything that Gray_Talg was a player irreversibly changed by this virtual reality after completing many Dark quests.

Before this, I couldn't understand how in-game events could so easily leak into the real world. Now things were clearer. The sensory realism equalized the two worlds. Many users of the Edge of the Abyss could no longer distinguish between the realities and behaved the same both here and there. They easily agreed to extreme measures without questioning the means needed to achieve the goal, anything to remove the obstacle and to snatch victory...

Who were these Shadows? What were they trying to achieve by manipulating the players?

While I was thinking, the squirrel pup, having successfully survived the frightening events, ran to the middle of the clearing, sniffed the ground, then turned and looked at Jeb and I in bewilderment.

He clearly didn't like the wilted purple grass. An unpleasant smell, like the stench of decay, emanated from it.

With a couple of leaps, the animal was back at the hut.

"Hey, buddy, did you get scared?"

The squirrel climbed onto Jeb's lap. He had an adorable face and his eyes glittered like onyx beads, as if saying, 'don't drive me away, okay?'

"What use will you be?" I grumbled, slowly

recovering from the unexpected events. I had acted calmly but had been sure that the Warrior of the Abyss would send us into respawn. And it would be back to that hateful dungeon, now probably full of Dark players looking for us.

"Dan, let's take him with us!"

"It's an ordinary NPC, not even a pet."

"So what?" Jeb said stubbornly. "He can always run off into the woods if he wants to."

"Hey, do what you like. It's up to you. Right now, we need to decide where to go next. Do we go and look for a working respawn point or return to the portal?"

"The portal? The wolf pack would certainly be back there by now! We barely survived them last time."

"We walk, then?"

"I saw an overgrown path running down the slope. It'll take us somewhere."

I was inclined to agree with him. The portal was a fast but very risky transportation method. It was impossible to know where it would send us. This way, we had a chance to keep leveling up since Level 30 players reached this place somehow, right? Not all of them, of course.

"All right. Let's go."

"Wait, what about the mine? There's lots of stuff in the basement, too. Maybe we'll find something useful?"

"I don't want to stay here. I bet the mine is a dungeon. And we don't need any more junk, you should change your habits."

Jeb wasn't offended but didn't agree with me either.
"I'll have a look anyway," he said and went back inside.
The squirrel pup followed him.

"Okay, wait. I'll help hold the torch, at least."

Chapter Thirteen

I T WAS DARK, damp and musty in the basement. The wavering torchlight revealed snatches of leaning wooden racks. This was where the mining equipment used to be stored. Bundles of wooden handles tied with twine, rusty picks, a broken wheelbarrow, cart wheels, broken pottery... trash, in short. We were wasting our time.

The squirrel pup was behaving strangely. It seemed to me like he could understood everything we were saying, and was now determined to prove his usefulness, standing still in the middle of the cluttered room and sniffing intensely.

While Jeber_Arium rattled around the different bits of metal, the animal jumped onto a shelf, tore through the cobwebs with his paw, scratched his claws along the wall and slipped into a narrow crack in the masonry.

"What a weasel!"

"Who?" Jeb turned back to me.

"The little squirrel. He's found a burrow."

"Weasel, huh?" Jeb's eyes flashed merrily. "I like it! Good name!" he lifted a rusty pick off the floor and began to tap it along the wall, at the spot the squirrel had indicated. "Wow, there's a hidden cache here!" Jeb exclaimed excitedly, knocking off the layer of clay that someone had used to carefully cover up the hole in the wall. "Hey, get out of the way so I don't get you by accident!"

Weasel jumped onto a rotten shelf and sneezed. He looked smug, as if saying, 'Well, what did I tell you? I'm useful, right?'

I smiled despite myself. What a cheeky devil. I looked at his frame, thinking of writing an article, but it turned out that there was already a Wiki entry.

Rock Squirrel. An endangered species found only in the foothills of the Dark Frontier. These creatures have an excellent sense of smell, are smart and possess a rare magical ability to see what is hidden, which helps them to survive and unerringly find caches of food stored for the winter (it is well known that ordinary squirrels often forget where they buried the nut, which helps to preserve forests).

...

So that's how it was?

"Dan, look!"

Jeb had removed all the clay and pulled several bricks out of the wall. The first alcove turned out to be fake, but there was something really interesting behind it!

We immediately opened the small wooden box, darkened with age. In the light of the torch, I saw a handwritten book bound in leather and a set of burins[5].

We turned the pages with interest. The yellowed parchment contained images of magical symbols and their combinations.

"Is this valuable?" I asked.

"Oh, yes!" Jeb nodded energetically. "It must have belonged to the dwarf rune master. These are mainly protective and enhancing symbols, but we can find other books."

"Wait, how does it work?"

"You don't understand? If you carve runes into wooden supports holding up the mine roof, for example, they will become stronger! A pickaxe with magic symbols engraved on it will split the stone more easily."

"So, using these tools, you can make items that increase stats or add magical affixes[6] to normal items?"

"Yes, but you need a special skill. I can't remember

---

[5] Burin - a steel cutting tool used for working with metal, wood, bone, stone and leather.
[6] Affix (from the Latin 'affixus' meaning attached) – the additional property of an object.

what it's called."

I took the book and set of instruments and added them to my inventory.

"Weasel!" Jeb called.

The animal immediately squeaked in response. The sound came from the depths of a damp room.

"Well, where are you?" I raised my torch higher.

"Did you find anything?" Jeb spoke to the squirrel like it was a person. "Dan, there seems to be another cache here!" he exclaimed.

This time, Weasel was trying to dig a hole in the far corner of the basement.

"Come on, get out of the way!" I grabbed an old pickaxe and churned up the dirt floor with a few blows. Something jangled. It was a small clay pot, filled to the brim with copper coins.

"Well done!" Jeb stroked the animal's fur.

I looked at his frame and read in surprise.

Weasel. Level 5.

"Jeb, did you see that?"

"Yeah. My interface is now showing him as an NPC companion. A separate tab has appeared! All his characteristics are at baseline, and he has a Level 1 ability to See What is Hidden."

We thoroughly explored the basement but didn't find anything else.

Jeb rewarded Weasel with a piece of boiled rat meat and stated adamantly that he wasn't going anywhere until he had searched all the buildings of the abandoned mine. It looked like he was seized with treasure hunting again.

I wanted to get out of there as soon as possible after the visit of the Warrior of the Abyss since the place was clearly not safe, but I didn't argue, just warned them not to go into the mine. I then picked up a split dwarf shield, sat down in the shade of the flimsy awning and began to study the book we had found, not forgetting to glance around from time to time.

The day turned out to be hot and sunny. Birds were singing. Midges hovered over the meadow grasses growing around the mine.

My thoughts flitted uneasily from one thing to another. Where was I going to find the remaining money to pay for Sasha's treatment?

We had to reach the regional capital as soon as possible. Walking no longer seemed quite so sensible. Although using a portal without first changing the anchor point was also incredibly risky.

I flicked through the parchment pages, lost in thought. Each page showed a magic symbol. There

were handwritten explanations below. The auto-
translator didn't work in this case. Even though
players from different countries could understand each
other, bypassing the language barrier, one had to
actually learn the ancient magical language.

Aha! Here was a familiar rune. The same one that
provided phantom protection.

I took a suitable burin from the set and decided to
conduct an experiment. I remembered creating a
makeshift spear by attaching a knife to a staff. Then
there was the staff that I had made out of moss and a
stick.

What if I carved a magic symbol on the old dwarven
shield?

Why not? VR was adaptive. It was easy to obtain
the baseline skill. All you needed was interest, just like
in real life. But to develop it, to gain a certain level of
skill, that required considerable effort.

I plugged away at it for about half an hour, carefully
removing the metal shavings but ultimately creating
only deep scratches in the beaten metal surface. The
rune ended up looking crooked.

"Ugh," I wiped the sweat off my brow and studied
my creation, hoping that the shield would gain a new
characteristic, but alas, the system's verdict was
harsh.

Useless piece of metal. Hit points 0.

...

What was the matter?

The image that I had scratched onto the shield was suddenly enveloped by a ghostly light and the metal began to corrode as if someone had splashed acid on it. I barely had time to fling it away from me when there was a flash and the shield disappeared, leaving behind a burnt patch of grass.

A message appeared:

You have destroyed an object.

You have angered the air elementals (negative effect: you cannot use spells or abilities relating to the element of Air for 24 hours).

Be careful: clumsy experiments with magic can have a fatal outcome.

...

That was a serious debuff! If I had been a Mage or an Archer, such a ban would have seriously complicated my life for the next 24 hours!

My life?

I caught myself on that thought.

That was quick... Less than a week had passed and yet the authenticity of the surrounding world had already won me over, gradually replacing concepts. The border between realities was being rapidly eroded and my mind was beginning to perceive VR as a fully-fledged world.

It was hot. The forested slopes and the Dark Frontier cliffs towering above them were wavering in the sultry haze. I understood that the Land of the Chosen truly was a blessed place. It was a pity that it had been broken, reshaped and given over to human passions and vices. Nobody wanted a beautiful but static world anymore. It was we, with our thoughts and actions, that were breathing real life into it...

I suddenly felt overwhelmed. It turned out that my nephew's words had struck a chord but I had gotten used to keeping my emotions in check.

Yes, he was right. I had been left homeless. But surprisingly, the worry about this crossed my mind and disappeared like water through sand.

Why, you might ask? I'd answer honestly.

I had no regrets. What kind of future did I have waiting for me in the real world? A tiny automated apartment in the metropolis? Gray days. Annoying, constant reminders of past wounds. You can't even imagine how terrible it was to feel weak and to understand that this wouldn't pass in time.

Here, I felt young and full of energy again... I wanted to stay. To experience the full depth of immersion, to travel along the unknown trails of neurotechnology.

"Dan, what are you doing over there?" Jeb called me over voice chat. "I found a cave in the cliff. Weasel showed me that the back wall in one of the sheds is fake."

"Hey, don't go anywhere without me!"

"I've already ripped away the boards, I'll just take a peek!"

"Don't go in there without me!"

"Are you coming soon? What are you doing?"
"I'm busy. Wait a bit, I'll be right there."

I did have some unfinished business. There was no escape from the problems of the real world.

After checking that there were no signs of any danger, I shifted to my personal digital space, from where I had access to the global web.

You have three unread messages.

I opened the first one. A notification from the auto real estate agent. The construction company was willing to buy my house and land for 20,000 credits. This was more than I had expected!

I agreed because the second letter contained a contract for the provision of paid medical services attached to it.

I approved it with my electronic signature and created a daily auto-payment to the specified bank account. Now, even if I couldn't exit to the real world, the banking system would automatically make payments for Sasha's advanced treatment.

Now all that was left was to obtain the missing amount.

The third message was a short one, from Denis.

Sorry I overreacted yesterday.

Fine. We'll work things out later. I simply didn't

have time for family dramas right now.

I quickly wrote a short reply and suggested that we discuss it all a bit later. And now, back to the Edge of the Abyss. Jeb and I still hadn't found a working respawn circle to change our anchor point. This bothered me the most at this point, while the other problems seemed solvable.

Nothing had changed in the few minutes that I was away. Passing by a flooded gap that indicated the entrance to the old mine, I looked at the reflections on the dark water. They formed a distorted inscription in an incomprehensible ancient language.

I took pictures. This was certainly an instance, which had never been explored. It was a priceless find. We wouldn't be able to go through such a dungeon. We would need lots of underwater breathing potions, plus, we couldn't handle the specifics of battling monsters in a narrow, flooded labyrinth. So, the information would go on sale.

I found Jeb by following a pointing marker. Weasel was also showing up on my minimap now, as a cheerful green spark. Both signals were showing up against a shed huddling at the edge of the cliff.

The impressively large doors were open. Boxes were piled up inside. They had probably been neatly stacked in the past, but the timber had rotted over time and the stacks had collapsed. Rays of light cut through the gloom, coming from the gaps in the roof and illuminating the motes of dust spinning lazily in the air.

I studied the contents falling out of the broken crates and worn-out bags. It was some kind of ore. I had no idea if it was valuable or not. I tried to get a hint but the interface wouldn't provide me with any details, simply labeling the find as 'rocks'. Perhaps I needed a special skill to identify them more accurately.

There was a break in the far wall, where Jeb had pulled away several boards. I could see a faint glow from a torch.

This place only emphasized the realism of the digital world. The design of neglect had arisen due to natural processes. I wasn't attacked by mobs, which (if the location was planned) would have certainly been nesting in the abandoned buildings and guarding some valuable items.

Nothing like that. The mine had simply been abandoned. The clearing was full of bushes and young saplings. The buildings were dilapidated. The mine had been gradually flooded with rain and groundwater. Virtual reality was living its own life. I thought that if all the users had suddenly disappeared, this virtual reality and the NPCs living in it would continue their everyday activities, and would maybe begin to develop themselves...

"Well, did you find anything?" I climbed into the gap and looked around.

"Nope," Jeb replied with disappointment and added as he raised the torch higher, "It looks like the dwarves had unearthed something valuable here," he pointed to marks made by mining tools. The ceiling was low and angular. The limestone was riddled with cracks, yet I couldn't see any supports. The cave wasn't large overall, as if the miners had indeed stumbled across a small deposit of valuable ore, extracted it and abandoned the space, without even using the resulting cave for storage since it was safer to build a shed than to reinforce the unreliable ceiling.

"Weasel didn't find anything either," Jeb sighed and then jerked his head up, staring at me, "Dan, what's happening to you?"

I felt suddenly dizzy. My breath caught and my mind went fuzzy.

I didn't understand what was going on myself! Jeber_Arium's face blurred, the torchlight became a distant spark and then...

...

You have discovered a new region, Path of the Doomed.

...

I was bathed in cold sweat and barely kept my balance. I clung to the cliff instinctively. A crumbling, unreliable ledge lay under my feet, clearly created by something other than nature!

Streaks of fog (or cloud?) slowly floated past, touching me and briefly obscuring the view, encasing everything in a gray shroud.

It was hard to breathe and my legs trembled with the strain. I had to spread my arms out along the stone surface.

How could this be happening again?

A sudden gust of wind nearly threw me into the chasm below. The white haze was torn into shreds and driven away. Looking around brought on an attack of vertigo.

Far below, I could see the foothills of the Dark Frontier.

Suppressing the wave of nausea, I tried to assess the situation. I took pictures automatically. I was very high up, between two gloomy and weathered fortifications. A road used to run between them. I could see miraculously preserved supports here and there in the rock, which used to hold up the planking. Most of them had been snapped off. Vultures sat on some of them. The path that the system notified me about had been created using elemental magic.

The stone looked like it had been melted. I had come across this before, when the people above had mistaken me for a necro. The narrow recess looked like a very long niche cut into the rock. It was the only thing connecting the two ancient towers.

There was a flash on the left as I was studying my surrounding. A portal! The special effect had the familiar purple shade.

Confirming my guess, a player appeared on the stone staircase. A Dark Warrior, judging by the aura and presence of armor. He confidently descended to the path. He was followed by a line of shuffling figures who were chained to one another. Prisoners. I counted fifteen of the unfortunate folk. A Dark Mage made up the rear.

Only two guards! I couldn't read their frames yet because they were too far away and the smoky aura also got in the way.

Remaining in the middle of the trail was madness. I wouldn't save anyone and would likely perish myself. If I was to take up the fight and try to free the prisoners (why else would I have been teleported here by some unseen force?), then I needed to do this from the nearby tower.

Who knew what was in there?

Overcoming my natural fear of heights, I began to make my way to the right fortification. It was awkward going. I had to put away my weapon and keep my hand in constant contact with the wall, otherwise, I would panic and fall.

The scraps of cloud came back. They floated by, hopefully masking my presence.

A little more. Some twenty steps and I would reach a small platform with a stone staircase ascending from it.

The vultures were suddenly disturbed by something. I could see them spreading their huge wings, pushing off from the wrecked wooden beams with their talons and soaring up on the streams of rising air.

I hoped that I hadn't scared them and that the

tower was empty...

There came the distinct clunk of a crossbow and a heavy, short bolt, capable of penetrating metal armor, struck the stone above my head.

Forgetting about my vertigo, I dashed forward, reached the staircase, ran up the steps and hid behind my shield.

The upper platform was windswept, with a lot of bones scattered about and two archers standing by the loophole — skeletons in rusty armor!

A bolt struck my shield with a dull thud, not causing any damage but using up some Stamina. I automatically rolled to avoid the second shot — my training with Jeb hadn't been for nothing! As I regained my feet, I chopped off the undead's head, with the skull clattering across the cobblestones.

The second archer scampered off to the side and was hurriedly reloading. I dispatched him quickly since they were weak enemies, only Level 15.

One dropped a soldier's crossbow and the other one dropped five ordinary bolts.

I glanced through the weapon characteristics. Shooting range was 30 meters. Damage was 4-5 with scaling according to Strength. Ideal for me, except for the fact that I had no practice in firing this sort of weapon.

I hid beside the loophole and peeked out. The prisoners were moving slowly. A Dark Warrior, Level 35, walked at the front of the line. He was wearing light leather armor that didn't restrict his movements, and was armed with a pole axe. He moved confidently. A dangerous opponent. The Dark Mage, on the other hand, was nervous and lagged behind, clinging to the rocks and clearly unfamiliar with the narrow path.

They hadn't notice me for sure! I lifted the crossbow and aimed at the Mage. I hoped that the very first shot would disable him and ideally, cast him into the abyss. Hopefully, the captives would realize what was going on, otherwise, there was a risk that they would fall too. One clumsy movement could be a death sentence since they were all chained together...

All the characters (except the two skeletons) were players.

I took aim and fired, but the heavy bolt seemed to snag in the suddenly dense air so that it flew only a few meters and dropped below.

Damn it! I had completely forgotten that the air elementals were still mad at me because of the failed experiment and the debuff was still active.

A sudden chill touched my back.

There was a grinding of stone slabs shifting aside. The ancient fortification vibrated.

I turned sharply.

The creature that climbed out of the gloomy depths of the tower could hardly be described. It was twice as tall as a human being. Skinny, with stooped shoulders, two legs and very long arms. It wasn't wearing any clothes. The pale skin was patterned with a bluish network of veins, in some places stained with flaking purple patches, as if this creature's distance ancestors had been covered in scales but now only rudimentary areas remained.

A bare, elongated scalp, small, watery eyes, a sunken nose, with the mouth framed by fine, constantly moving growths with suckers on the ends.

Obviously, players had met such creatures before, but I could see only question marks in the red frame, and, *Poacher, a creature from the Abyss*. I shivered. So, nobody had published any information about these beings.

"What have we here?" there were notes of disgusted surprise in the hoarse voice. "A Guardian, eh? But too small... Too small..." he grinned creepily, quite pleased with himself. "Things can't be going very well since the defeat if your masters are willing to send anyone these days."

I covered myself with the shield, preparing for the fight.

He laughed huskily, "Really?! You want to try?"

In the next instant, a crushing blow of the long, thin arm swept me into the chasm below, together with a section of the ancient masonry.

I was falling, my breath stuck in my throat. Everything froze inside me and my mind went dark.

"Dan, what's the matter with you?"

I lay on the cave floor. It was hard to breathe, and even harder to speak.

"Was this a portal summoning again?" Jeb persisted.

"Yes," I croaked as I stood up. I could taste blood and felt like I'd had my breath knocked out of me. "Let's get out of here."

We climbed out of the cave. The sun's warm rays dulled the nasty sensations a little.

Weasel immediately scampered off into the nearest bushes, probably looking for something to eat. I drank the cold spring water until I felt full. Then Jeb and I sat down in the shade of the awning, and I briefly told him what had happened.

"I don't understand. Why wasn't I sent into respawn?"

Jeb sat and thought for a while.

"Maybe they simply returned you to the starting point?" he suggested. "They didn't let you fall to your death."

"I don't like these unannounced summonings. Do you know anything about the Guardians?"

"No idea," Jeber_Arium shrugged. "Dan, you have to finish the quest The Secret of Forest Hill, remember?"

"Yes, of course, I remember. But how do we reach Anchor?"

"We have to go west. I checked this morning. The sun rises over the Dark Frontier. If we keep the mountains at our back as a guide, we won't get lost."

"Maybe we should risk returning to the portal?"

"Where will it take us?" Jeb hunched down at once, his shoulders drooping. I understood his feelings. He had felt normal again, had escaped not only the darkness of the underground but also the shroud of encroaching madness and he cherished it and was afraid of a repeat.

"Let's try it, at least." I insisted. "Think about it, the portal now features the usual rune sequence. Maybe it has a normal interface, too? Like a 'pick your destination'?"

Jeb nodded with some effort. We hadn't had time to check the arrival point since we had immediately rolled down the slope and were then attacked by the wolf pack.

"Let's not delay then. Call Weasel."

"Right, just wait a minute," he paused, focusing on the interface tabs and probably reconfiguring it again to give him quick command access to our NPC companion.

I left him to it. I was overcome with questions and doubts. The sudden teleportation had left a very bad taste in my mouth. Who was using me for their own ends, pulling my strings whenever they wanted?

Yes, I had to admit, I did wonder if I should get rid of the stone and the amulet. Or at least block their effects. I had enough of my own problems.

Weasel was dashing toward us across the clearing. The squirrel pup was dragging something long behind him. A hazel branch, full of nuts!

Jeb patted the animal and gathered a handful of hazelnuts. Weasel immediately snatched one of them, ran a little distance away and bit into it.

Wow, what a breadwinner! He had filled his belly and even brought us a treat. His sincere care touched my soul and made me ashamed of my earlier thoughts. Yes, I had plenty of problems. But would I not have tried to free the captives myself if I had the chance?

I shouldn't blame some unknown force when I'd failed. Last time, when I managed to help the novice player, I didn't feel this annoyance.

Jeb was right. The Secret of Forest Hill was a priority. As soon as we got out of here, I'd sell the portal coordinates to the mapmakers. If that money wasn't be enough for Sasha's treatment, I'd take out a loan. We'd make it.

Chapter Fourteen

T HE SUN HAD PASSED the zenith when we finally
finished packing and left the abandoned mine,
heading up the slope in a roundabout way,
towards the portal.

I still had questions but was now thinking in a
different direction.

I acutely remembered the sudden summoning. I
had seen the frames of the captives. They were all
players. Why were the Dark ones taking prisoners to
the tower? The remains littering the platform, the
repulsive appearance of the creature from the Abyss,
particularly the tentacles with suckers framing its
mouth, evoked some creepy suspicions. What if *it* feeds
on the victims?

It sounded crazy even to my own ears. How could
this be possible? Surely the admins were monitoring

what happened in virtual reality! It was terrifying to imagine what a person would feel if the beast began to devour them alive.

What other options were there? Why were they being led there?

A scarlet marker suddenly flashed at the edge of the minimap.

"Dan, it's the wolves!" Jeb warned me nervously.

"Yes, I can see them. Up the tree you go!"

I reacted more or less calmly to the appearance of the mobs. After the morning's visit by the Warrior of the Abyss and the subsequent summoning, the appearance of the wolf pack didn't produce such acute emotions as the day before.

Separately, we could handle each one of the opponents. Even the pack leader. Jeb and I had discussed tactics in advance and now the main thing was to stick to them.

But the NPCs had learned something too! Their mental agility was striking! The pack was in no hurry to attack. Having spotted me, the wolves began circling at a distance. The red markers moved further and further apart, forming a circle, and only the trembling of shrubs occasionally revealed the position of the predators.

"Dan, I can't take aim! They're too quick!"

"Try to aggro them!"

A fireball pierced the forest gloom and the burst of flame briefly illuminated two swift silhouettes. Jeb missed them. At best, he had slightly singed their fur.

This was bad. The mobs were going to rush me from all sides, knocking me down and ripping out my throat. They had attacked alone or in pairs yesterday!

I couldn't see the smoky wolf yet. He kept away, filling the forest with his lilting howl.

"I'm retreating to the mine!" I had to change my plans. "Jeb, try to reach it without going down to the ground."

"I will!" came his answer.

I rushed back to the cliff. It was worth remembering that most NPCs were based on neural network technologies, so they could learn and change their approach, depending on the circumstances. Cyberspace developers had managed to recreate real wild nature... It was time that I learned that.

Branches smacked me in the face. There was a flash behind me as Jeb tried to draw the aggro towards him, but unsuccessfully as he probably missed again.

The line of markers broke. My unexpected rush made two predators stop on the spot (they were hoping to catch me at the cliff) and the rest to launch in pursuit. The green mark of my only ally quickly retreated to the edge of the minimap.

A long howl swept over the slope as the Aura of Fear — the leader used one of his abilities, which slowed me down slightly but couldn't inflict serious damage due to the distance between us.

Jeb and I were still too weak for these dangerous

locations. I couldn't help but remember the coordinated defense of the Dark players, who had killed the Protorat.

The ravine soon brought me to the cliff. A gray shadow darted across my path and a strong jolt almost knocked me to the ground. Teeth gnashed against the shield that I had just managed to hide behind when I detected the mob. It leaped back, avoiding a retaliatory strike, but where was the second one?

A scarlet marker rapidly approached from behind. I didn't have enough time to turn around and meet the enemy face on. I had only one risky option still left. I charged forward until the edge of the rocky ridge, pushed off with all my might and jumped...

The old boardwalk barely withstood my weight. Bits of rotten wood showered down. One of the mobs managed to leap after me. I quickly straightened up and turned around, but the beast found itself in an unfamiliar situation and at high altitude. It dropped down to the dilapidated boards and howled anxiously but received only a plaintive whine in response. One wolf had fallen into the ravine and the others hesitated at the edge of the cliff, shuffling nervously and considering a jump.

I couldn't let them do that! Hiding behind my shield, I began to push the mob back, blocking the blows from its paws. He shrank back and then jumped, trying to knock me down using a tried and tested technique, but the rotten planking trembled, one of the cracked vertical bars suddenly snapped, unable to bear the weight, and the old dwarven construction began to lean dangerously. It wouldn't take much for it to collapse completely and then we'd both be in trouble!

The wolf sunk his fangs into the edge of my shield, hanging off it like an unbearable weight and forcing me to expose myself. His claws slashed across my leather breastplate as we teetered on the edge...

The fight did not last long. The wolf tore open my shoulder and cut my head, but was pierced twice by my sword. I staggered. The pain was unbearable. Blood from the laceration poured into my eyes. To avoid losing my balance on the dangerously leaning platform, I had to cling to the wooden gate of the lift, dark with age.

The pain clouded my mind... Where was Jeb?

The wolves were still darting along the cliff edge, not daring to jump onto the listing planking.

There was my partner! The green marker approached rapidly. Did he ignore my advice and came down from the tree? Nope! The fireball struck downwards and sideways, exploding at the edge of the cliff and pushing three mobs into the abyss. They fell, their fur emitting a stinking smoke. A moment and the impact on the sharp rocks sent them into respawn. Only one wolf was left, plus the smoky pack leader, whom I couldn't see.

"Jeb?"

"Everything's great, Dan!" he responded recklessly,

releasing a string of flaming spheres. The last wolf in the pack shared the fate of its fellows.

"You got here quick!" I said, wiping off the blood and breathing quickly and heavily. My head was spinning like crazy.

That's all right... I had to be patient. Natural regeneration was slowly but steadily restoring my life points, gradually easing the pain and returning the ability to move and think clearly.

"I moved through the treetops! Weasel showed me the way! I would have had to climb down without him, since I couldn't know which branch would stand my weight and which one wouldn't." Jeb's voice still rang with the excitement of the short battle. "Dan, you won't believe it, but the smoky one ran away."

"You're right, I don't believe it." Feeling a little better, I began to cautiously descend along the rickety structure. My Life bar trembled at a quarter full. "Stay in the tree! I'll take the long way up."

As I scrambled up the barely noticeable, winding and steep path laid by the dwarves, the former owners of the abandoned mine, Jeb kept watch, but it was as if the smoky pack leader had disappeared into thin air.

My Life bar had managed to regenerate to half-full by this time.

"What's the situation?" I tried to spot my companion, but he was well camouflaged among the thick foliage.

Weasel slipped down on the ground from the stout tree, followed by Jeb.

"Quiet for now. Shall we go to the portal before the wolves respawn?"

"Send Weasel ahead to check. By the way, how do you communicate with him?"

"I have a set of commands. I've been reading that you need to master the ability 'Animal Friend' to establish a mental connection."

"Are you going down the multiclass path?"

"Yes, in the end, everything rests on it. Only elves naturally possess this ability, but with high Adaptability and the presence of an NPC companion, I'll definitely be able to master it!"

"Let's make a note of it," I agreed. "There must be other options, like books with skills and abilities. The main thing is to reach the town. Hiking through the Wild Lands is not an option. We're still weak for such adventures. We've only got four hours and we have to figure out the portal in that time..."

"And deal with the smoky wolf," Jeb added.

True, a large crimson marker had appeared on the minimap.

The leader of the pack was hiding near the portal. He didn't pay any attention to the nimble little animal moving through the trees.

Weasel turned out to be an excellent scout. His speed and the ability to see what is hidden allowed us to avoid an ambush.

Strangely, even as we cautiously approached the portal, located at the top of a small forest hill, Jeb and I couldn't see anything.

I raised my hand in warning and Jeb stopped obediently.

"Do you see him?"

"No," he answered in a husky whisper.

"Don't move. How much mana do you have?"

"Seventy-five. It's at maximum. I have enough for seven fireballs and I can also cast a minor healing spell."

I just shook my head. Our abilities were still very limited. I only had two types of attack in my arsenal: lunge and slash. I hadn't managed to learn any combinations. I also couldn't parry properly with my shield.

"Withdraw."

"Why?" Jeb asked in a whisper.

"Weasel can see the smoky wolf but we can't. Something's not right. Call the squirrel."

We retreated ten paces and disappeared into the hazel. I took the lump of resin that I had found in the cave from my inventory. It concentrated elemental energies. Perhaps I could use it to buff my weapon.

Weasel was already here, winding between our feet. I wished that we could communicate with him properly.

How could we find out where the pack leader was hiding?

Jeb squatted down and began to question his companion in the hope that he would understand why we were concerned.

I rubbed the resin against the blade but so far with no effect.

Weasel turned out to be surprisingly quick-witted. He disappeared into the shrub for a few seconds, then came back with a small flat stone, which he threw under Jeb's feet and began to ruffle the grass around it.

"What is he trying to say?"

"The stone is the portal. The wolf is hiding in the grass?" Jeb supposed.

"Seriously?" I laughed ironically. "The leader is too big to hide like that!"

"We have to check!"

"Fine."

There were plenty of tall trees growing around the hill. We climbed one of them and saw the portal. The stone circle was still emitting a faint golden shimmer, but there really was something wrong with the grass. Why wasn't it moving when the leaves on the nearby shrub rustled in the wind?

I looked closely and spotted a faint haze clinging to the ground.

An illusion? Or was the Abyss-altered wolf capable of metamorphosis?

My right hand prickled. I inspected my sword. It didn't look any different but why did I feel a slight tingling, as if from a weak current?

I concentrated on the weapon and read its properties.

Long sword. 8-10 damage with scaling according to Strength.

Additional lightning damage 1 with scaling according to Intellect.

...

I couldn't understand why the lightning damage was so small.

A hint popped up immediately:

Air elementals are still angry at you because of the way you treated their magic symbol.

...

What a pain! I'd be smarter in the future.

"Jeb, will the fireballs reach the hill from here?"

He nodded vigorously.

"Then you're staying here. See the mist in the grass near the portal?"

"Yeah."

"That's the leader. He metamorphosed or used an illusion — we won't know until we disrupt his ambush. I'll go first. Attack on my command."

"Okay," Jeb clearly didn't like my risky plan, but he didn't argue because there were no other options. Fire damage was the most powerful, and therefore the mage had to be out of reach of the enemy's claws and teeth.

I climbed up the hill. My goal was to aggravate the pack leader and force him to materialize and attack, thus exposing him to Jeb's fireballs.

It seemed simple. Yesterday, the smoky wolf was sent into respawn quite quickly since he was extremely vulnerable to fire. When we watched the recording, we noticed that the fireballs stunned him, disrupting his attack and forcing him to stand still while his fur burned. This would give me a good opportunity to inflict physical damage and retreat.

There was the top of the hill. I could see the faint golden glow of the teleport and the misty substance spread over the grass.

Why wasn't the creature reacting to my approach? Was he waiting for me to cross the boundary of his trap? What did this haze mean? It was a shame that we hadn't managed to discover all his abilities. The pack leader had left something in reserve.

The buff on my sword was still holding. I stepped forward and swept the sword over the ground, knowing that the steel was unlikely to inflict damage to the disembodied form but the lighting would at least sting and annoy him.

I was right!

The mist rose in swirling geysers and most of them instantly curved, throwing smoky tentacles in my direction. I recoiled, feeling very dizzy.

My Life bar wobbled and suddenly dropped!

...

You have discovered a new ability, Focused Mental Attack. Damage 75 HP (resistance depends on the Intellect score).

...

The smoky tendrils intertwined, forming the huge and creepy otherworldly figure of the wolf.

"Run, Dan!" Jeb screamed. A fireball pierced the ghostly mob but the damage inflicted was ridiculous, only 10 HP.

The haze billowed and suddenly spread out along the ground again, like the wall of a blast wave.

...

You have discovered a new ability, Mental Attack Over Area. Damage 55 HP, radius 7 meters, negative effects: Stun 3 seconds, Aura of Fear 5 seconds.

...

I lost my balance, fell and rolled down the slope, barely finding the strength to get back on my feet.

"Jeb, heal me!"

I wasn't far from the tree where he had hidden with Weasel. The mist crept back, coalescing into the shape of the phantom wolf again.

The minor healing restored some of my health but I had absolutely no idea what to do next.

"Dan, attack him and withdraw immediately. He's exhausted!"

Why would that be? Why would Jeb think that?

I bounded up the slope again. I kept having the nagging feeling that a melee fighter had little chance to stand against the ghostly creature unless you had special equipment or buffs that gave you high resistance to mental attacks. I also needed special weaponry...

The mob grew indistinct again, phantom tentacles shooting towards me. I dodged them with swift rolls. One of them brushed past me. My Life bar dropped disturbingly.

"Retreat!" Jeb hollered.

Again, I went head over heels down the slope, followed by the Mental Attack Over Area.

"Yes! It's done. I told you that he'd run out of steam soon!" Jeb screamed exuberantly.

Before I could even catch my breath, I climbed up the hill again. A fireball flew through the air ahead of me.

The phantom disappeared. Only shreds of darkness could still be seen here and there, while the leader of the pack stood in the flesh beside the portal.

His fur was smoking — Jeber_Arium hadn't missed his chance and had fired several times. The wolf's Life bar was shrinking in spurts and a Confusion debuff hung over him.

I took advantage of this and showered him with a barrage of strikes enhanced by Rage. I gave it my all.

The smoky wolf howled imploringly. Blood poured

from his wounds and the burned parts of his skin blistered.

A second more and he fell to his side, shuddered convulsively several times and was still.

I sat on the flattened grass, breathing heavily. Weasel scampered up to me, sniffed the air and snorted. He clearly didn't like the smell of blood.

Jeb followed him up the hill.

I was consumed with pain. My Life bar was almost empty.

"Just a second!" Jeb quickly cast several minor healings in a row.

"How did you know that the wolf would resume his usual form?" I asked hoarsely, feeling the pain ebb away and my muscles ache with fatigue.

"He was expending mana at a huge speed and not replenishing it. The ghostly appearance and the mental attacks were gobbling it up! He's an Abyss mutation and was previously drawing energy from the portal. But now that the portal has become a normal one, the leader was left with no way to recharge."

It was a logical explanation, proving once again that levels were one thing but without normal weapons, equipment, potions, and most importantly, without the ability to obtain and level up combat skills, we would not last here long. Twice, we'd won by the barest of margins, had nearly been sent into respawn and back to the dungeon.

"Let's loot him and get out of here."

The smoky wolf gave us two vials of blood marked as a 'rare alchemical ingredient' and a ring made from an unknown alloy. I was immediately alarmed by its rippling outline.

...

A metamorph ring. Item from the Abyss.

Strength +5.

Dexterity +5.

Special feature: The wearer of this ring is endowed with Level 1 Metamorph Ability. Effect: You can transform into a disembodied form. Conventional weapons (dealing only physical damage) pass through your body without causing harm. Duration 20 seconds. Cooldown/recharge 1 hour.

Restriction: Can only be used by a Warrior of the Abyss.

...

Such a ring would be so handy for me right now! Perhaps I would be able to ignore the class constraints at high levels of Adaptability but who knew when that would happen?

Jeb showed little interest in the finds, glancing at them briefly and then going to study the portal.

"Any luck?" I placed the ring and vials in my inventory.

"The standard interface is working again now!" Jeb declared happily. "There used to be access to five destination points from here but now only two are active. We don't really have much choice. But now we know the name of the town that the Ifrit burned down!"

Looking at the portal interface, I understood what Jeb meant. A menu bar appeared before my mind's eye.

Flooded Mine Teleport. Active.

Select a destination:

~~*Cloud Shelter*~~ *(no response).*

~~*Griffin Breeding Grounds*~~ *(no response).*

Dungeon of Noogard (active)

~~*Noogard's Pass*~~ *(no response).*

Rabbit Junction (active).

...

Yes, that certainly wasn't much choice. I'd have to look up information about Noogard but now we had to be on our way.

Jeb nodded to me, confirming that he was ready to travel. Weasel had crawled under his shirt and was peeking out of there.

With a flicker of my pupils, I selected the destination and reality became distorted for a moment.

...

You have discovered a lost stone teleport (+1 to Fame if you list the coordinates on a public map).

You have discovered a lost location, Dryad Stow.

...

"Jeb, stay on your toes!"

I gazed around with surprise and concern.

The place looked nothing like a junction. Nor like an ordinary forest. It was hot and humid, as if we were in a jungle. The trees around us were mighty and gnarled like old oak trees but they were all dried up... The sky was gloomy with low-hanging storm clouds promising imminent rain.

Thick grass pushed through the traces of an old fire. The area was covered in narrow flooded ditches, connecting small ponds covered with swamp duckweed. Streaks of thick fog floated over the canals. The whitish haze severely hampered visibility due to the lack of wind.

The teleport stone must have shifted here when the Abyss invaded, and was stuck obliquely in the ground and covered in withered leaves. Not only had it changed location but it must have served as a conduit for harmful mutations for a long time.

The magic symbols on it were barely glowing. The normal sequence was working now and I called up the interface, hoping that it would show new destination points.

...

Rabbit Junction/Dryad Stow Teleport (change or confirm the name).

Select a destination:

Northern Frontier (no response).

Mercenary Tavern (no response).

Flooded Mine.

~~Snake Catcher Oasis~~ *(no response).*
~~Unicorn Forest~~ *(no response).*
...

Was this a dead end? This portal could bring us back to the mine, but no more than that...

I wondered what 'stow' meant. It sounded ominous but I wanted to find out the exact meaning.

A search produced immediate results. It turned out that a stow was a natural boundary, such as a swamp in the middle of a field, a rock ledge or a ravine that separated parts of a forest. Although, I suspected that it had another meaning here...

Weasel dropped down to the ground and disappeared into the fog, but then came straight back and clambered up Jeb's clothes to his shoulder, as if scared of something.

"Come one, let's look around and try to find a respawn circle," I wasn't in the mood to stand around.

It was muggy. The canals were shallow, only knee-deep. We crossed several of them easily and reached the nearest pond.

"Dan, look," Jeb whispered shakily, pointing to a tree torn out with its roots. Only a fragment of its massive trunk remained. What kind of strength was needed to pull such a giant out of the ground?

"Shh!" I felt a regular vibration in the soil. Someone enormous was stomping around nearby.

There were muffled sounds of creaking, sighing and rustling.

We hid behind the remains of the fallen tree and watched but the mysterious creature didn't appear, hidden by the fog.

Lighting flashed in the distance and thunder rumbled. The heavy clouds released their first drops and soon the rain was bucketing down.

It grew much darker and the rising wind chased away the mist. The rolls of thunder drew closer and closer, becoming clearer and more deafening.

We had nowhere to hide and were instantly soaked to the skin. There was nothing to do but to keep going, since we didn't know when the downpour would stop.

A branched lightning lit up our surroundings, revealing an enormous mossy figure.

...

Wood Giant. Guardian of the Stow. Level 105.

...

He was stomping around in one place, packing down the soggy earth and paying us no attention.

"Get lost! Get lost! Get lost!" his creaking voice was even louder than the thunder.

Something was moving beneath the giant's feet!

I took a closer look when the next lighting flashed. The ground and fallen tree trunks were completely covered in a carpet of insects. I focused on one of the frames,

Black Woodborer Beetle. Mutation of the Abyss. Level 35.

...

There were hundreds of them! So that's who had turned the uprooted trees into dust. The insatiable horde was probably slowly migrating from the portal.

"Jeb, could we help the giant?"

"Are you crazy? We still haven't changed our anchor point!"

He was right. The massive beetles look menacing. Their shells were black and glossy and were probably as hard as armor. Their powerful mandibles easily bit through branches as thick as my arm.

"Fine. We'll go around them for now. There must be a respawn point here!" I turned around and spotted the squirrel hiding in my companion's shirt. "Weasel, scout it out, off you go!

The animal didn't listen to me but Jeb's request had the desired effect. Weasel briskly leaped to the ground and disappeared among the inclement weather.

"I see him on the map."

"Does Weasel uncover the map for you?"

"Yes. Let's follow him. Keep up, Dan!"

The downpour continued and the ground beneath our feet turned to slush. The shapes of dead Wood Giants appeared out of the haze — they had held the line of defense but had lost the battle. The giants had literally been gnawed away. Their bark was completely gone and their gnarly branch-like arms had gone black in the rain.

This place spoke of tragedy. It was clear that this area used to be a dense forest. But who had the giants been protecting?

The realism was taking its toll. I shivered, but not from the cold. I wanted to turn around and, defying common sense, rush back to help the last defender of the stow.

"Keep going, Dan! I don't think it's far now, look!" Jeb pointed ahead.

He was right. Living trees began to gradually appear. Many had been damaged by something and had partially dried out but didn't die. Soon Weasel's path brought us the edge of a mossy thicket. The oak trees here grew so close that their canopies intertwined.

The respawn circle could be seen beside the oldest tree. This relic had survived centuries and the attacks of the Abyss-altered creatures, but things weren't looking good for it. Its bark was peeling and the leaves had shriveled.

"Quickly," Jeb hurried me along. His attention was focused solely on the respawn circle.

A few more steps and we left the wall of rain behind us. Only the large drops, flowing down the leaves, reached the forest floor here.

A respawn point... finally!

Another step and the long-awaited sign appeared

before me,

You have discovered the respawn circle of the Dryad Stow.

Would you like to change the anchor point?

...

I answered 'Yes' without hesitation.

Farewell, the underground! We had finally broken free of you!

The crowns of nearby trees were suddenly disturbed as if by a gust of wind. There was crackling and rustling. The branches dipped lower to the ground, as if someone hiding among the leaves wanted to take a closer look at us.

I saw the dim outline of a being step away from the dying oak. A moment later, it turned into a gaunt woman wrapped in a dense leaf cloak.

Dryad[4], Level 152.

Her frame was yellow so she was neutral to us.

"You are too late, Guardian. It is too late to fix anything," she said with quiet reproach, then added, "If you had closed the Abyss portal a bit earlier..."

"You are mistaken," I didn't want to lie to her. "We are simple travelers. We're moving from the Dark Frontier in search of a road to the Peaceful Woods near Anchor."

The Dryad looked at me closely. "Yes, you are not a

---

[4] Dryads – in Greek mythology, forest nymphs that protect the trees. They could control plants and subdue all flora.

Guardian," she sighed in agreement. "And who knows if you will become one. Nevertheless, I would thank you for your help since one of you has closed the Abyss portal. I can feel it there is no point denying it!"

"I accidentally acquired two artifacts," there was no point in dissembling for the Dryad could see right through us. "We restored one portal with their help," I answered. "But it was far from here."

"Distance doesn't matter. There was a chain of events. I'm afraid, traveler, that you won't be left alone. Have you seen the Abyss? Have you seen its creations and their minions?"

"Yes. We barely escaped death."

"You are still weak. Why are you so eager to help the last defender of the Stow?"

Wow, she could read thoughts? I was indeed listening to the distant sounds, trying to determine whether the Wood Giant could cope with the horde surrounding him.

"No, he will not be able to defeat them. Our time is up. The portal has spread its pestilent mutations for too long. Nothing is precious or sacred in our world to the creatures of the Abyss. The cradle of the Dryads has been destroyed. The special trees with which we are inextricably linked have been lost. Our natural magic is distorted and weakened by the long influence of the Abyss."

"How can we help?"

I noticed that Jeb nodded in approval since our

dialogue with a high-level NPC clearly presumed a rare quest, but to be honest, I had completely forgotten that we were in the digital world in that moment. War had left a deep scar on my soul. The feelings and memories that I had tried to keep locked away suddenly stirred under the overwhelming atmosphere of hopelessness and despair surrounding us.

"Where does this bitter force inside you come from?" the Dryad flinched as if she had mentally touched something hot.

"My past." I only shrugged because she would not understand the explanation. "How can we help you?"

"Tell me, how did you obtain the Guardian's Amulet?"

"I found it in the Peaceful Woods. To be honest, I took it from some remains."

"This means all the Guardians are dead." the Dryad stared into my eyes. "Yes, you can help me. Find out who that person was. And take this," she stretched her arm out towards me.

I saw a grain. A tiny insignificant grain.

"What is it?"

"A seed of the Dryad tree. I have no one else to turn to!" she begged. "Find a safe place where it can grow. Only then will we be reborn in this world. Everything is finished here. This battle has been lost..."

As if confirming her words, the earth shuddered.

"The last giant has fallen. Go!" the Dryad pointed to the path leading into the thicket. I could have sworn that a solid wall of trees stood there a minute ago. "Hurry. I'll delay the creatures of the Abyss."

...

You have received a new quest: Cradle of the Dryads.

Find a safe place where the seed of the Dryad tree can grow. Look after it until it starts to bear fruit.

Reward: hidden, variable.

Penalty for refusal/failure: the forces of nature will become hostile towards you.

...

You have received a new quest: The Last Guardian.

Return to the Peaceful Woods and find out whom the remains where you found the amulet belong to.

Reward: hidden, variable (depending on the results).

Penalty for refusal/failure: none.

...

"Now go and don't look back. Quickly. I won't be able to hold them for long!"

Jeb and I stepped onto the narrow and dimly lit path. The rain had grown stronger and we could hear its rustle, although not a single drop penetrated the mossy wilderness, through which we were shown the way.

If only we knew where the path led.

Chapter Fifteen

THE DAY WAS WANING. It rapidly grew darker in the dense forest. My first impression was deceptive — it wasn't the trees themselves but their lower branches and the dense undergrowth that parted before us, forming a narrow track.

We walked quickly, at the limit of our endurance. The vegetation was setting the pace, with the thicket closing up behind us, as if urging us onwards and whispering, 'Faster, faster, faster'.

Thunder faded in the distance. The trail turned several times, led us to a ford across the river and then back into the depths of the forest.

"Jeb, I've long wanted to ask, what's your level of realism?"

"Seventy-five," he was breathing heavily and looked like he was about to fall behind.

"Yeah, I thought you were gaining experience points faster than I am." I tried to distract him from the monotonous and exhausting hike. Weasel was feeling the best, perched on Jeb's shoulder, glancing around and sniffing the air.

"I wanted to reduce it to fifty percent, but I can't."

"Is your VR capsule working OK?"

"I have no idea. I don't know how to check."

"What about your memories? Are they coming back?"

"Nope... It's like I've always lived here. Sometimes I see fragments of the past, but they seem dull, as if they're not real."

That was a problem that we'd have to deal with. As soon as we found a genuinely safe place where we could rest properly, we'd take a look at it. Surely Jeb's interface would show some data? For example, I had indicators showing the state of my VR capsule and they were all growing green. I also had a separate window showing my IP address. It could be used to find out the real location of the device.

"Light ahead!" Jeb said huskily.

We stopped. It had gotten dark. The sky was clear and filled with stars, the moon peeking through the gaps between the tree branches, its cold dim light flooding the clearing.

"Are we out?" I was delighted.

"Looks like it." Jeb glanced around him nervously.

I checked the map. The 'fog of war' covering the

unexplored regions was pierced by the thin thread of our passing.

"Send Weasel off to explore. He's been sitting on your shoulder the whole time."

The animal eagerly leaped to the ground and disappeared into the gloom. I switched to the local area map. Immediately beyond the forest edge, appeared the crossroads and a symbol indicating a tavern. Two emerald circles denoted the respawn point and an active portal. The name 'Mercenary Tavern' appeared as well.

A large scattering of red dots around the structure lit up a moment later.

Mobs, judging by the markers. User signals looked slightly different. The dots were motionless, but Weasel was rushing from side to side, as if dodging attacks, as he skirted the tavern building.

He completed the circle and sprinted back at once.

Fifty-four scarlet marks! They surrounded the respawn point and the teleport stone in a particularly tight circle.

"What are we going to do? Shall we go around or try to fight our way through?" Jeb asked.

"Let's at least find out who's hiding there?" I suggested. "The markers are static, did you notice?"

"Yeah."

The grass rustled and Weasel reappeared.

Jeb squatted down and stroked the animal's fur. "Well, who's hiding there?"

Weasel opened his mouth wide in response, as if yawning, then snapped his teeth sharply.

Whoever those creatures were, they had big, toothy mouths!

The markers on the map remained still. I set out a route in my head.

"Let's go."

The glove on Jeb's hand glowed with crimson streaks. He was ready for battle although it was obvious that he was deadly tired and had no desire to participate in another fight.

Yes, it had been a long day. All the more reason to find a safe place to rest. After all, we were somewhere on the border between the Wild Lands and low-level regions. I hoped that we'd make it.

The moon was shining brightly enough. I could see the outline of the tavern up ahead. The silence was extraordinary. There was only the faint rustling of leaves disturbed by a light breeze and the repetitive creaking of the sign at the entrance to the abandoned building.

The tavern roof had collapsed. Everything was overgrown with weeds. A weak glow came from two places — the respawn point and the teleportation stone.

Where were the mobs?

Weasel jumped off Jeb's shoulder, ran forward, stood up on his hind legs and began to gnash his teeth again.

Understood. It was dangerous to go any further. But who was waiting for us here?

In the moonlight, I could see only strange vine-like plants with large (the size of my head), elongated fruits hanging on long grassy stalks.

No matter how closely I looked, I couldn't see any frames. Who was hiding in this thicket? The unusual plants had climbed over every surface, their shoots twining around the walls of the dilapidated building, the shadoof of the well, the crooked gate posts and the separately growing trees.

The teleportation stone exuded a golden shimmer so it was working in normal mode.

I gestured for Jeb to step back. A fireball could fly about twenty meters. There was no reason for the mage to be in the thick of things.

I picked up a heavy stone and threw it right into the midst of the strange plants.

No response. Well, I was just going to have to risk it. Hiding behind my shield, I slowly walked forward toward the respawn circle, crossed the line that Weasel had indicated and then everything became clear. The nearest fruit suddenly split open, dividing into petals covered in large, sharp teeth!

I managed to deflect several rapid attacks with my shield, cut down the closest stalk, it's mouth spitting caustic juice, and fell back, yelling, "Jeb, burn them!"

The wall of vegetation moved threateningly. The vines were much more dangerous than they had seemed at first glance. Their flexible green trunks peeled away from their supports and reached for us! The plants were like a tangle of snakes, eagerly pursuing their prey!

...

Exoral. Level 25.

...

The frames seemed to indicate that we could take on the plants. They posed a serious threat only to the lonely traveler. Imagine if a player had passed through the portal and immediately found themselves surrounded by a dense network of predatory flora from the Wild Lands?

Odd that nobody had cleaned them up yet.

Jeb and I worked quite well together. While I distracted the Exorals, deflecting their blows and corrosive spit with my shield, he successfully burned them with fireballs.

The problem was that his store of mental energy was still not very big. He had destroyed only a third of the predators when his mana ran out.

"Dan, retreat."

I followed his advice and withdrew to a safe distance. The vines had roots, after all, so they could only extend to a certain length.

"What are we going to do?" I puffed.

"Give me the Intellect ring," Jeb asked.

"Here you go."

"Awesome!" he perked up. "Now, as soon as I regain

some mana, I'll serve them something special! I've got this one spell that will be perfect."

The Exorals wouldn't calm down. The fireballs had left large burnt patches in their midst but the greedy plants continued to extend dark green shoots in our direction.

I watched them. A hint appeared in my mind's eye with a link to an Encyclopedia article.

Exorals are carnivorous flora from the Wild Lands. They posed little danger before the invasion of the Abyss but they then mutated somewhere on the border of the Dark Frontier. The new type of Exoral became much larger and what's worse, they began to gain levels with every consumed victim. Individual Exorals can reach Level 50-60 and can pose a serious threat to even a group of explorers.

Features: spit toxic juice to weaken their opponent.

Respawn after death and lose levels. A colony of these plants can be wiped out.

Particularly aggressive during the fruit ripening period. Ripe fruits (that fall to the ground) serve as food for some birds and animals that contribute to the spread of their seeds.

Article author: Curious_Michael, a famous explorer.

...

"Ready, Dan. Look at this," Jeb used the glove to launch a small ball of fire into the midst of the plants, which turned into a puddle of lava as soon as it touched the ground. This type of pyromancy would be no threat to a mobile mob, but was fatal to carnivorous vegetation, with many of the trunks crumbling to dust.

"We'll gradually make our way to the teleport this way. I don't want to spend the night here!"

I nodded in agreement. Mobs respawned after four hours. We wouldn't have enough time to rest properly before the regenerated plants surrounded the tavern again. So that's why the building stood abandoned.

It was almost midnight. Jeb and I were dead tired after fighting our way to the portal. The burning hot lava puddles required a lot more mental energy than a simple fireball and my companion had to rest often to restore his mana.

"We need potions." he sighed.

"We'll buy them when we get to the town."

"They're expensive. I'd rather go into herbalism and alchemy." Jeb replied dreamily. "I'll wander through the Peaceful Woods, collecting herbs and recovering my skills."

"You can see them?" I was surprised.

"Yeah, but they're nearly at zero because I lost so many levels. Alchemy is on 1 and Herbalism is on 2 right now," Jeb stood up, the fiery streaks on his glove glowing brightly again.

I got ready as well. We'd worked up quite a sweat

over the past hour, cutting down the toothy fruits and trying to widen the path leading to the portal. The Exoral colony was like the mythical Hydra. We'd chop down one maw, and another couple would appear on the fresh shoots. It was the pits! The red markers kept multiplying as the plants used their life reserves to grow clingy brown tentacles. They then tried to grab me and drag me into the thicket.

Curious_Michael did not mention such an ability so I would need to update his article.

Jeb threw a lump of lava. The flash was bright in the darkness and a viscous crimson puddle spread over the ground, burning the soil and snapping the knobbly tree-like trunks.

I cut off a tendril with my sword. We were nearly there...

"What are you doing here, unkind people?"

The voice made us turn around.

"Can't you see? We're clearing the way to the portal." Jeb snapped.

Two villagers appeared in the light of the rapidly cooling lava. An old man leaning on a crooked staff and a dashing hero holding a blacksmith's hammer in his mighty arms.

They were clearly NPCs.

"Is there a village nearby?" I hazarded a guess.

The blacksmith glared at me from under heavy brows. He seemed to be waiting for a sign to attack. Both frames were red so they were hostile towards us.

Why would that be?

"Don't be angry with us, father," I decided not to escalate the situation. "I thought we were doing a good deed."

"Yeah, a good one, right," the old man muttered. He looked at us intently and meanly. "We went into the dark forest, collected the seeds, planted them and now you're burning them down!"

"Wait," I was completely taken aback. "You're growing these things here on purpose?"

"That's right."

"Why?"

"To keep scum from wandering through here!" the blacksmith boomed, throwing his hammer from one hand to the other.

Something wasn't right. The portal seemed ordinary enough. I could clearly see its golden glow. It wasn't connected to the Abyss in any way.

"What did the other people do to displease you?"

"They're not people, they're bandits!"

"Mercenaries, you mean?" Jeb asked.

"Bandits, mercenaries, hunters, knights — they're all the same!" the old man replied darkly. "They were nothing but trouble. They'd go into the forest to hunt the animals but couldn't manage. And what do you think they did then?"

"They ran away?" I guessed.

"That's right! Of course, they ran away. Through our fields and our crops. And they dragged the beasts after them, so that the village guards would have something to do. And when they got drunk at the one-eyed's tavern? We'd get no sleep, no rest! How are you supposed to live if it's after midnight and people are knocking on your door, asking, 'Do you need any help, esteemed elder?' Yeesh... Why would I need help when I'm sleeping?"

"So, you decided to plant carnivorous plants beside the portal?" Jeb had accumulated a bit of mana and the glove on his hand smoldered ominously.

"We did," the old man nodded. "And we won't let you burn them! We're going to make a fence like this around the village, too!" he promised darkly.

"Look, we need to get into town," I decided to make another attempt to smooth things over. The NPCs here had clearly started developing and weren't keen on players.

"See the road? Off you go. Sixty versts and you'll reach the town."

"Have you lost your mind?" Jeb exploded. "How many days will that take?"

"Well, you asked for it," the old man lost his temper too and quickly cast some kind of buff on the blacksmith, who raised his hammer and rushed at me.

"Jeb, stay back!" I yelled as I automatically performed a roll to get out of the way. The blacksmith was strong but clumsy. The hammer had barely left a deep dent in the ground and I was already standing behind him, my blade pressed to the nape of his neck, warning him, "Don't move or you'll be in trouble."

The old man uttered an inarticulate curse.

"We're going through the portal," Jeb snarled. "Whether you like it or not!"

"Fine, fine." the elder backpedaled. "Lower your sword, will you? Let's find a peaceful solution."

"That's better," I noticed that both character frames became yellow and thus neutral.

"Don't burn the toothies," asked the village elder. "There is another way."

Well, I wasn't too surprised. I had guessed at once that they were still using the portal somehow.

The lava puddles had long died out. The moon was barely peeking out from the massing clouds. It was quiet and cool. Two village women appeared from the darkness. Each one was holding a canvas bag. They approached the carnivorous plants and started throwing them pieces of meat, making the vines stretch away from the portal. Then, incredibly, when the two bags were empty, the sated Exorals slumped to the ground.

"Check them," the elder said to the blacksmith.

He fearlessly entered the thicket but the carnivorous plants didn't react as they were full.

"Go on!" the old man wanted to get rid of us as quickly as possible. "Leave and don't come back. Just look at you, burning our toothies!"

He didn't need to say it twice. Jeb and I had been on our feet all day and the fight against the Exorals had taken everything out of us.

We followed the blacksmith to the portal. The teleportation interface switched on immediately.

Mercenary Tavern teleport.

Select a destination:

~~Rabbit Junction~~ (no response).

~~Mansion of the Chosen~~ (no response).

Anchor, capital of the region.

~~Over the River~~ (no response).

~~Old Ford~~ (no response).

...

I activated the only available route and reality turned hazy for a moment.

...

The city wall offered stunning views. It was the middle of the night and the sky shone with stars, an unsteady flickering surrounding the respawn circle...

I recognized Anchor.

We had returned! We had escaped the Dark Frontier!

Jeb was staring around him in surprise.

"Come on," I patted him on the shoulder. "There's an inn nearby. Let's get some dinner and then sleep."

I woke up at first light the next day, but in a far from cheerful mood. Jeb snored softly and Weasel was also still asleep. I decided not to wake them, but rather went into the common room, ordered porridge for breakfast and sat there, thinking.

The Mongooses weren't replying even though I had tried to contact the clan several times. They turned out to have four other castles. Max had disappeared into thin air. He wasn't listed among the dead, so did that mean he was hiding from someone?

It was only now that I truly became aware of the gravity of the situation. I had become homeless in the real world. All that was left was cyberspace and I was nobody here. Just an ordinary character.

Fine. Let's try again. In real life, I could rent an apartment and a VR capsule. I had enough money for that. But where would I get the money for Sasha'a treatment and for Denis' loan repayments?

Once I finished eating, I asked the inkeeper for directions to the Guild of Mapmakers and went outside.

The town was waking up. My route took me along twisting streets to the Central Square, where people were already bustling about. Merchants were laying out their goods, the herald of a local NPC faction was reading out a decree, a small group of citizens gathered around him. The sun rose above the horizon, bathing the roofs in light. The stained glass windows in the Town Hall sparkled.

"Dan?" someone called out to me in amazement.

The guy in the basic knight armor seemed vaguely familiar.

I read his frame, remembered and smiled, holding out my hand, "Sir_Lans? Good to see you!"

He shook my hand firmly. "You were unavailable. I wanted to add you as a friend but the system froze, can you believe it?"

"It must have been the distance. My friend and I were traveling through a different region."

"Listen," he hesitated for some reason, "are you really a Guardian?"

"I don't know yet," I replied honestly. "I accepted one quest, but where will it lead me?"

"A unique mission? Wow!"

I liked Lans. I could sense his simple and uncomplicated sincerity.

"I can't tell you about it yet. You've leveled up, I see?" I changed the subject. I didn't want to answer questions when I myself didn't know the answers.

Lance raised his head proudly. He was now on Level 27, which meant that the fellow had been working on his character continuously, with only short rest breaks. An enviable persistence, considering he was not being stalked by deadly circumstances.

"Dan, we found a cave nearby and we're planning

to go and explore it today. Do you want to come with us?"

"I can't, unfortunately. I have business to take care of. But I've added you as a friend."

"Yeah, I can see that. I've accepted! Well... see you around?"

"Of course. Send me a message if anything."

"Super!" he was genuinely glad to see me. "Once you've sorted out your affairs, pop into the tavern in the evening. I've been promised a map of the Wild Lands!"

"All right."

My mood improved significantly as if Lance had given me an emotional boost. Why was I freaking out? Had I made any mistakes?

I shook my head in response to such thoughts.

When you walk into enemy fire or run into a burning house, you don't think about the consequences. You just do it.

So, nothing to hang my head about. Life went on. There was no point drowning in my problems. I needed to turn them into tasks to solve.

It's true what they say, 'A person is as young as they feel inside.' I approached the Town Hall in a completely different mood.

On the right stood a branch of the World Bank and on the left was the Mapmakers' Guild, which rumors said was controlled by players. This was where I needed to go.

The door was already open, and I stepped resolutely into the cool of the lobby.

There weren't many people inside. Dignified NPCs sat at individual tables. I could hear the creaking of quills and rustle of parchment.

An elderly clerk approached me. He looked at me appraisingly from a distance. My shabby leather armor didn't win him over but a client was still a client, so the guild member tried to appear extremely interested, "What does the venerable sir desire? Have you returned from a dangerous journey and possess new information about our world? Or would you like to purchase maps of the regions? We have a wide selection."

"I'd like to do both," I replied.

"Please." he indicated two armchairs. Between them stood a small table with drinks and a writing implement.

"So?" he looked at me inquiringly.

"I have been in the Dark Frontier and have discovered several active portals. I want to sell their coordinates."

"They haven't been published anywhere?"

"No."

"Tell me more. Were you able to use them? Are they

normal teleports or Abyss ones?"

I faltered.

True. Why didn't I think of that? Without knowing the exact sequence or possessing the artifact key, who would be able to visit the Scorched Lands or the Deadly Crag that Jeb and I discovered? The Dark players had come through the portal in the abandoned dwarf settlement so someone already knew its coordinates. There were probably single-use artifact keys that the mysterious Shadows had given their minions.

Moreover, the caravans of the unknown NPC faction also passed through the Abyss-altered teleports, which meant they also had access. What could I offer? Myself as a key and a guide?

It was a shame, but nothing could be done. I had to set aside the unique regions for now. I would be able to sell only the coordinates of the restored portals to the mapmakers.

"Will you tell me?"

"Yes. There are three teleports forming a chain. One on the border of the Wild Lands, the second in the foothills of the Dark Frontier, and the third in the dungeons below Noogard. All portals are working in normal mode but most destinations are blocked. Only the route that I mentioned is active. I can't reveal any more until I find out the price that the guild is willing to pay."

Greed flashed for a second in the clerk's eyes. I definitely noticed the gloating spark.

"We pay five thousand gold coins for each destination," he replied.

"No discussion?"

"It's a lot of money!"

"I know. But I would like some special conditions."

He looked away, angry.

Fifteen thousand gold really was a lot of money in the game world. But I needed real credits and the exchange rate for in-game currency was 10:1. Which meant that, at best, I would only get 1,500 credits.

"I will have to consult with management," the clerk had gottten a grip on himself and spoke in a kind tone again. "It is a delicate matter since it concerns the Dark Frontier. Could you come back in a couple of hours?"

"Yes, of course. Do you have any maps of Noogard and the pass located nearby?"

"Only old maps, unfortunately. A map of the town, the way it was before the Abyss invaded, plus the surrounding area, of course. Although things have probably changed there a lot. The scrolls cost 10 gold each. Will you be buying them today?"

"Later. Once we've dealt with the sale of the portal coordinates."

"Very good. I will be at your service again in two hours, but I must warn you that the offer is unlikely to change. I have told you the maximum price for this kind of information."

My visit to the Mapmakers' Guild did not fill me with optimism. The clerk was acting suspiciously. I couldn't explain it but I could feel that something was off.

I went into a nearby tavern, sat down at a back table, ordered a beer and thought about it. The way of the Explorer would have suited me. It meant adventure, fame, danger and good money by the standards of cyberspace. If I traveled a lot, I could even earn enough money for the real world but I was now facing a crisis. I needed 13,000 credits right away, which was 130,000 gold coins in gaming currency! There was no way I could gather so much unless I sold my services, using the artifacts to lead groups of players to unique locations.

Even this would take time. Besides, I had no idea how to attract serious clientele, and where was the guarantee that I wouldn't be killed for my artifacts?

I had to leave the game for a little while. I suspected that the empty mug of strong beer was the reason for my lack of focus.

That's what I did. Without leaving the VR capsule, I exited into my personal space.

...

You have two unread messages.

...

The first message was from the hospital. Sasha had

regained consciousness. He was getting steadily better.

I was glad but it also meant that I didn't have much time to find the missing amount!

Well, what about the second message?

Wow! He could already send e-mails?

...

Andrey Dmitrievich, I tried to get in touch with you but the system wouldn't deliver my messages. I'm assuming you're still in the catacombs of the Dark Frontier. That's why the messages aren't getting through. Please contact me as soon as you get out. We have a lot to discuss. Thank you for everything... I'm not sure that I would have done the same for a stranger.

Sasha.

...

Well, what would I say to him?

'Hold on, Sasha, maybe I can get some more money?' How would that cheer him up and help him recover? No. I'd get in touch when I acquired the missing amount. He mustn't worry right now.

There was still nothing from Max.

Fine. I returned to the Edge of the Abyss. I would look for a way out of this situation even though I was no good as a man of business.

I had been away for only a few minutes, yet someone had already sat down at my table.

A stranger sat in front of me, dressed in a cloak with a deep hood. Their face was hidden from view.

"Have we met before?" I asked rather harshly. I was on edge. My head was full of issues requiring an immediate solution. I wanted to sit and think in peace.

"Of course," he said, throwing off the veil of secrecy. The frame *Alexander Lourier* immediately appeared.

"Lourier?" I asked, mentally going through my rather limited circle of online friends. "I don't remember ever meeting you."

"Andrey Dmitrievich, this is my alter."

I see. Does this guy know me from the real world?

"An alternative character?"

"Yeah."

"Max, is it you?"

"No. It's me, Sasha."

"Sasha!" I was surprised, delighted and angry. "How did you end up here?"

"What am I supposed to do, die from boredom in the regeneration chamber? I've regained consciousness."

"All right, but how? How did you get in here?"

"The hospital's local network has poor security," he waved his hand dismissively. "I'm here on business. I want to say thank you in person and help you, too."

"Sasha, wait," I sighed. "Not everything's so rosy. I've only paid for part of the required course of treatment and I'm broke."

"I know. That's why I broke the rules. I'm an interested party, right?"

I had nothing to say to that.

"I was watching you, Andrey Dmitrievich..."

"Just call me Andrey."

"OK. I followed you in stealth mode. Well done for not falling for the mapmaker's offer. Many players in that guild pretend to be NPCs. He was just trying to get information out of you for very little money."

"Yes, I noticed how eagerly he was watching me. But I have no idea where to go and whom to turn to. Will someone else offer me more money for the portal coordinates? You heard everything, so come on, spit it out!"

"So, I can steer things here?"

"Yes, go on. Show me where I made a mistake and what opportunity I missed. Just tell me where to go and what I to say."

"We won't go anywhere. Do you have access to the auction?"

"Yes, there is such a tab, but I've never used it."

"Open it. Go to the 'Information Lots' section."

"Got it."

"Pay the fee to register as a seller."

"A thousand gold pieces? I don't have that much

right now."

"Here," he transferred the required amount of in-game currency to my account.

I didn't argue. It wasn't the right time. I ran my eyes over the text. There was a lot with portal coordinates in the Wild Lands. The price was 10,000 gold coins. It was twice as much as the mapmaker had offered me but still too little for the amount that I needed for Sasha's treatment. After all, I had the coordinates of only three portals while the rest opened in my presence using artifacts.

"Thirty thousand gold won't be enough," I pointed out. "I need more."

Sasha grinned.

"Tell me the details. I'm mainly interested in the surroundings of each portal."

I ordered another beer. Sasha declined a drink and listened to me carefully, his gaze occasionally dulling during my tale as he searched for information online.

"Cool. Really, really cool." He summed up at the end. "I think we'll be able to get the required amount and even a bit extra. It's just that you don't have experience in this kind of thing. I'd do it myself, but I don't know how long I can stay here."

"It's not going to hamper your treatment?"

"Nah... I came here on 10% of realism. All right, I'm going to create three lots. Your task is to place them. When they're sold, the money will be transferred to your account, and you can shift it into the real world through a branch of the World Bank. Here's your contact. I trust this guy. He has an advanced account. Now give me a bit of time, okay?"

I nodded, although couldn't imagine what he could squeeze out the coordinates of three portals.

Sasha got to work. He sat still.

Half an hour passed and I was beginning to worry when he sent me a message.

"Read it."

I opened the message.

...

Lot No. 1. Flooded dungeon. First passage guarantee. Unique loot. Minimum requirements: raid levels 50+. Starting price is 50,000 gold.

A flooded dwarf mine + portal coordinates. The respawn point is faulty, revival will require a support mage with an Intellect of 40 and the ability 'Carver of Magic Runes'. Nobody has explored the dungeon since the invasion of the Abyss. A screenshot of the security seal is attached. Number of underground levels — unknown. Level bosses — unknown. There is a chance of finding a path to the legendary flooded dwarf city with its countless treasures.

...

Lot No. 2. Hunt for the Ifrit. The portal coordinates for the Dungeon of Noogard (Dark Frontier) + first kill guarantee. The Ifrit (Level 50) has escaped from an unexplored region of the Abyss and has destroyed the town of Noogard. Attention, there were powerful elemental mages present in Noogard at the time of the Ifrit's attack but they have died, and so has the population of the town. Dangerous! Raid recommended. Starting price is 30,000 gold.

...

Lot No. 3. Farming creatures from the Abyss (Levels 35+). Guaranteed drop of unique alchemical ingredients + unique (smoky) chitin for making armor. Exclusive: coordinates of the portal + active respawn point. Starting price is 25,000 gold.

...

Sasha didn't just surprise me. I was in shock. A hundred thousand gold instead of fifteen thousand? Everything was set out clearly and attractively. I certainly didn't possess such a talent and hadn't noticed or appreciated the potential of the discovered areas...

"Sasha, even 100,000 won't be enough."

"This is only the starting price. Not many people have gone beyond the foothills of the Dark Frontier, which means our offers are very 'tasty'. The clans will fight over them and drive up the price. Leave it to the pros at the auction. They don't charge their percentage for nothing."

"Got it. I'll post them now. One question, though. I have an open quest related to the Ifrit. I've told you about it."

"Yes, I remember. But where does it say you need to personally destroy the creature? It says, 'find a way to banish the Ifrit'. It doesn't matter who gets rid of it, the quest will still count for you."

I placed the lots, and Sasha and I sat in the tavern for a bit longer since he was in no hurry to leave.

"Why didn't the Mongooses help you and why won't they answer me?"

"They're in crisis right now. The idea of concentrating their forces in the real world turned out to be dumb and dangerous. Can you imagine what's happening in the Clan's other regional centers right now? They're frantically changing locations, and people are dispersing so as not to repeat the tragedy at Mainstream."

"So, they just abandoned you? What does it all mean? Why are virtual wars spilling out into the real world?"

"I can't explain it. I don't know where this sudden outburst of cruelty came from and why the problems are being projected onto the real world."

"Fine. Don't worry about it. We'll figure it out in time. Speaking of the real world. Do you remember Jeber_Arium?"

"Of course."

"I managed to bring the guy back to his senses and he started communicating again. We're in a party now.

We escaped from the Dark Frontier together. There is a problem, however. He remembers almost nothing about his past life and can't even tell me where he lives. His VR capsule is preventing him from logging out for 'medical reasons'."

"We need to get Jeb out." Sasha perked up.

"That's what I'm saying... but how? I can't even call the emergency services since I don't know where he's based. He could be on the other side of the globe."

Lourier pondered the problem, then dug around in his inventory and gave me a tiny pin.

"Pin this to his clothes."

"What for?"

"I'll be able to track his communication channel."

"Back to the VR capsule?"

"If Jeb isn't heavily encrypted, then yes."

"He won't get banned? This must be illegal."

"It's an admin thing. I'll be quick so there'll be no ban. You'll then return the pin to me. I have nothing to do right now anyway, while the regeneration is taking place. I'll try to find out who he is, where he's from and how we can help him."

"Great. Thank you. We really need to rescue the guy."

"If he has the latest VR capsule model, you don't need to worry too much about him. It has a rehabilitation exit system. I'll try to find out everything."

"Right. I will go out into my personal space from

time to time. But you shouldn't risk it."

"You mean, I shouldn't log into the Edge of the Abyss? I'll go mad with boredom."

"Read something. It helps. The world is more than just virtual reality."

"Fine," Sasha sighed. "But don't you disappear, either. Keep me posted on how the lots are going, okay?"

"Agreed."

"And another thing," he hesitated for a moment. "I don't want to return to the Mongooses."

"I understand."

"Will you take me?"

"Into my group? Of course, I'd be happy to."

He cheered up visibly.

We shook hands and a few seconds later, Alexander_Lourier vanished into thin air.

Chapter Sixteen

I RETURNED TO THE tavern close to noon.

Jeb was still sleeping. Poor bastard. I had read on the forums and in guides that sleep was vital for a person fully immersed in virtual reality. Our brain couldn't work twenty-four hours a day, seven days a week, in a state of constant wakefulness. This led to irreversible and harmful consequences.

While he had been surviving in the dungeon, Jeber_Arium could only sleep in snatches, so I decided not to disturb him.

Weasel had found something to occupy him by sitting on the windowsill and watching the passers-by. What a quirky, nimble and quick-witted little animal. A great example of how artificial neural networks, which formed the basis of NPCs in the virtual world, could begin to sporadically develop.

I pinned the tracker to Jeb's clothing and wrote him a note, asking him not to leave the inn before I get back. The coins that we had found below Noogard and in the basement of the Miner's Hut would be enough to live comfortably for several days.

The Secret of Forest Hill kept gnawing at me. I was planning to go there and start digging. I thought I'd be done by evening.

I went down to the main hall, briefly spoke to the innkeeper, paid for another day of accommodation and asked him to feed my companion when he awoke.

Now, into the woods!

I hadn't even realized how intensely I was interested in the first quest that I had received in the Edge of the Abyss.

I passed through the town gates, used the map to find my old route and turned decisively into the forest. I was no longer afraid of meeting an adult bear since we were now on equal levels. I'd seen worse mobs since we had last met.

I was in an excellent mood. Sasha's a champ. That's what it means when a person known the virtual world well. To figure out what to do so quickly!

I didn't end up meeting the bear. Maybe someone had dispatched it?

I cut through the brambles, following an animal track the meandered through the prickly bushes. Low-level mobs were studiously avoiding me. It was all part of the gameplay. While you were weak, even trying to catch a hare was a whole battle. As soon as you leveled up a bit, obtaining a piece of meat and a pelt suitable for clothing wasn't so simple either. You'd have to work up a sweat, chasing the prey. Nothing was easy here.

Ah, I was back in familiar territory. Nothing had changed below the wooded hill. The dead tree immediately caught my eye. I wondered where I had crossed the border of the instance, without even noticing that I was entering a personally generated location.

Roughly hewn stones jutted out from the ground. Yellow bones lay in the grass nearby, covered with scraps of decaying clothing. This was where I had found the Guardian's Amulet and the Soul Crystal.

Had it really only been a week?

I squatted down and examined the remains. A light breeze ruffled my hair. Judging by the shreds of clothing, a mage had died here. I didn't notice any weapons or armor but found a decomposing bag and a fragment of a wooden staff.

All right, let's see... I used my dagger to carefully peel away the scraps of old fabric. The contents of the canvas bag had been heavily damaged by rain, insects and a brown mold. A waterlogged book, a pouch with five silver coins and two vials containing a reddish liquid. Not much, really. I read the description,

Minor regeneration potion. Restores 3 HP/sec, counteracts the negative effects of poisoning and bleeding.

This would come in useful. The vials shifted into my inventory.

Now the book. I gently turned the soaked pages but couldn't make out a word. Most of the text and drawings had blurred and were damaged beyond repair. The ink must have been of poor quality and unable to withstand moisture.

I managed to find a couple of well-preserved pages in the middle of the tome. One page depicted a battle scene, done in the manner of a child's sketch. Many figures armed with something like short rods that emitted multicolored energy sparks. I hadn't come across magic like this before.

There was a clear difference between the warring sides, which even the clumsy artist had managed to emphasize. Some were wearing Guardian Amulets while the others were enveloped in a gray aura.

Perhaps the text on the second page would explain what was going on?

I squinted at the blurred lines. The handwriting was hard to read. The book seemed similar to my field diary.

Gradually, by deciphering the remaining sentences, I discovered that the remains belonged to an NPC, who had survived the invasion of the Abyss.

He had never been the mysterious Guardian. He must have taken the crystal and amulet from a dead body.

There was a curious note. Some of the words could

not be read but I understood the meaning.

'...dying from wounds... gave him tisanes... he awoke... told me about the forest hill... gave me the key and amulet, asked me to go there...

Died...

There must be treasures hidden there... rich and move to town... My abilities should be enough... I will rob the treasury and then throw away the amulet and key...'

The following picture formed in my head: there had been a battle between the Guardians and the equally mysterious (to me, at least) Shadows during the invasion of the Abyss. It appeared that the Guardians had lost. A local resident, probably a novice magician, found one of the wounded Guardians and tried to heal him, but unsuccessfully. The Guardian told him about the treasures hidden in the depths of the forest hill.

So, the Soul Crystal is a key. The entrance must be somewhere nearby. I had no idea what could be hidden inside.

...

The Secret of Forest Hill quest has been updated. You found out who the unknown prospector was.

Find the entrance to the treasury and try to use the Soul Crystal as a key.

...

Fine. I would start with the roughly hewn stones sunk into the ground. They had to be removed. What alarmed me was that the mage, who had gone in search of the treasure, hadn't succeeded with such a simple task.

Who killed him?

It obviously wasn't a person or they would have taken the money, amulet and crystal.

As I stood there thinking, the remains of the unfortunate prospector suddenly grew hazy and disappeared.

There was nobody around, the sun beating down on my head. An unnatural silence hung over the area.

Seeing no obvious signs of danger, I turned back to the stones and began to remove the turf, surprised to find an unusual type of soil underneath. It consisted of black grains with an abundance of solid glass pellets and small metal fragments. A very strange kind of soil for a wooded hill!

The soil was loose and easy to shift. I dug into it with my dagger and moved it out of the way with my hands. There were frequent lumps of rust, among which I suddenly spotted a flash of silver.

...

A tiny and shapeless mithril ingot. It must have been part of a weapon but is now only good for selling due to its value as 'true silver'.

...

It looked like the site of a grand battle and maybe some serious magic had been used?

Considering the softness of the soil, I expected to finish quite quickly. I thought to loosen the stones so that they would roll down the slope on their own, but soon the obsidian-colored sandy loam[7] ended and firmly packed slag lay beneath. My dagger was no match for it, I needed a more serious implement.

After resting a little and having a drink of water, I returned to the dried-up tree, found a suitable bough and broke it off. My high Strength allowed me to do it without using an axe.

I sat down in the shade and used a knife to carve out a rough handle, to which I attached the rusty pickaxe that I had found near the mage.

Why hadn't he used elemental forces rather than digging manually?

After about an hour, I managed to topple and roll away all the stones protruding from the slope. I was left with an elongated, asymmetrical excavation site. I tried to dig deeper but the pickaxe only produced sparks as it bounced off the hard surface.

I sat down on the pile of dug-up soil and wiped the sweat off my brow.

The new obstacle looked like pavement. The closely fitted blocks formed a surface that ran deep into the hill but didn't match the angle of the slope.

---

[7] Sandy loam – loose rock or soil, consisting mainly of sand particles

Perhaps it was time for me to use my head rather than my hands? I could dig and break up the stone for the rest of eternity. What was hidden below? How did this elevation form, anyway?

The quest, which had seemed simple at first glance, was becoming more and more interesting and difficult.

Also, my Life bar had dropped slightly. Just a little, by a couple of percent, but in recent days I had learned to pay attention to such 'small things'.

I expanded my system messages window.

...

You have been working at maximum endurance for a whole hour.

You have dug up two cubic meters of soil.

New skill available: Miner. Effect: +1 to Strength, +5% to Stamina (when using the skill). Level 1 of the skill enables you to identify the most common minerals and ores.

...

You are exhausted. Negative effect: Strength is reduced by 1 point. Regeneration slowed down by 5%. You will lose 1 HP every 10 seconds until you rest and regain your strength.

...

Ain't I delicate...

My fingers were bleeding from the scratches on them and blisters had appeared on my palms. I didn't really have time to sit around since evening was fast approaching. I could remove the debuffs another way.

I drank one of the regeneration potions that I had found and waited for my cuts to heal, then started climbing to the top of the hill.

I wanted to study my surroundings before it got dark. Perhaps the overall picture would help me to understand what was hidden beneath the mysterious mound?

The slope turned out to be treacherous. It was strewn with shallow ravines formed by rainwater. I couldn't hear any beasts or birds, the oppressive silence continuing to hang over the area. I often came across the shoots of young trees that had found shelter in the terraces, of which there were many. I couldn't help but think of an architectural structure, covered in ash and slag, which had turned into a hill...

The sun was beginning to sink towards the horizon when I finally reached the flat top.

Impressively large granite fragments lay scattered around. I examined the mossy surfaces and realized that they were pieces of enormous statues. They had once formed a square but were now broken and meaningless... except one figure.

A strange creature clad in armor stood on a massive pedestal. It reminded me of a lizard, vaguely similar to a Tyrannosaurus Rex, with a huge elongated head, its torso leaning forward, the front limbs short and similar to human arms, while the rear ones looked very powerful. To my surprise, the tail was long but thin and covered in spikes. It looked more like a natural weapon than an extra support point.

The creature held a staff in one hand and a huge sword in the other, which made the human great swords look rather modest in comparison.

The presence of a sword and staff, as far as I understood, was the symbol of a multiclass character.

What a death machine! I wouldn't want to run into such a thing. Not at my current level, at least.

Someone had scratched a crooked inscription on the pedestal,

Watch the sun. Think.

I squinted and looked west. The fiery drop reaching for the horizon looked like a ball of primitive chaos, flooding the surroundings with crimson and making all the objects cast long shadows.

I had no idea what the inscription on the pedestal meant but it confirmed my suspicion that the hill was actually a formidable artificial structure. Too tall and compact for a town, too small for a castle. It was most likely a single building with a terraced architecture forming five tiers. It used to be surrounded by squares, with roads leading to it, but now the base of the hill was densely overgrown with grass and shrubs, as well as the occasional tree.

It was now obvious that I had to direct my work forward rather than down. This way I would move deeper into the hill until I stumbled across a preserved room. It was likely that my coveted goal was close. I could probably dig another couple of meters today.

Glancing askance at the statue of the armored lizard, I shrugged and headed back down the slope.

The sun had not yet set when I lifted my pickaxe again, gently tapping along the wall of pressed slag at the far end of the excavation site.

I started at the left wall. A few loud ringing strikes, followed by a dull one. Fine, what if I shift more to the right? Another dull thud and then a loud one! Higher? The pickaxe struck stone again.

I imagined an arched doorway in front of me, filled with slag and ash. Let's check!

Now that I knew where to strike, I drove the pickaxe hard into the compressed slag and then leaned on the handle, using it as a lever. The layer of soil soon cracked and then collapsed. I could now see the outline of the arch along the edges and at the top. Well, it meant that I'd keep moving in this direction.

Several more blows and my tool struck stone again.

Was it a piece of debris caught in the landslide?

Alas, it soon became clear that the archway was blocked by a monolithic stone slab, with a small recess in the center. I examined the cavity and couldn't help but shiver. It looked like the Soul Crystal would perfectly fit into the space!

It worked! As soon as I placed the crystal into the

recess, there came a dim flash. I was subconsciously waiting for the screech of the slab moving aside and the vibration of the counterweights, but nothing happened.

Why?

The Soul Crystal became completely transparent, so that I could see a flame trembling in its depths. Maybe the ancient mechanisms had jammed?

I had to try again. Take the key out and insert it one more time. Or should I try to turn it?

The hill shuddered suddenly. Cracks appeared in the walls of the excavation site from the powerful jolt and rivulets of black sand poured down from above. The slab didn't move an inch but I sensed a measured, heavy tread in the earth's trembling.

I dropped the pickaxe and grasped my sword before I turned around.

There was nobody behind me but the steps, like the aftershocks of an earthquake, were clearly coming towards me.

I climbed out of my excavation site and saw the colossal figure of the armor-clad lizard warrior in the light of the setting sun.

The creature was heading right at me!

...

Havl. Shadow Warrior. A creature from the Abyss. Cursed guard. Level ???

...

His roar made the leaves tremble. His heavy, confident footfall shook the earth. He noticed me and stopped, slightly tilting his head and examining me as if I was a bug.

There was nowhere to retreat to, so I rushed at him, but only managed to take a couple of steps.

There came an eerie guttural growl. Darkness descended rapidly.

I couldn't move! The system messages window flashed with scrolling lines of text:

You have been affected by the Aura of Petrifaction. Effect: immobilization for 30 seconds.

You have been affected by the Aura of Fear. Effect: you cannot attack creatures whose level exceeds yours for 30 seconds.

You have been affected by the Aura of the Abyss. Effect: random damage to all living things.

You have been affected by Crushing Roar. Effect: all types of armor is reduced by 50 hit points.

...

The earth stirred. Shaking off the black sand, the remains of long-dead beings began to arise around me.

The eyes of the lizard glowed with an otherworldly flame.

"The Guardians have been destroyed!" it growled. "So it is and so it shall be!"

In the next moment, the giant sword swung through the air and one-shotted me.

A second of unbearable pain and my mind went dark.

...

YOU HAVE DIED.
Lost: 2,753 Exp.
Items lost:
Rusty pickaxe.
Torn leather jacket.
Outfit hit points: 0.

I regained my senses, crouching in the respawn circle.

For the past fifteen minutes, my mind had been in a terrifying emptiness, lacking thoughts, emotions or a will.

A painful wheeze came out of my mouth with the first exhale.

The town guard standing nearby glanced in my direction but didn't say anything. Perhaps they were used to players appearing in such a state?

I still hurt. My thoughts were jumbled. My body continued to convulse but the warm light of the respawn circle gradually stripped away the remaining debuffs.

I stood up, swaying and leaning on my sword, took a few unsteady steps and slumped against the battlement merlon.

I couldn't stop shivering.

The first thing I did was open my inventory. The Soul Crystal and Guardian's Amulet were still there. They were the type of items that couldn't be lost.

...

You have one new event.

...

I opened the tab.

...

Your information lot 'Farming creatures from the Abyss' has sold for 37,000 gold coins.

...

Not bad! Almost twice the starting price. I was glad, of course, but the emotions were dim, the thoughts tumbling around in my head like boulders. I had to get back to the tavern...

I didn't go out into the real world that evening. I lay in our room, rambled about what had happened to the concerned Jeb, ate and fell asleep.

We held a council of war the next day.

"That wasn't supposed to happen!" Jeb insisted. "If the system gave you a task, it must be doable!"

"Did you see the video?"

"Yes."

"What are my chances? The lizard didn't even need

to lift its sword. Did you see how much damage was inflicted by the Aura of the Abyss?"

"You clearly missed something important!" Jeb replied stubbornly.

"Jeb, I did everything right! Everything was fine until I tried to open the 'door' with the crystal. Could it be a glitch of some kind? Or is the quest intended for high-level players?"

"Then you wouldn't have been let into the instance. You wouldn't have noticed it or you would have received a warning that the location is designed for players with Level 100+, for example."

"Fine. I'll go there again and take a closer look. Maybe I need to destroy the statue so that the lizard can't come alive?"

"It's an option." Jeb nodded. "Oh, it's such a pity that I can't go there with you!" he looked upset. "I'm tired of sitting indoors."

"Well then, take a walk around the town, check out outfits and skill books, if you can find them."

He cheered up visibly. "What about you, Dan?"

"Business first, then I'll go and buy some kind of sledgehammer and head over to the hill to try to smash up that statue."

"All right. Then I'll go to the library. There must be suitable spells that destroy stone. Perhaps you could buy a scroll and use that?"

"Sure, have a look."

"Dan, aren't you going to change your gear?"

"Not yet. What's the point of spending money on it? If the lizard attacks me again, it'll wipe out my armor with its growl. I'll just walk around in what I have for now."

"You should still visit a craftsman, let them restore ten percent of the durability at least," Jeb advised. "You never know whom you'll meet in the forest. Dark players, for example."

"Yes, I think I'll do that."

Jeb and I went down to the common room, had breakfast, and went about our business.

It was a five-minute stroll from the tavern to the Main Square, where the local branch of the World Bank (they didn't even change the name) was located. There were a lot of people on the street but nobody paid me any attention, not players nor NPCs. I didn't stand out from the crowd, except perhaps for my tattered clothes.

I did look quite unpresentable and might not have been allowed into the bank. I thus heeded Jeb's advice and went into a workshop where I was, frankly, dumbfounded by the variety of goods for sale.

Wooden mannequins were dressed in sets of armor made completely from leather. Nobody came out to greet me but I could see the workshop yard through the open door, the craftspeople busy at work beneath the awning.

I looked around and studied the details in surprise. The design of the leather creations seemed limited only by the master's imagination. I had expected to find simple, cookie-cutter products but instead saw works of art.

They must cost a lot and offer poor protection.

I was drawn to one particular set and wanted to touch it, but my hand encountered a viscous resistance.

"Good day. I will remove the security in a moment," said a voice behind me. "We have to set it to discourage thieves."

I turned around.

"André, at your service," a lean old craftsman shook my hand. His frame immediately appeared.

André_Ilgard, famous master leatherworker. Level 135. Profession Level 30.

"A good choice, Dan. Leather armor is light, comfortable, does not restrict movement and at the same time protects from arrows, chopping and stabbing blows, although it fails against crushing damage, but this can be corrected."

"Leather against a sword?" I gestured to my pitiful and tattered outfit.

"Peasant copies and real armor are completely different things. I use several layers of leather crafted from the skins of rare creatures. Believe me, leather is my passion. I know all about it. Arrows get stuck in my armor. Sword strikes ruin its appearance but this is easily fixable with a special enchanted repair kit. Until you reach Level 100 and obtain sufficiently high Strength, my armor is the best choice. I could talk about its advantages for hours but I won't. Realism is everything. Many people think that metal will make them invincible. But it looks like you have already been in some skirmishes and know how important mobility is?"

I nodded in agreement.

"Several layers of carefully selected leather, taken from different creatures, will provide protection to equal steel."

"How expensive is this set?" I indicated the armor that I had been considering.

"A hundred gold. But it won't wear out. I will give you the repair kit for ten gold. It is a powder based on magical techniques, a pinch of which completely restores the appearance and strength of the armor."

I thought hard.

The price was steep. Yesterday I would have just sighed and walked away, hoping to someday farm enough for such a purchase, but now, thanks to the information sold at auction, I had money. I wasn't planning to splash it around but the master's words inspired trust. He wouldn't have reached such a level in the profession without his products having the proper quality.

"What about protection against magic, poisons, acids and toxins?" I asked.

"Plus twenty to your resistance," André responded proudly. "The armor can also be further enchanted. If you buy it, I will give you recommendations for whom to contact."

"Can my armor be repaired?"

Surprisingly, he reacted normally. He didn't grimace disdainfully but smiled slyly instead, "A second set?"

I nodded.

"I can give you light and unassuming armor made by my apprentices for 15 gold. It doesn't have the same level of protection but it will serve as a replacement."

"Can I try it on?" I turned back to the armor set that I liked best.

"There's no point. These are display samples. Your armor will be made to order according to your measurements. Any requests for the finish?"

"I'm happy with this model."

"Excellent. That'll be one hundred and ten gold. You can pick up the completed set and repair kit tomorrow. A day's wait is worth the comfort that an individually tailored suit of armor provides. I have already taken your measurements."

I counted out the required amount and gave the master a heavy pouch. Incredibly, the gold weighed nothing in the inventory but instantly acquired all its physical properties in my hand.

"Do you have anything suitable for a mage?"

"Certainly. Bring your friend and we'll talk. And now, a small bonus from me," he took a small box out of his pocket and threw a pinch of sparkling powder over me.

Master André_Ilgard has restored the durability of your leather armor.

...

"Thank you, master," I thanked him sincerely, appreciating the quality and convenience of the enchanted powder. I should keep several such repair kits on me.

"The enchanted powder cannot restore armor that wasn't made by me," André said as if he had read my mind.

"But you just..."

"I can. Someone else can't. The repair kit works only on my own creations."

I see. It was just business.

"Until tomorrow. I'll come with a friend."

"Always happy to meet new clients," the craftsman smiled warmly.

The Main Square was bustling with people. There were tents, stalls and counters everywhere I looked. Only the center of the square, with a fountain and a huge sundial, had space for a guard patrol and players resting on the benches when they got tired of shopping.

I looked at the time. It was almost noon. The

gnomon's[8] short shadow lay between the markings for 11 and 12.

I didn't stop and continued toward the bank. I still had to reach the forest hill.

I told the clerk in the lobby the nickname of the employee I needed, and I was immediately taken to a separate room, where I was soon joined by a dwarf.

Frugal_Tibul, Merchant, Level 73.

It was the first time that I saw a player who had picked a race other than human or elf.

He got straight to the point, "Donation or withdrawal?"

"I need to withdraw 30,000 gold to the real world," I replied.

"No problem. Tell me your statcard number and get 3,000 gold ready. I charge 10% for withdrawal."

Well, that was something! But I had no choice. I suspected that the other 'bankers' charged even more, otherwise Sasha wouldn't have recommended Frugal_Tibul.

The transaction was complete in a matter of minutes. My balance increased by 3,000 credits (with a conversion rate of 10:1 for in-game gold).

"Thank you," I said and gave the dwarf his interest.

---

[8] Gnomon – an ancient astronomical instrument, a vertical object (obelisk, column, pole) that allows the angular height of the Sun to be determined using its shortest shadow (at noon). The shortest shadow also indicates the direction of the true meridian. The gnomon is also the part of a sundial, whose shadow indicates the time.

I had a little less than 4,000 gold left. I hadn't received any new messages from the auction but I was hoping that the 'Hunt for the Ifrit' and 'First Passage' of the treasure-filled dungeon would interest someone.

Right, now I had to buy a sledgehammer, pop into the tavern, grab something to eat and head over to the forest hill! I had to deal with this statue somehow, otherwise, I would never get inside the mysterious structure.

With everything that had happened, I didn't even remember that I had spent more than two days in the VR capsule. This must be how reality was replaced?

I'd have to log out, eat some real food and sleep, otherwise, I'd turn into Jeb...

Passing by a pile of weapons, I noticed a sledgehammer of impressive size. The description read:

Warhammer. A crushing weapon. 15-20 damage with scaling according to Strength.

When placed in an equipment slot, gives the owner the skill 'Shield Crusher'.

Minimum requirements: Strength 15, Stamina 15.

...

I currently had Strength 13, Stamina 12.

Fine. I'd have to take a look at the jewelry. In any case, I was going to buy rings with stats for the main characteristics, to switch them around as required.

It might have looked like I had made some easy money, thanks to Sasha's help and some lucky coincidences, which I was now in a hurry to spend.

Not so. I had become very angry at my nephew's words but he was ultimately right. I had nowhere to go in the real world. Either I learned how to survive in the Edge of the Abyss or my interest and abilities would soon run out, and then I would truly be left with nothing.

These expensive purchases that I could currently afford were an investment in my future. André was right. A reliable outfit, weapons, additional bonuses from rings — they all counted for the sensory realism.

Chapter Seventeen

I DIDN'T REACH the forest hill until five o'clock in the evening. It tended to get dark at nine o'clock so I would have enough time to climb to the top and test the lizard statue for durability.

My arsenal now boasted a war hammer, a long sword enchanted for Chaotic damage and two identical sets of rings providing +3 to the main characteristics. I had paid a tidy sum for them but felt no regrets. If Jeb and I had possessed such rings, surviving in the dungeon of Noogard would have been a lot easier. In addition, I had bought a wide, comfortable belt with pockets for three vials of healing potion.

I approached the excavation site cautiously, observed it for a while from afar, but there was nobody around. The undead raised by the Aura of the Abyss had long disappeared since these creatures couldn't stand the light of the midday sun.

The archway was closed. The tunnel leading into the bowels of the hill was still inaccessible to me, since the lizard would appear as soon I placed the crystal into its intended recess.

'What if I can sneak inside in time?' came the stray thought. 'The beast has to descend from the top of the hill and that takes several minutes!'

No, I wasn't going to risk it just yet. I would try and smash the statue into pieces first.

Armed with the war hammer and wearing the Stamina, Strength and Accelerated Regeneration rings, I began to climb the slope. Unfortunately, I could only use three rings at one time, according to the number of slots in the character's outfit tab.

I reached the statue in about twenty minutes, having carefully examined several ravines along the way, carved out by the flowing rainwater. I was hoping to find an access hole of some kind, but to no avail.

Fine. I'd stick to the original plan.

I circled the enormous sculpture. The sign on the pedestal drew my attention again.

Watch the sun. Think.

I looked to the west. The sun had not yet touched the tops of the trees. I understood that the inscription was there for a reason but what could it mean? Yes, sunlight inflicted damage to the undead, burning through the Aura of the Abyss. I knew that already.

Perhaps Jeb wound find something in the library?

After all, he had spent the whole day among the ancient manuscripts. It was a pity that the invisible border of the instance blocked all types of communication, leaving me alone with the Secret of Forest Hill.

'Well then, creature,' I approached its head, took aim and slammed my hammer as hard as I could between its eyes.

The metal bounced off the granite with a sharp clang. Well, nobody said it would be easy. Drenched in sweat, I landed blow after blow, aiming for the same spot, until the first crack appeared in the stone surface.

Yes! I could do this, even if I had to return here day after day, chipping pieces off the statue!

I was on the right track to solving this puzzle.

Another blow! And again!

The surface of the huge statue suddenly rippled with distortions.

There came the sound of rumbling and a crash. A cloud of dust shot up into the air as if the giant had come to life, shaking off pieces of its stone shell.

It had!

I retreated and switched weapons. My hammer went back into the inventory and now I held the shield and the enchanted Chaotic sword.

The dust slowly settled. The lizard shook its head. A bleeding indentation could be seen in the place where I had struck it repeatedly with the hammer and the creature appeared to be stunned.

Its frame popped up:

...

Havl. Shadow Warrior. A creature from the Abyss. Cursed guard. Level 62.

...

To say that I was surprised was an understatement. Yesterday, I could only see question marks in place of his level. Did that mean that he used to be 3-4 times stronger than me but today was only twice as strong? Had I leveled up somehow?

The lizard rushed at me with a roar, not bothering to use auras or magic. He was enraged but his movements remained hesitant, as if a debuff was affecting him. The blood continued to ooze from his split forehead, obscuring his vision.

I managed to roll out of the way and deliver several strikes to his legs. I had read in the guides that this was a proven technique against large monsters. I had to stay out of the way of his weapon, roll between his legs and inflict damage from the side and back.

Havl howled in pain. Fury swamped his mind and his movements grew more abrupt. Never mind. I was doing quite well. The huge blade whistled through the air over my head and I blocked his staff with my shield, losing almost all my Stamina in the process. However, the Accelerated Regeneration ring quickly restored my Stamina so I had time to circle behind the creature, accumulate a little Strength and use the Rage ability, which gave me +5% to absorbing damage and the same to my attack. Now, if only I could find the armored giant's Achilles heel, I would stand a chance!

The lizard growled and spun around. I didn't expect such deft and rapid movements from its hulking body and almost went into respawn. At the last possible moment, I managed to use my shield to block the blow from its massive sword.

My Stamina dropped to zero. I was knocked down and thrown several meters. My Life bar halved. I got back up and threw myself under the lizard's feet, using up the pitiful crumbs of my slowly regenerating Stamina.

My sword dealt not only physical but also random elemental damage, flaring up with fire or icing over, then stinging with lightning. But Havl's armor and skin were thick and his resistance to damage was high, so the attacks only served to aggravate him.

During another risky roll, I noticed loose folds of skin on the lizard's neck. It was a vulnerable spot! One of the armor joints was poorly fitted.

I increased the distance between us, drank one of the healing potions, pretended to lunge to the left and then rapidly rolled closer to the lizard and drove my sword into the narrow gap.

...

You have been hit by Crushing Roar. Effect: all types of armor is reduced by 50 hit points.

...

I was thrown back again. The attack failed. The

beast had finally regained his senses and was using his abilities again.

I mustn't miss these attacks! I drank another healing potion and approached from the side, hiding behind my shield. I had only wiped out half his Life points. My Stamina had recovered sufficiently for a roll and a sharp thrust.

I was going to get that brute!

I almost couldn't feel the pain in the heat of the battle. I was dragging my foot for some reason and something hot and sticky flowed down my thigh.

The lizard raised his staff, intending to stun me with a murderous aura. It was the perfect moment. The lizard was built in such a way that his massive, elongated head was always held parallel to the ground. Now, to roll closer and crit it! It wouldn't kill him, of course, but it would interrupt the casting and inflict significant pain...

The creature laughed wildly.

The staff never lit up with an aura, instead, he unexpectedly struck with his whip-like, spiked tail.

Reality spun before my eyes, losing its clarity.

"The Guardians have been destroyed! So it is and so it shall be!"

...

You have died.
You have lost one level.
Item lost: war hammer.
Item lost: torn leather breastplate.

Access to virtual reality is temporarily blocked. Emergency exit initialized for medical reasons.

...

I spent the rest of the evening and the following night in the real world. I had a normal meal, sent Jeb a message so he wouldn't worry and went to bed.

I had nightmares. The enormous lizard was constantly on my heels, sending me into respawn again and again. I would wake up in a cold sweat, think, 'It's only a dream' and gratefully sink back into sleep.

The real world

Early morning.

I wasn't asleep any longer. I simply lay in bed and listened to my body. I didn't feel exhausted and depressed after all those nightmares, which was surprising.

Oh, so there was the answer. As I had previously mentioned, the neural interface was now always with me, only the active icons changing depending on where I was.

...

The third metabolic correction has been successfully completed. You can now remain in the VR capsule for up to seven days with no risk to your health.

Such ominous but compelling technology.

My muscles ached. True, I had traveled a lot in recent days, performed heavy physical labor such as digging and shifting boulders, fought with a lizard, and all the while, the 'smart' sensory gel changed its density, sending microcurrents to my muscles and making them contract. This was called electrical myostimulation. Basically, the VR capsule was not only a transmitter of realistic sensations but a complex medical device that maintained the body in good shape.

To date, the record for continuous immersion in virtual reality was one hundred and fifty-seven days. Wow. We used to talk about how long a human could stay in space, and now we were conquering the depths of fictional cyberspace...

I kept thinking about the lizard. Why did his level decrease? What was the reason?

Watch the sun. Think.

The sentence scrawled on the pedestal kept running through my head. I was sure that it held the answer to the Secret of Forest Hill.

It was clear that pummeling the statue with a sledgehammer was not an option.

The bed was crumpled. I threw the sheets into the laundry chute, ordered breakfast and went into the shower. I stood under the hot jets of water for a long time, until I heard the beeping of the delivery service.

The VR capsule had unblocked itself by this point. I didn't feel overly hungry. I picked up a juice, mentally activated the huge wall screen and it immediately lit up, showing me a view of the metropolis.

The city was drowning in a haze of fumes. The clouds floated by at different heights. The sun's morning rays could hardly break through the stone jungle.

What would our future look like? A couple more metabolic corrections and I'd be able to fully entrust my mortal body to the life support system and plunge into the digital world forever.

Only recently, such a possibility would have repulsed me but now, staring over the metropolis, I asked myself, 'Where would you go now and what would you do?'

What had happened to me? It was like my life had been crumpled up and replaced with a different reality. Which world did I belong to now?

'There are no more open spaces here. No new emotions. No wildlife...' whispered my imagination.

'But nothing is real there, in the dream world!' my common sense protested.

The sun rose majestically over the city, carving long shadows from the buildings.

The shadows!

I felt like I'd been electrocuted.

The lizard was a Shadow Warrior! But how can there be shadow without light?

Watch the sun. Think.

I immediately remembered the town square of

Anchor and the sundial at noon.

This was the solution! I didn't know what happened at dusk or at night, but in clear weather, shadows were longest in the morning and evening but shortest around noon, when the sun passed through the zenith.

My thoughts raced ahead.

I had first met the lizard at around nine o'clock in the evening, when the shadows were long and deep. Yesterday, I clashed with him at about six pm, when the sun was higher and the shadows shorter. My adversary's power, expressed in levels, had been significantly lower.

So, the higher the sun and the shorter the shadow, the weaker the lizard?

Could it really be so simple? I had to use the Soul Crystal closer to noon. Who would come to me then? A small lizard?

I didn't think so. The Secret of Forest Hill was not an easy quest. I would bet that even at noon, the lizard would be a worthy opponent, probably equal to me in levels.

I had to thoroughly prepare and kill him. I already knew my enemy's approximate range of magical and physical attacks, and this would give me a significant advantage. Although I still had to test my hypothesis about the relationship between the position of the sun, the length of the shadows and the lizard's current level. I could be mistaken, just like when I thought that I could smash the statue into pieces.

It was decided. There was no time to waste! I had to rejoin the Edge of the Abyss.

I hastily ate my breakfast, transferred 3,000 credits to Sasha's treatment account, received a confirmation of payment and climbed into the VR capsule with a clear conscience.

Because of my character's death, I appeared in one of the respawn circles on the town wall.

"Jeb, where are you right now?"

"I'm having breakfast at the tavern," my companion responded at once through the group voice chat.

"I'll be there soon. Did you find anything useful in the library?"

"Yes, there are a couple of elemental damage spells that can be scribed on a scroll. They'll definitely break granite!"

"Forget about them. I longer need them. Can you look for any information about an ability called the Crushing Roar?"

"Sure."

After speaking to Jeb, I opened the auction tab. The lots hadn't yet been sold. Nobody was interested in the 'Hunt for the Ifrit' while 'First Pass' had increased slightly in price. It meant that people were beginning to fight over the information about the dungeon but not very eagerly.

Fine. I still had time.

I had to visit Master André so I descended the stairs and turned into a side street.

A sign caught my eye at the entrance to a vast estate surrounded by a towering wall.

...

The Arena of Long-armed_Kyle.
We prepare fighters. Expensive.
First consultation is free. Find out what you're capable of, right now.

...

I couldn't resist and knocked on the gate.

A player opened the door.

...

Goodnatured_Bolg. Warrior. Level 35.

...

"Here for training or a consultation?"

"Consultation."

He looked me up and down, led me inside and pointed to the grounds surrounding a modest house, "Coach is over there."

I decided not to pester him with questions and proceeded down the stone path. A familiar picture. The house had suffered significant damage and had only recently been restored. The cobblestones also showed evidence of repair, and the round sandy training areas had been created on top of ruins. I could see the remains of foundations overgrown with grass in some places. This was clearly one of the sites where the Abyss had invaded. The manor house had been destroyed, the place was considered unlucky, and the current owner had probably bought the ruins at a bargain price, as soon as the town mages had succeeded in destroying the portals.

There was Long-armed_Kyle, a tall, muscular Level 75 Warrior.

Seeing me, he beckoned invitingly. "Here for a consultation?"

"Yes."

"Excellent. Straight from respawn?" Kyle asked, noticing the deplorable state of my incomplete set of leather armor.

"Yes."

"The shield's a good one," surprise flashed in his shrewd gaze. "I would say the affix is unique. Have you been to the Dark Frontier?"

"Unfortunately."

"Did you get out on your own?"

"Together with a friend."

"Respect. Show me your weapon."

I pulled out my sword.

"Nice toy," the coach chuckled, glancing at my Chaotic blade.

"What do you mean by 'toy'?" I was taken aback.

"You'll see. Ivan, come here!"

A player ran up to us. He wasn't wearing any armor, just a loincloth. He held a wooden shield and sword in his hands, similar in length and quality to mine.

"Enter the circle. I'm setting 10% of realism."

"Hey, I'm not going to reload!"

"You don't have to," the coach replied. "The arena options allow you to change the level of realism without reloading. GO!"

My opponent attacked at once. I dodged and reached him with a retaliatory lunge but with minimal result. The damage was very small. Ivan suddenly slung his shield across his back, grabbed the sword with both hands and performed a combo, first wiping out my Stamina and then halving my Life bar with the final blow.

"Break up! Thanks, Ivan, you can return to training," Kyle turned to me and gestured to the magic eye displaying the combat logs.

"Study the numbers and remember them well. The first lesson is free. These are the basics. Any character, be it a player or an NPC, has several types of defense. First, against physical damage, and second, against magical attacks, and, of course, resistance to all kinds of effects, such as poisoning."

"Yeah, I know."

"Now look. When your sword was enchanted, 70 points of Chaotic damage were added. Acting according to the formulas, the system compensated for the addition, reducing your weapon's physical damage by 35 points to avoid the appearance of an imbalanced sword. The result? The total damage increased. Now, this is important: Ivan's defense against magic is 50. His physical defense, due to the high level of Strength, is 65. This means that he received 40 points of physical damage and 20 points of magical damage from your attack. A total of 60 damage instead of the 175 that your sword supposedly delivers! By dividing the damage into physical and chaotic, you've allowed your opponent to use two defenses at the same time. Mind you, Ivan wasn't even wearing any armor!"

"Yes, I see now," I said dejectedly, remembering my battle with the lizard.

"Don't feel bad," the coach encouraged me. "Just keep in mind for next time that if the weapon doesn't have high scaling for Intellect, or if you haven't leveled up your Intellect, then enchanting a sword with different types of magic makes no sense. It might look pretty but it's just hot air. Don't listen to the merchants. You have honest steel in your hands. Squeeze the maximum physical damage out of the sword since you are a Warrior."

"What do I do with creatures that are vulnerable to fire, for example?" I asked.

"There are oils and resins for that. You can always use them to buff the sword at the right moment, depending on the situation. Such a buff doesn't last long but it doesn't reduce the main physical damage, adding to it instead. Got it?"

I nodded.

The coach handed me a training sword. "Get into the circle. I'm attacking. Let's see how you move. Ready?"

"Yes!" I replied, watching Kyle carefully. He grinned, obviously planning to carry out a crushing combination of blows. It was clear from his stance. He held the sword in both hands at approximately shoulder height and with the sword tip pointing at me...

I didn't hesitate and rolled to avoid the anticipated the combo.

The coach easily shifted his weapon into one hand and struck me twice on the back with the flat of his sword, as if with a stick. "You're in too much of a hurry! You need to roll beneath a strike and not its imitation. My stance doesn't mean anything! Got it?"

"Yes."

"Ready to train?"

I mentally assessed the events of the last few minutes and nodded grimly.

"Good. I'll make a strong swordsman out of you but I'll charge a lot in gold and blood. Training is six hours per day. The course runs for two weeks. Do you agree?"

I nodded again. In only a few minutes, Long-armed_Kyle had demonstrated my, to put it mildly, mediocrity.

"Then let's not waste any time," he got straight to the point. "Today, we'll study the basics. Remember that levels and abilities are good, but the real combat experience that you obtain here is unique. It will stay with you forever. You cannot develop it by farming mobs. Only fights with other players will show you what you are truly worth. I'll work with you myself. You might want to warn your friends that you'll return in the evening angry, battered and starving," he chuckled.

I sent a message to Jeb and entered the circle.

The Secret of Forest Hill could wait. I had no intention of letting the lizard send me into respawn for the third time.

Over the next two weeks, I lived by the rules of the arena, setting aside all my current affairs.

The harsh training didn't give me a single new level. Even adaptive leveling up didn't work there, but every day, I discovered something new, learned to endure pain and fought until I was exhausted. I went to sleep in the real world at the insistence of the coach.

Jeb settled down in the library. I had paid for a room at the inn for the entire training period and so wasn't worried about him.

The 'Flooded Dungeon' lot sold for 110,000 gold. The 'Hunt for the Ifrit' remained in limbo. I asked the coach for some time off, went to the bank and transferred 10,000 credits to the real world, using them to pay for the remainder of Sasha's regeneration treatment.

Max still hadn't shown up. My hope that he had survived was fading.

Having taken care of urgent business, I returned to the arena of Long-armed_Kyle.

I could barely keep up with the pace of the training. I lost most fights. In the evenings, after clambering out of the VR capsule, I had trouble getting to sleep as my whole body ached.

On the fifth or sixth day of exhausting bouts, I suddenly felt young again, as if I'd gotten a second wind.

Kyle had been observing me closely, often shaking his head and pointing out my mistakes, but now he only nodded in approval as he watched the sparring. My combat acrobatics quickly became automatic. I listened attentively to advice and instructions, and learned to predict enemy attacks by the type of weapon, direction of gaze, movements and tensing of muscles.

I felt the difference that the coach had mentioned straight away. NPCs were very predictable. Their attacks could be studied. Players were another matter entirely.

So many little things that I had previously ignored now allowed me to survive in intense fights.

The training was incredibly tough. Kyle forbid us from using regular healing potions, giving us minor ones instead, which removed debuffs caused by wounds and slightly increased our health points. This motivated us to be attentive and not miss any hits. If we did receive damage, we had to rapidly put some distance between us and our opponent and heal ourselves so that the pain didn't impair our Stamina and reaction speed.

I learned how to ration my energy and use it efficiently. My Stamina no longer plunged to zero in frenetic but ineffective attacks. I constantly monitored my characteristic bars, not letting them drop to critical levels.

I appreciated the affix of the shield found on the

Deadly Crag. The reduced consumption of Stamina allowed me to block several blows while preserving the energy for a sudden counterattack.

By the end of the training course, I was winning five bouts out of ten.

"That's all," Kyle looked pleased. "You have learned the basics, and the individual art of combat will come only with long practice."

"Thank you," I shook his hand firmly.

"You will always be welcome here. If you need work, come and see us. We often get contracts."

"I'll keep that in mind, although I don't want to become a mercenary just yet."

"Will you go solo?'

"I have a companion, a mage. We're going to travel."

"A good activity. And profitable. Geographical discoveries are in demand right now. I have added you as a friend. If you suddenly find yourself in need of help, send me a message with the coordinates. I always have teleportation scrolls at hand and can send over a few fighters in a matter of minutes. You know the rates."

"Agreed. Is there a next level of education?"

"Only from Level 100, once you have filled in all the ability and skill slots. It is very individualized, depending on how the character has been leveled up."

After leaving the arena of Long-armed_Kyle, I went to the tavern. Jeb and I had seen each other only briefly over the last few days. I needed to take him to Master André and order an outfit suitable for a mage, and collect my order at the same time.

To my surprise, the rented room was empty. It was almost evening but Jeb still hadn't returned.

Looking at the map, I immediately saw his green marker. What was he doing outside the town, alone in the Peaceful Woods and, moreover, close to the blackberry bushes where the adult brown bear had made its den?

I became worried.

I tried to call him via voice chat but there was no response. 'Maybe it's the Dark players?' came the uneasy thought. They were always sneaking about nearby!

"Jeb?"

He didn't answer again, and my anxiety grew.

There were no teleports in the Peaceful Woods. Not even in the surrounding villages, since they had yet to be rebuilt after the invasion of the Abyss.

'Why would that be... Of course! Teleportation would interfere with robbery. There must be corrupt NPCs in the courts and in the Mage Guild, in the service of the Dark ones,' spurred on by such thoughts,

I ran out of the tavern and sprinted to the nearest gate, alarming the respectable citizens of Anchor and arousing the interest of other players.

I briefly switched to walking once I was outside the town walls, to regenerate my flagging Stamina. The star metal shield (Kyle had identified it for me) worked not only when blocking blows, as it turned out. The Tireless affix was activated by any prolonged effort. I had slung the shield over my back so that it wouldn't get in the way, but it still reduced my consumption of Stamina by 10%.

I started running again. Jeb's marker was close and hardly moving. Naturally, this didn't put me in mind of anything good. A small clearing was the typical place for a robbers' camp. How many of them were there? If two or three, I could handle them.

The forest rustled quietly. I couldn't hear any voices but the smell of smoke from a fire drifted between the trees.

There were no crimson markers. Had they spotted me and gone into stealth mode?

I held the sword in a two-handed grip and activated Rage. Not all Dark players leveled up Stealth, so I was going to send into respawn the first one I spotted, and then act according to the situation.

The element of surprise was a bonus in any fight, hence I didn't hesitate and rushed into the clearing.

The turf in the middle had been removed. A small fire crackled in the circle of loosened earth. Beside it stood a lopsided hut and an equally unassuming lean-to, with walls made of poles and a roof covered with fir branches. Jeb sat on a tree stump in front of the fire. A rag was spread out on the ground before him, various jars were scattered around and a pot hung over the flames, hissing and giving out the scent of herbs.

A reddish shape flashed through the branches of the nearest tree and my interface displayed detailed information about the friendly creature.

Weasel, Level 10.

Active ability to See What is Hidden, Level 3.

Current quest: search.

...

I lowered my sword and breathed a sigh of relief.

Jeb hadn't even noticed me, absorbed in leafing through the pages of an old book and occasionally stirring the herby brew.

I stepped closer to the fire and asked sternly, "Why aren't you answering my calls?"

He didn't even startle, only turned around, "Oh, hey there, Dan! Sorry, I turned off the sound and minimized the messaging window so it wouldn't distract me."

"Is that your work?" I indicated the hut and lean-to.

"Yep," he admitted proudly. "I spent all day making them. I discovered the skills Naturalist and Natural Philosopher and now I'm leveling them up, together with Herbalism and Alchemy."

"You're making potions then?"

"I'm collecting plants, brewing potions, and developing Weasel's ability to See What is Hidden at the same time."

"How are you doing that, if it's not a secret?" I sat down by the fire.

"He climbs up a tree and looks for the ingredients that I need. They're mostly hidden, either in the thick grass or underground, if they're roots."

"What about robbers?"

Jeb arched an eyebrow. "What are they going to do to me? Yeah, two tried to sneak up on me yesterday. Weasel spotted them a mile away. I've fully restored my Intellect after my trips to the library, to the detriment of other characteristics, of course, but I'm a Mage, not a warrior of necessity, like before," he grinned.

"So, what happened to the Dark ones?"

"I entangled them in poisonous vines."

"You sent them into respawn?"

"Yep. They didn't even know who offed them. They blamed the blackberries, I heard one screaming to the other, 'It's mutated!'"

Only now did I look at my friend's frame in surprise. *Jeber_Arium. Battlemage. Level 40.*

...

"There's also a bear that keeps hanging around here," he continued, as if nothing had happened. "The woods are cool. I can breathe more easily and I'm sleeping better."

"The bear," I reminded him.

"It's a bit dumb," Jeb shrugged. "It can't seem to understand that it can't win against me. I found several powerful spells at the library. Look at this," he put the book down, stood up and rapidly cast a spell. A flaming sphere appeared high over the clearing. It hung immobile, crackling and shimmering in shades of red.

The grass stirred at the edge of the meadow. Five or six small clumps of flame immediately split off from the fireball and each one struck a target.

"Perfect, that will be dinner," Jeb laughed and went to one of the scorched spots. He returned with a rabbit.

Well, Jeb certainly hadn't wasted any time after the morbid dungeons of the Dark Frontier. He had restored his Intellect, went up ten levels, discovered new skills and was training Weasel. And here I was, still trying to protect him out of habit...

"How is it at night?"

"It's quiet. Just the forest rustling and the stars in the sky." he replied dreamily. "I built the hut to have a safe place to rest. Sometimes a werewolf howls nearby but it doesn't bother me."

"You're not sleeping in the tavern, then?"

"No, it's too noisy there. I much prefer it here."

I didn't have the heart to reprimand him for his carelessness. Thirty-five points of Intellect, powerful spells, plus Weasel as an early warning system were very impressive for the Peaceful Woods, but if a gang of, say, ten Dark players had appeared, Jeb would already be chained up in the dungeons of the Dark Frontier.

No, I didn't scold him. The guy had only recently found himself again and began to believe in his own abilities.

"Let's make a deal that we sleep in town, okay? If we leave the protection of the town walls, we do it together."

"Okay. But can we stay here tonight?" he nodded in the direction of the makeshift building, already surrounded by an Aura of Immunity.

We ate dinner and sat by the fire. Jeb poured the finished elixir into vials and fell asleep on a pile of hay in the lean-to, blaming fatigue.

I sat looking at the stars for a long time.

Two very important events were going to happen tomorrow. First, Sasha's active regeneration would be complete. Second, I was going to go to the wooded hill at noon and test my theory about the position of the sun and the Shadow Warrior's level.

But what would happen next?

Max had disappeared. I didn't want to believe that he was dead.

The moon was peeking through the trees, its cold light flooding the clearing. Jeb was snoring softly. Weasel was curled up in a ball beside him, also asleep.

The air was clear and heavy with the smell of herbs.

Which world did I belong to now?

Maybe I should stop, find out where Jeb's VR

capsule was located and emerge from the world of digital dreams?

Yeah, right. If the 'Hunt for the Ifrit' information lot sold, I'd be able to buy or rent a modest apartment and then what?

I never found a definite answer that night.

In the morning, Jeb and I returned to town. The clearing would now be our temporary camp. This was convenient since it was not far from Forest Hill.

We went to see André first. I apologized to the master for the delay, collected my order and left Jeb to choose his outfit while I exited the game and went into my personal space.

Sasha hadn't yet left the regeneration chamber, but he was completely healthy. He still had a few days of rehabilitation left so we spoke online.

"Andrey Dmitrievich, I can barely recognize you!" Lourier appreciated the change in me.

"It's thanks to the Arena of Long-armed_Kyle."

"What percentage of realism?"

"Seventy-five over the last two weeks. All very grown-up," I joked, although I had also noticed that my extra fat had disappeared and I was moving more confidently. The forces that I was being exposed to through the VR capsule's unique sensory gel technology were clearly benefiting my body.

"Sasha, do you have a place to go once you've been discharged?"

"Yes, of course. I have my own apartment although I'm still paying it off."

"What are you planning to do?"

"I'll return to the Edge of the Abyss. I have to make money, and it's interesting there. By the way, I have enough space for a second VR capsule, if you need it."

"Thank you, I might take you up on your offer. Still, nobody is driving me out of Max' apartment just yet. He hasn't reappeared?"

"No," Lourier sighed heavily.

"Did you learn anything about Jeb?" I moved away from the topic that was upsetting for both of us.

"That's why I called you."

"Did you trace his location?"

"That's the thing, I couldn't."

"Why? Did the admin device not work?"

"I traced his data exchange channel. It led me to one of the World Space Agency servers. It's a dead end. I can't get through their defenses and it would be dangerous, anyway."

"This means that Jeb logged into the Edge of the Abyss through the WSA's local network?"

"Yes. And logically, his VR capsule should be supervised."

"Then how was he allowed to get to such a state?"

"One possibility could be an experiment to

determine the limits of human capabilities," Lourier replied. "I've heard of such experiments. Records for continuously staying in a VR capsule and such. Jeb is probably a volunteer and knew the risks."

"But he doesn't remember anything from his real life! His mind has clearly swapped such concepts around!"

"Andrey Dmitrievich, we can't pull him out of there. Not with our level of influence and contacts. Not unless he remembers something himself."

"All right," I sighed. "I won't force him but I'll try to stir up his memories."

"How are things going with the Forest Hill quest?"

"I'm going there today. I think I've found the solution."

Chapter Eighteen

THE NOON HEAT shimmered over the land.

The grass had wilted in some places. Not a drop of rain had fallen around Anchor for the past two weeks and I had heard the farmers complaining about the unusual drought.

The longer I spent in the Edge of the Abyss, the thinner the line between the two realities.

My dig was a mysterious dark spot on the slope.

In my youth, I had dreamed of becoming an archaeologist and looking for traces of lost civilizations but life had decided differently. Now, it seemed, my dream was coming true.

Something ancient and undiscovered was lurking here. I jumped down into the narrow space and approached the melted and cracked stone slab that blocked my way.

The sun was directly overhead.

Well, shall I?

I took the Soul Crystal out of my inventory and placed it in the recess. My fingers prickled as if from a discharge of current. The magical key fitted perfectly into the niche, just like last time, and became transparent, revealing the flickering flame inside.

I listened but nothing was happening.

The ground didn't shake and I couldn't feel the heavy tread of the guard. I quickly climbed out of the excavation and looked around.

Where are you, lizard?

I was ready to fight. I wore my old leather armor restored to its full durability. It should be enough to withstand a single Crushing Roar. My star metal shield hung across my back. My wide belt contained three vials of healing potion and two scrolls purchased from the Mage Guild, which I could quickly access. I held a bastard sword in my hands, with scaling according to Strength. It suited my character's current characteristics perfectly.

Silence. Only a faint breeze carried the heady scent of meadow grasses.

Was the beast not going to show up at all? I refused to believe it.

The branches of a briar bush shifted suddenly. A gap appeared in the thorny thicket, yet I couldn't see the enemy.

The grass was compressed by a chain of footprints.

He was moving in Stealth mode, probably another ability of the Shadow Warriors. How did they remain invisible in the bright midday sun?

I kept completely still, pretending not to notice the approaching enemy. The lizard was moving almost silently, clearly intending to sneak up from behind and perform a critical strike out of Stealth.

I didn't react, only shifted my pupils to follow his movements by the stirring of the grass.

The tread was too light for a massive opponent encased in armor! The cicadas sang annoyingly loudly, drowning out the rustle of his steps.

I could sense him behind me already. A chill ran down my spine.

One second...

Two...

There was the hoarse exhalation!

I ducked rapidly, simultaneously performing a spinning strike, which I had practiced until it had become completely automatic. The bastard sword spun in a blurred silver circle and produced an angry howl of pain.

I rolled to get out of the way.

A shimmering outline appeared a few steps away from me. The sudden attack and resulting damage dispelled the invisibility.

...

Havl. Shadow Warrior. A creature from the Abyss. Cursed guard. Level 32.

My guess about the position of the sun had been correct!

My opponent was only a little taller than me now. The right greave was sliced right through and the leg was bleeding. Excellent! A deep dent was visible on the helmet, evidence of my failed attempt to break the statue into pieces.

He lunged and I dodged easily. We circled, getting a sense of each other. Did you think of me, lizard? I thought of you hundreds of times while training in the arena, mentally working through possible combat scenarios.

Havl was massive and strong. His sword was longer than mine and inflicted more damage but the Shadow Warrior's abilities were the greatest threat. I first had to annul and survive his abilities. I slowly retreated up the slope, which angered the lizard. He couldn't end the fight with one blow as he had surely hoped and was now forced to expend his energy by hobbling after me.

He was going to snap...

Exactly! There was a short cast, followed by a hollow roar.

A smoke-blue haze spread over the slope. The earth moved and my Life bar dropped by a third.

...

You have been affected by the Aura of Petrifaction. Effect: immobilization for 5 seconds.

You have been affected by the Aura of Fear. Effect: you cannot attack creatures whose level exceeds yours for 5 seconds.

You have been affected by the Aura of the Abyss. Effect: random damage to all living things.

You have been hit by Crushing Roar. Effect: all types of armor is reduced by 50 hit points.

...

A moment earlier, noting the movement of the staff, I had managed to jump back, increasing the distance between us.

Five seconds!

The earth churned. All around me, shaking off the sandy loam stuck to them, arose the remains of long-dead creatures, summoned by the Aura of the Abyss.

They weren't only animals. Unable to move, I could only numbly watch as skeleton warriors in rusty armor and liches[1] in ragged robes stood up here and there...

The limping Havl snarled and tried to rush at me, but the crowd of summoned beings got in his way. This hill had seen too many deaths.

Four seconds... Five seconds!

The debuff stopped working. I could move again, sweeping aside the ancient, slow-moving undead, chopping my way up the slope, with enough time to pull a scroll from my belt and break the magical seal.

...

You have cast the Stone Skin spell.

Absorption of all incoming damage is increased by

---

[1] Lich – an undead mage.

25%. Duration: 3 minutes.

...

The midday sun was on my side. Its blazing light made the yellowed bones smoke and the liches howl as they hurriedly cast protective spells on themselves.

The gray haze caused the grass to crumble into dust. Leaves wilted on the sparse trees. The bushes curled and blackened, beginning to resemble coils of barbed wire.

Havl was having trouble clambering up the slope as he tried to reach me, ruthlessly trampling the undead in his way.

Soon this flood of creatures would boil away. The sun's rays would incinerate the long-dead beings, dust to dust.

I drank a healing potion while on the move. The wound on the lizard's leg was gradually healing since the Shadow Warrior's regeneration was very fast and powerful.

Havl's figure was suddenly enveloped in gloom. He tried to enter Stealth mode again but I didn't let him, attacking at once with a combination of strikes. He was lower down the slope than me and most of the damage landed on his head, making the lizard stagger and fall back.

"You will not get inside!" he wheezed.

I rolled under the whistling blow of his sword. It grazed me but the pain was bearable.

"What's inside?" I asked as I got him with a

stabbing lunge.

Ash swirled around us.

"You shall never find out!"

I mustn't delay. The buff compensating for my armor's reduced hit points would not last forever. If Havl was to use his auras again, I'd be in trouble.

I intensified my onslaught, spending all my Stamina and not giving him a moment's respite, forcing him to retreat to where a fragment of ancient masonry protruded from the ground.

The lizard stumbled, lost his balance and tipped onto his back. I saw the loose skin under his chin again, where the breastplate didn't fit properly, and leaped forward, intent on finishing him off.

Havl reacted at the last possible moment. Something immaterial blocked my blade, there was a ringing sound and the steel shattered into tiny fragments, but I could not stop the movement. The lizard's teeth clashed, it's reeking breath washed over me and a piercing pain nearly made me lose consciousness.

I managed to escape, leaving my punctured left vambrace and a piece of flesh in his mouth.

He was already back on his feet and rushing at me!

I barely avoided the vertical slash and rolled away from the whistling spinning strike. Havl was furious and desperate to finish me off in any way possible: crush me, tear me, bite my head off...

He finally stopped, exhausted, his eyes bloodshot.

I had enough time to drink a healing potion and change weapons, grabbing two one-handed swords from my quick access panel — the one I had found at the Deadly Crag and the Chaotic one bought by mistake, since I didn't have anything else at hand right now.

The lizard took a deep breath and rushed to attack again.

I used my two blades. Long-armed_Kyle had taught me this technique. Havl was a large, strong but not very mobile opponent. I waited until he ran out of Stamina, performed a series of short 'spamming' blows, then rapidly retreated.

The extreme combat acrobatics produced a wave of dizziness but I had been successful in making the Shadow Warrior slow down. His armor had been pierced in numerous places. Blood flowed freely from the shallow but extremely painful wounds.

Havl was quickly losing strength. His regeneration could no longer keep up with the damage.

I snatched up the second scroll that I had bought from the Mage Guild. My fingers broke the seal and we were enveloped in a heavy and tangible silence, as if the air around us had suddenly solidified.

Havl raised his staff but with no result.

The Silence affected us both. Neither of us could use magic.

The lizard realized this and flew into a rage. His blows could cleave me in two but would I let him? I evaded his attacks again and again. My left hand grew numb and no longer obeyed me while sweat and blood dripped into my eyes.

I couldn't keep up this pace for much longer. Havl sensed my weakness and redoubled his efforts.

Seizing a free moment, I drank the last healing potion. My wounds closed but the Silence would soon stop working and then I would lose for certain.

The lizard attacked again. Only a third of his Life points remained but his longer sword prevented me from coming any closer.

Wounded by the Chaotic blade, I threw it at the lizard. Havl instinctively recoiled, which gave me a couple of seconds to move the shield to my left hand and activate Rage.

Now my defense and inflicted damage both increased by 5%.

This was the decisive moment in the battle. The Silence continued to work.

The lizard roared, threw away his staff and held his sword in a two-handed grip, beginning a deadly combo of three spinning strikes.

I didn't retreat. I blocked the first two attacks with minimal damage and parried the third one.

A sharp swing of my shield knocked the sword out of his hands.

Havl staggered and dropped to one knee. His Stamina was at zero, for he had spent it all on the failed combo.

The lizard was immobilized for a moment and I

thrust the blade into his head, aiming for the dent in his forehead.

There was a dull thud, the screech of pierced metal, a deep roar...

His figure became indistinct. With the last of his effort, Havl managed to slash me with his claws, leaving five deep wounds on my chest, and then fell sideways.

I vomited blood. My internal organs were pulverized and my Life bar flickered in the red zone.

My mind went fuzzy. My legs gave out from under me and everything doubled before my eyes.

The HP bar shuddered, growing and then dropping down due to the Bleeding damage.

I don't know how long I lay unconscious beside the defeated Havl but eventually, my natural regeneration triumphed and my wounds began to heal.

Once I recovered a little, I went into my inventory. I had used up all the healing potions in my quick access panel, but there were others in my bag.

Damn it... A strange brown liquid was bubbling in the vials! Either the merchant had tricked me or this instance had certain restrictions that the system hadn't warned me about.

There was nobody around. Only a light breeze

mixed the stench of decay from the Aura of the Abyss with the scent of meadow grasses.

The wilted grass was blackened in places and splattered with blood. I could see rusty armor and scraps of clothing scattered around.

The staff of the Shadow Warrior lay a little to the side. He was still clutching the sword.

My throat was parched. I took a long, deep drink from the flask (water also restored a small number of HP), then changed my outfit, putting on the armor made by Master André.

I slung the shield across my back. In my hand, I held the long sword found on the Deadly Crag.

I opened the message window.

You have completed the Cursed Guard hidden quest.

You have defeated Havl, thus removing an ancient curse. The last statue has now been destroyed.

You have received 20,000 Exp.

You have regained the lost level.

...

What about the Secret of Forest Hill?

I quickly scrolled through the system messages, then checked the traveler's diary. Not a word about the main quest!

Fine. I picked up the staff and examined its characteristics.

Shadow Staff. Cursed product by an unknown craftsman.

Charges remaining: 15 out of 200.

Available spells:

Aura of the Abyss (primary effect — damage to all living things according to the formula: ten times the owner's current level of Intellect. Secondary effect — summoning of creatures who have previously died and whose remains are in range of the aura).

Aura of Petrifaction (effect — enemy immobilization; duration: 1 second per 1 staff charge spent).

Aura of Fear (effect — enemy cannot attack you if they have a lower level than you; duration: 1 second per 1 staff charge spent).

Recharge: kill any creature that is under the influence of auras to restore some of the staff charges.

Permanent effect: Dark regeneration.

Restricted for use only by cursed beings.

...

Hmm...

My fingers began to tingle unpleasantly, so I hurriedly put the staff away in my inventory. When I was buying scrolls at the Mage Guild, I saw special tubes and cases for storing dangerous artifacts. I would have to purchase one.

I gathered Havl's loot.

The sword was easy to take. The lizard didn't drop anything but I noticed a thin chain hanging around his neck and poking out from under the armor. I pulled on it and gaped in shock.

A Soul Crystal dangled at the end of the chain!

Unlike mine, this jewel was filled with darkness and the black flame of the Abyss flickered inside.

Who was he?!

I would probably never know the answer. The Shadow Warrior's figure began to fade away. I looked at the time. A little more than twenty minutes had passed since our fight.

But mobs respawned after four hours! Did that mean he wasn't an NPC?

My guess sent shivers down my spine. No, I couldn't believe it. It was surely a glitch. It was a very odd instance, after all. The potions went bad, Havl disappeared...

I had to go and see if the entrance to the hill had finally opened.

Before returning to my dig, I carefully inspected the enormous (by human standards) blade.

...

Sword of the Shadow Warrior.

Forged from meteoric iron by one of the Guardians.

Damage 30-35 with scaling according to Strength and Intellect.

Permanent effect: gives the owner the ability to use Crushing Roar, which destroys the durability of enemy armor (50 hit points per use, cooldown/recharge 10 minutes).

...

A very unusual weapon! It was the first time that I'd seen an unenchanted blade with Intellect scaling. But most of all, I was surprised and alarmed by the mention of a Guardian who had forged the sword.

Aren't the mysterious Shadows their polar opposites? Although the lizard could have found the blade, bought it or obtained it in battle...

Right. Like the Soul Crystal. And then Havl became petrified and turned into a guard for this hill?

Deep in thought, I returned to the narrow manhole. The stone slab was still there, blocking the way. My crystal remained transparent and I could see a normal flame burning inside, only slightly edged in black.

I touched the precious stone. It was fixed firmly in its recess.

I tried to turn it like a combination lock on a safe, but nothing happened.

What was I supposed to do? Why wasn't I provided with any clues?

What if I tried this? I pressed firmly on the jewel and a grating sound suddenly came from inside the hill.

I quickly removed the Soul Crystal from its recess, noticing that the stone slab was slowly moving upward and rivulets of black sand were cascading down the archway.

The barrier shifted about a meter and stopped. The

rumble died away.

Crouching down, I squeezed through the gap with some difficulty. The air was stale. I couldn't see anything in the darkness, only the pale outline of another archway far ahead.

My inventory contained a rope, a torch, a hammer and metal pitons with eye holes. I had come to the instance thoroughly prepared, although I had very limited knowledge of caving.

Special skills weren't required at the start, however. I lit a torch and discovered that I was in a tunnel made of roughly hewn stone blocks.

The walls and ceiling were thick with cobwebs and a layer of dust lay over the floor. I couldn't see any side tunnels.

I walked forward slowly, my shield on my back, the torch in my left hand and the sword in my right.

Every step raised a cloud of dust.

I supposed that I should be careful of traps. It was a shame that Jeb and Weasel weren't with me.

I saw a square hole in the flickering torchlight. One of the floor slabs was missing. I could see rusty spikes at the bottom of the stone well, with ancient bones scattered among them.

I wondered who had been here before me. I immediately remembered the three broken statues at the top of the hill, and the scratched inscription about the position of the sun.

There had probably been numerous attempts made

to get inside the hill but none of them had ended well.

The short passageway strained my nerves.

Twice, I inadvertently stepped on trap triggers, hidden under the layer of dust. First, I was nearly crushed under a pile of rocks. I jumped back just in time, as soon as I heard a suspicious screech. The next time, a slab dropped treacherously underfoot, but the rusty falling grate became jammed and slipped down only a third of the way.

A little further along, crossbows were mounted behind narrow slits, but fortunately, someone had already unloaded them.

A thick layer of cobwebs covered the archway where the dim light was coming from. I guessed that the creature that had spun them was long dead for the sticky threads were decorated with a fringe of the ubiquitous dust.

Tearing down this heavy curtain, I found myself at the threshold of a spacious dome-shaped hall. Its roof had cracked and partially collapsed.

The floor was powdered with ash and broken in the center. The walls were covered in a strange pattern of lines, geometric shapes and strange symbols. The ancient frescoes were seriously damaged by the traces of a fierce battle, with gouges and scorch marks visible everywhere.

The light source turned out to be a respawn circle, located near the entrance. The far side of the hall lay in darkness.

Something wasn't right. My path inside the mysterious construction had been too simple.

Yes, the fight with the lizard hadn't been easy. But it felt like the rest of the way had been prepared for me. I couldn't forget what kind of world I was in. Where were the innumerable enemy NPCs, where were their bosses and why was this place so desolate?

The respawn point was very strange. It was formed by two intersecting circles. The distorted runes were barely smoldering...

All of a sudden, a gust of wind from the tunnel behind me swept away the layer of dust, disturbing the years of oblivion, and an incredible sight opened up before me.

It turned out that the floor of this huge room was made of a clear, glass-like substance, with a landscape visible in its depth, as if I was looking at the world from above!

A mountain range ran beneath my feet, a plain visible a little further on with lakes, rivers, forests, towns, villages, roads, many portals, respawn circles, and the tiny figures of people and animals.

I took a few steps forward, admiring the realism of the panorama enclosed in the glass, until I saw a network of cracks that gradually widened and ended at the jagged Edge of the Abyss — a gap full of tangible, swirling darkness.

A feeling of icy hostility emanated from it.

I drew closer and brought my arm with the torch forward, hoping to dispel the gloom and see what was hidden in the breach in the center of the hall. The uneven light couldn't penetrate down far enough but I could clearly see that the well of darkness exuded a blue-gray haze that was slowly eroding the edges and destroying the glass-like material. Right before my eyes, a piece at the edge collapsed, and the tiny figures of people, animals and plants fell into the Abyss together with their part of the firmament.

I hoped that the sinister processes taking place here didn't reflect reality.

I didn't dare to come any closer. The cracked surface didn't inspire much trust.

What else could I do? Explore the hall's perimeter in the hope of finding a way deeper into the strange structure?

Yes, this was probably the most sensible option.

The torch crackled, dispelling the gloom only slightly. A thick layer of ash shifted underfoot. The gust of wind had blown away only part of it, revealing a tiny fragment of the virtual world.

A smoke-blue haze trickled out of the Abyss breech. Motes of dust swirled in the musty air.

I walked slowly along the wall, stepping over cracked and collapsed columns of green marble. I was hoping that the other side of the huge hall would contain a door or a corridor that would lead me to other rooms in this mysterious building buried beneath the hill.

Nobody blocked my path, which continued to unsettle me. I was expecting a trick.

The strange geometric pattern and the inscriptions in an unfamiliar language peeked disturbingly out from under a layer of soot. They bore no resemblance to known runes or magic symbols, but I didn't think that the frescoes were there just for decoration.

The wall curved gently. I could see the vague outlines of some shapes up ahead.

I nearly tripped over the edge of a wide step protruding from the ash. The shallow staircase led to a group of statues on a separate platform.

There were four sculptures, arranged in pairs, with a huge archway visible behind them, sealed by a shimmering barrier.

I ascended the steps, keeping the torch in front of me so as not to miss a single detail.

The statues seemed to be people. Two men in armor and two women in loose-fitting robes. Their faces had been obliterated and their arms were covered in slashes — a clear act of vandalism, mixed with fear and hatred.

As I had already seen, some statues could come to life!

I approached cautiously.

The mysterious hill had taught me to be careful. I was Level 30 now and wore good-quality armor, but I was out of healing potions and my sword left a lot to be desired. Common sense dictated that I needed to return to town, thoroughly prepare again, and only then try to pass through the magic barrier inscribed with a glowing string of unfamiliar symbols.

I took another few steps and found myself between the statues.

A book lay at the base of each sculpture! I could swear that they had been hidden under the ashes a moment ago, but had suddenly and inexplicably rose up, as if an invisible force had pushed them out of oblivion.

Without touching the books, I read the names stamped on their leather bindings:

The Carver of Magic Runes. A Skill Book.

Wow! I shifted my gaze.

Blade Master. A Skill Book.

I turned slowly.

High-Level Magic. A Skill Book.

And finally, the fourth one.

The Portal Wanderer. A Skill Book.

What was I supposed to do? It was possible that they were activated by touch so I had better not be hasty. How could I check? I couldn't develop all four skills, especially since two of them required a very high level of Intellect and I would ruin the character if I got too greedy. It made more sense to take them with me and use them as necessary, but was such a thing possible?

I could use the Blade Master book, and the Carver of Magic Runes wouldn't hurt either. I'd certainly do well in the Edge of the Abyss with a profession like that! There must be countless faulty portals, respawn circles and other devices around that needed restoration.

Which one to choose...

Either way, I had to take a risk. If just touching the book didn't activate the skill, then I would place all four volumes in my inventory and use them wisely as needed.

I approached the statue of a warrior and touched the Blade Master book. Nothing happened. The ancient manuscript was safely transferred to my inventory, followed by the others.

The system messages window popped up at once.

The Secret of Forest Hill quest has been updated.

The quest status has changed from personal to group/clan. Level 50+ is recommended.

You have stopped at a magical barrier. To open it, you must recreate what was lost. Discover the identity of these four and most importantly, what happened to the artifacts that they were holding.

You will able to proceed further only after you find

the four items and return them to their place.

...

I had mixed feelings about this, to be honest. The skill books were cool, of course, but after everything that I had been through, the mysterious hall made me feel melancholic. Or was it the tiredness talking?

I studied the statues again. Who were they? I couldn't see any obvious clues. Someone had tried very hard to de-identify them. The inscriptions on the pedestals had been erased.

I took detailed photographs of the sculptures in the torchlight so I could show them to Jeb and Sasha. We'd ponder the mystery together.

I couldn't cross the magical barrier. A force pushed me back gently.

Well, it was worth a try... Or maybe not! I suddenly heard distant footsteps in the gloomy depths of the hall.

I turned sharply.

The steps came closer and closer. A large mob was approaching, without even bothering to hide its presence.

Havl. Shadow Warrior. A creature from the Abyss. Level 32.

No way! I had dispatched him!

The lizard was unarmed, not counting the sharp and steely claws that the beast had used to nearly send me into respawn.

I stuck the torch into the compressed ashes and

prepared for battle.

I had no intention of retreating or running away. We'd see who got whom! Without the auras that the sword and staff had produced, he was just a thick-skinned, strong and incredibly dangerous animal.

I had no healing potions left but Havl could no longer use Dark regeneration.

His eyes were bloodshot and there was a gaping hole in his helmet.

The clang of armor, the nervous tapping of the spiked tail, the metal plates dully reflecting the light of the torch — he was barging at me like a tank...

I brought up my shield, watching my opponent carefully.

Havl stopped abruptly and wheezed, "Give me back my sword!"

"As if! Maybe you want the staff back as well?"

"I do not need the staff anymore. You have lifted the curse. I am thankful for that!"

He wasn't going to attack me? Did he come to say 'thank you'?

"Please, give me back my sword."

"First tell me, what is this place?"

"No."

"Why not?"

He sank down on a dusty step, wrapped his spiked tail around his legs, demonstrating his peaceful intentions, and growled, "A long time ago, I took an oath and made promises that I once broke, for which I was cursed. I do not intend to repeat my mistakes. If you return the sword to me, I will stay here voluntarily, guarding the hill against robbers and rogues."

"I don't believe you. You're a Shadow! A creature from the Abyss."

The lizard fixed me with an unblinking gaze. "And you are a human!"

This was turning into a bizarre conversation. We were both hiding something.

"Are all humans the same?" Havl asked hoarsely.

"Of course not," I smiled crookedly.

"Then do not judge! Shadows are different too. It is up to you. I will not beg. If you change your mind, you will find me at the top, by the wrecked statues."

He stood up and walked away, his head drooping.

It was evening when, tired and hungry, I finally reached the inn where Jeb and I were renting a room.

I'd had a lot of time to think on my trip back to town.

No matter who Havl was, he had spoken sincerely. What did I need this heavy sword for? I doubted that I could wield it even if I spent all my time leveling up my Strength. It would be a shame to sell it. At least the mysterious hill would have a guard this way.

I'd go and talk to him again tomorrow, but today I

just wanted to eat and sleep. I was very tired.

The revealed story arc of the Guardians would require me to painstakingly gather information. Whose statues stood in the enormous hall? What exactly had they been holding in their hands and where was I to look for these undoubtedly powerful artifacts? And most importantly, with what forces? Jeb and I alone wouldn't be able to handle this quest but did I have any other friends in the Edge of the Abyss? Oh yeah, Sasha would join us soon, but it still wasn't enough. I needed a group of at least five people.

Was I getting too carried away with this game?

I couldn't shake the feeling that life has spun me around like a twig and was carrying me in the current of somebody's invented storylines. Where would this raging torrent of game events spit me out? Wasn't it time to take a break, sort out my business in the real world, take a good look around and think things through?

Jeb wasn't in the room, so I went down to the tavern's central hall. Yep, there he was, sitting at a table with a weird person swathed in black. His frame was hidden but it appeared as soon as I came closer, Alexander_Lourier.

"Hey, Jeb. Sasha, what are you doing here? You still have a few more days of rehabilitation left, right?"

"I have news, Andrey Dmitrievich."

"Go on," I sat down at the table, winked at Weasel and pounced on the food.

"I received a message today."

"From whom?"

"From Max."

I nearly choked on a piece of meat. I chewed and swallowed, then looked up at Sasha, "Tell me. What does he say?"

"It's not clear at all. That's why I came here," he passed me a piece of parchment with letters and numbers scribbled on it.

"Where did you get it?" my stomach dropped when I saw the clumsily scratched line of letters and numbers. No wonder Sasha had no idea what it meant, but I understood at once.

"I entered the game in the morning because I had some stuff to sort out. A beggar handed me this piece of paper in the marketplace, whispered 'from Max' and disappeared into the crowd. I thought it was some kind of joke.

"No," I said hoarsely.

"Then what does it say?"

"The first group of numbers is Lieutenant Maxim Pekhov's personal number." I underscored it with my fingernail. "This here is an alphanumeric code meant for communication, and it says 'have been wounded and captured'. The last group of numbers is probably coordinates."

"Let me check," Lourier caught on straight away. "They don't match anything in the real world," he said after a minute.

"Check the Edge of the Abyss," Jeb advised.

"I'm already on it. Got it!" Sasha ran a hand over the table, and the wooden surface changed to look like a map. "Here," he pointed to a mountainous area dotted with question marks.

"Where exactly is this?"

"The Half-blood Gorge. It's deep inside the Dark Frontier. None of our people have ever reached it. There are no known portals there. I took the information from public maps uploaded by the Guild. They tried to fly around the territory on mounts but then abandoned this risky activity."

A multitude of thoughts flashed through my mind in those seconds.

Max was a prisoner. Nothing else mattered now. We had to rescue him but how?

"We know where his avatar is," my voice sounded hollow. "But where is he in the real world? How did he end up with the Shadow Clans?"

"Don't you remember what was going on around Mainstream Center?" Lourier asked. "The wounded were transported to nearby hospitals, often right in their VR capsules. The ambulance doctor told me. It would have been easy to capture Max on that night," Sasha summarized and sighed. "Especially if it had been planned, like the attack itself. He was privy to many clan secrets."

"What are we going to do?" Jeb asked, bewildered.

"The ravine is a week's travel from Noogard," I

replied sharply. "Sasha, can you find out the real location of Maxim's VR capsule when we free his character?"

"Yes. I can." Lourier answered confidently.

"Dan, but you've already been there!" Jeb exclaimed. "A whole army won't be enough to break through!"

A heavy silence descended for a moment.

"Sasha, I'm withdrawing the 'Hunt for the Ifrit' lot from auction."

"Why?" Lourier looked surprised.

"I know whom to offer it to in exchange for help."

Jeb's eyes held nothing but poorly suppressed fear. He asked quietly, "Do you really want to return to the Dark Frontier?"

"Yes. Not with an army but with a small, powerful team. Participation is voluntary. Each person must decide for themselves. I have to go Forest Hill now," I stood up. "We'll meet here again in a day."

End of Book One

January — July 2018, Krasnodar Krai.

The Dark Frontier (*Respawn Trials* Book Two) is currently being written.

The Abyss Portal (*Respawn Trials* Book Three, working title) is under development.

Author's website: https://livadny.ru

VK group: https://vk.com/club84398682

Want to be the first to know about our latest LitRPG, sci fi and fantasy titles from your favorite authors? Subscribe to our **New Releases** newsletter: http://eepurl.com/b7niIL

Thank you for reading *Edge of the Abyss!*
If you like what you've read, check out other LitRPG novels
published by Magic Dome Books:

Level Up LitRPG series by Dan Sugralinov:
Re-Start
Hero
The Final Trial
Level Up: The Knockout (with Max Lagno)

Adam Online LitRPG Leries by Max Lagno:
Absolute Zero

**The Way of the Shaman LitRPG series
by Vasily Mahanenko:**
Survival Quest
The Kartoss Gambit
The Secret of the Dark Forest
The Phantom Castle
The Karmadont Chess Set
Shaman's Revenge
Clans War

Dark Paladin LitRPG series by Vasily Mahanenko:
The Beginning
The Quest
Restart

Galactogon LitRPG series by Vasily Mahanenko:
Start the Game!
In Search of the Uldans

**The Bard from Barliona LitRPG series
by Eugenia Dmitrieva and Vasily Mahanenko:**
The Renegades
A Song of Shadow

The Neuro LitRPG series by Andrei Livadny:
The Crystal Sphere
The Curse of Rion Castle
The Reapers

Phantom Server LitRPG series by Andrei Livadny:
Edge of Reality
The Outlaw
Black Sun

In order to have new books of the series translated faster, we need your help and support! Please consider leaving a review or spread the word by recommending *Edge of the Abyss* to your friends and posting the link on social media. The more people buy the book, the sooner we'll be able to make new translations available. Thank you!

Till next time!

www.ingramcontent.com/pod-product-compliance
Lightning Source LLC
Chambersburg PA
CBHW071641260626
47170CB00001B/186